The Thirteenth Unicorn

Book One

A Children's Fantasy

by

W. D. Newman

ISBN: 1460966201
ISBN-13: 978-1460966204

"The family - that dear octopus from whose tentacles we never quite escape, nor, in our inmost hearts, ever quite wish to."

~Dodie Smith.

CONTENTS

PROLOGUE

ZORN, 27 B.E. (BEFORE EVACUATION)

The small cottage seemed to crouch beneath the oak trees that stood about it like tired old sentries with their great shaggy limbs hanging protectively about the sides. Inside, a pathway wound from the front door through piles of books, scrolls, boxes, and crates to a large table tucked away in the corner. A mischievous breeze entered the front window and danced merrily around the room, teasing the scrolls and dusty old tomes before leaping out the back window and speeding across the meadow. In another corner of the room embers from last night's fire had ceased to glow, but still radiated heat into the small open area before the hearth. Here, the air shimmered then solidified, forming a one dimensional black hole six feet high and suspended a few inches above the floor. An old man stepped out of the dark hole into the room and the gaping maw silently snapped shut behind him.

Dressed in tattered rags and stooped with the weight of years upon his shoulders the old man, clutching an armful of

1

moldy parchments to his chest, moved through the clutter in the cottage with a spryness that belied his age. His gray hair stuck out in all directions and his beard, which would have been white except for the tobacco stains around his mouth, bristled like an angry hedge hog. When he reached the table, he hastily swept it clean with one arm and spread the parchments out before him. He absently mumbled some unintelligible word and a small white orb appeared over his head, illuminating the parchment like a miniature sun. With dirty fingers he traced over the runes, his lips moving silently as he translated their meaning. Suddenly he stopped, his finger poised over one of the designs with numbers and formulas scrawled all around it.

"That's it!" he cried, stabbing his finger down upon the strange design. "That's it!"

Scooping the parchments up into his arms the old man hurried back through the maze on the cottage floor. As he neared the small open area by the hearth, he spoke another strange word under his breath and the black hole re-opened before him, tall and wide, visible only from the front and rear and yet thin as a single sheet of paper if viewed from either side. Without missing a step, he strode through the front of the hole into the darkness and vanished. The hole started to wink out and then paused. The old man's wiry arm shot out from the rear of the hole and snatched a gnarled wooden staff from beside the fireplace and disappeared back into the darkness. The hole snapped shut and another merry breeze jumped through the front window and raced around the room seeking his brother. Finding the cottage empty, the mischievous wind shot up the chimney to shake the leaves and wake the old trees from their napping in the afternoon sun.

Now the black hole opened up onto a small plain situated high above the capital city of Zorn, among the barren windswept peaks of the Ironstone Mountains. These black holes were entrances to tunnels that traversed through space and time. The wizards of Zorn could create these tunnels, or pathways as they called them, at will and used them often to travel to and fro about their world. Once again the old man stepped out of the black hole, this time onto the lifeless plain where a cold wind threatened to rip the parchments from his arms. Powerless to stop the wind the old man crouched to the ground and placed a large rock on top of the parchments to keep them from taking flight. The wind howled in protest and the old man's tattered robe flapped violently against his bony frame. Defiantly he planted his staff into the ground and, with a voice that even the shrieking wind could not overpower, he began to chant.

A rumble, almost imperceptible, began to emanate from deep below the plain and then the ground beneath the old mans weathered boots began to shake, slowly at first, but quickly building into a crescendo that forced him to grasp his staff with both hands and lean heavily upon it to keep from falling. When he could hold himself steady no longer he raised his staff and struck the ground and cried out with a loud voice, "CEASE!"

The shaking immediately stopped and time paused. Even the wind momentarily ceased it's howling, as if waiting breathlessly to see what the old man would do next. Once more he began to chant, this time in a whisper, and before him a green sprout sprung forth from the ground and began to grow. In just a few seconds it had gone from a tender green sprout to a tall willowy sapling. The old man began rapping his staff upon the ground, beating a cadence to the rhythm of his chant and the tree began to grow even faster. Tall and thick in girth became the bole; yet the limbs, though thickened, remained short. The tree blossomed and then leafed. The leaves turned crimson and then fell. The seasons blurred by and with each passing season the tree aged with fewer blossoms each spring cycle and fewer leaves each summer. Finally the seasons halted and the tree, bare of leaves and twisted with age, cracked asunder with a tremendous pop. As if this were the cue for which they were waiting, the winds rolled off the mountains like an avalanche and caught the old man unawares, sending him sprawling to the ground. He struggled to his feet and, leaning into the wind, slowly made his way to the tree.

The crack in the tree's bole had not destroyed the tree, but had created an opening large enough to walk through in the very center of the tree. The old man, peering through this opening, could see the plain stretching out behind the tree and the steep granite sides of the mountains rising up sharply along the edge. Stooping down, he scooped up a rock and tossed it through the opening. As soon as the rock exited the hole on the other side, it vanished. Excitedly, the old man tucked his staff under his arm, took a deep breath, and marched through the crack in the center of the tree.

After centuries spent scouring the high mountain plain bare of vegetation, the wind took offense for this lone intruder and beat upon the tree with all its might. The tree stood fast against this assault, immovable and now hard and rigid as the mountains of granite from which the wind was born. Unable to shake the tree, the winds searched for an easier target; the old man. But, he was nowhere to be found.

* * * * *

Karnopia was the last remaining continent on Zorn, a dying world whose polar ice caps were melting. The governing body was comprised of twelve council members; one wizard from each district. Miles below the Ironstones, in the gleaming capitol city, eleven of these council members sat round a crystal table. They were arrayed in brightly colored robes of the finest silks on Zorn. Their hair and beards were neatly trimmed and their feet were shod in slippers of supple calf skin. Doran, head of the council, rose from his chair and lightly tapped his staff on the glassy table top for silence.

"I'm very sorry for the delay," he said, nodding toward the empty chair. "We'll give him a just few more minutes. I'm sure he'll be here shortly."

Mordred rose from his chair and pounded his fist upon the table. "That man," he shouted, pointing at the empty chair, "is a disgrace to this council. He is always late! And even when he is present his mind is always elsewhere."

"He's probably at his cottage with his nose in some dirty scroll," someone muttered.

"Here! Here!" came cries from around the table.

Nespar, Doran's closest friend and advisor, turned to the head wizard. "Mordred is right. He never contributes anything to our meetings anyway and we have many pressing matters to discuss."

Doran sighed and nodded. He cleared his throat to call the meeting to order and at that very moment the air shimmered and a pathway opened up before them. To everyone's horror the old man popped out of the black hole right onto the crystal table, his wild hair and beard shooting out in all directions, his dark eyes glittering madly.

The room erupted into chaos with everyone protesting at once. Recovering quickly from his shock, Doran banged his staff on the table in an attempt to restore order. When everyone had quieted, Doran glared at the old man who was still standing on top of the crystal table, with muddy boots no less.

"Merlin!" he exclaimed. "What is the meaning of this?"

"We're saved. Saved!" the old man cackled. "Follow me, quickly now."

Before anyone could speak, the old man leapt into the black hole and vanished. The council sat round the table, stunned at this breach in etiquette and appalled by the audacity of the mad wizard. They waited for the pathway to close, but it remained open.

"What now?" asked Jabal, "We cannot begin our meeting with a pathway open on top of our table!"

"I guess we go and see what mischief he has been up to," Doran answered, with another sigh.

"You do not expect us all to go traipsing off after that old fool, do you?" cried Mordred.

"No, I certainly do not. I will go. Nespar, you will come with me. I wager he has dug up another one of those scrolls."

"What?" Mordred asked, with disbelief. "Doran, you are becoming as big of a fool as he."

An uncomfortable silence hung in the air. All of the other wizards looked away, embarrassed by the awkward scene that was playing out before them. Mordred and Doran locked eyes and a contest of wills ensued. Seconds slowly ticked by until Mordred, finally realizing that he was the weaker, for now, snatched his cloak and stormed from the room.

Shaken, Doran leaned heavily upon his staff. Mordred's strength was increasing and the struggle had taken a toll upon him. Realizing that all eyes were now upon him, he straightened up and dismissed everyone. After the other wizards had left, Nespar helped him onto the crystal table and they entered the pathway together.

Doran and Nespar were expecting the pathway to take them to Merlin's cottage. They were quite surprised when they stepped out onto the desolate plain high up in the Ironstones. The wind cut through their thin silks and chilled them instantly. Merlin was standing by an old dead tree, wearing that stupid grin that often adorns the faces of mindless doddering old men. But Merlin was anything but mindless. Eccentric yes, even to an extreme, but never mindless nor doddering. Beneath those tattered rags, that covered what appeared to be a frail bony body, and behind those deep set black eyes, was a strength and cunning that had surprised many adversaries over the years. Doran knew this. All of the council members knew this. Merlin's power, coupled with his lack of respect for protocol and authority, was the root of all the resentment from his fellow council members. Yet they were powerless to reign him in, powerless to get him to conform, and powerless to get rid of him. And so it had been since he became a council member, and so it would continue until he stepped down or died. Most believed neither would ever occur.

"Merlin, why have you brought us here?" Doran shouted over the wind. "This is madness!"

Merlin cackled madly and strode through the gaping hole in the center of the old tree, and vanished. Doran and Nespar stood there with there mouths agape.

"Where did he go?" Nespar cried. "Merlin!" he called, "Merlin!"

"Come," said Doran, taking Nespar by the arm. "He intended for us to follow. Let's get this over with before we both freeze to death."

CAMELOT, 1231 A.E. (AFTER EVACUATION)

Sweat streamed down the horses' foam-flecked sides as its hooves churned up the forest floor. The cart bounced madly behind the terrified animal, while the dark, twisted trees flew by in rapid succession. Suddenly, the narrow trail dipped sharply and then exploded from the forest, spilling out onto a bleak and barren field. The witch cracked her whip across the animal's back, spurring it on even faster.

Stone Dog was in sight now. The castle was perched on the crown of a hill and stood small, squat, and black against the early morning sky. The horse and cart flew over the dismal plain in a plume of dust and thundered across the bridge and through the gates. The poor animal had run all through the night without rest, and as the sun peaked over the horizon, his great heart finally burst. In a flurry of legs and hooves the horse collapsed, sending both the cart and the witch plummeting toward the ground. The cart tumbled end over end across the courtyard and smashed into the base of the castle's lone tower. The witch, however, vanished in a puff of smoke and a clap of thunder, before striking the ground. At that very same instant, a light winked on in the top of the tower.

Thirty miles east of Stone Dog, two men combed the western slopes of a rocky mountain side. Though the sun had just risen, beneath the tall pines and hemlocks it was still dim and strangely quiet. The men were tall and clad in forest greens and browns. Their skin was fair and their raven hair was pulled back into a long thick braid that revealed high cheek bones and upswept ears. And yet the most striking feature about these men was their eyes; keen and stern, chips of blue ice burning like lamps in the gray morning light. These were elves from the Twilight.

"Do you still feel it, Gabriel?"

"Yes, Nicholas, I still feel it. But it is weak now and growing dimmer."

"That is what I perceived as well. We must hurry."

The two elves picked up their pace and began to lope across the rocky terrain, looking both left and right as they sped beneath the trees. They came upon a small clearing where the sun had managed to coax up some tender green grass. Here, they found what they were searching for, but they were too late. The witch had already done her work.

A great struggle had taken place in the clearing and all of the earth was churned up. Most of the grass was bent and broken and covered with a black substance that had a reddish tint in the morning sunlight. The coppery smell of blood hung thick about the area and the two elves covered their noses as they approached the large white horse in the center of the small glade. After confirming their worst fears, Gabriel looked away quickly as Nicholas dropped to his knees and wept bitterly.

"What shall we do now?" Nicholas moaned.

"Go home. There is nothing we can do here now," Gabriel replied.

"The Sickness, Gabriel. It will spread faster now."

"Yes. It has always done so with each murder."

"I say we must act, before it is too late."

Gabriel pulled Nicholas to his feet and clasped his shoulders with both hands. "I feel the same as you, brother. But, you know the Keeper's prophesy the same as I. We must wait."

Nicholas looked back at the horse. The animal had been savagely torn apart. Yet, the thing that sickened both elves the most, was the gaping hole in the center of the animal's forehead, just above the sightless blue eyes.

"Then we shall return to the Twilight and wait," Nicholas responded. "But we must redouble our watch. That was the twelfth unicorn."

Gabriel turned to the north and shaded his eyes against the morning sun. Dark clouds were rising there and thunder rumbled low in the distance. The storm was coming. A storm always came with the death of a unicorn, and every storm had been worse than the one before it. Turning his back to the gathering darkness, Gabriel left the small clearing with Nicholas falling in behind him. With a bit of luck, and a little speed, they had a slight chance of making it back to the Twilight before the storm hit. The two elves loped into the forest and silently disappeared among the trees.

1 SCHOOL IS OUT

Dust motes floated lazily in the warm May sunshine that streamed through the window of Ben's seventh grade history class. Soon school would be history. For the summer anyway. All of the text books had been collected, final exams were over, and five minutes were all that remained of seventh grade at R.C. Johnston Middle School. At twelve years of age Ben, was a small boy who had not yet hit a growth spurt like most other boys his age. Being smaller than the other boys, Ben shunned sports and other physical activities and spent much of his time reading. His sister Casey was just the opposite. While Ben was a handsome boy with big brown eyes and dark brown hair, he was shy and the glasses he wore gave him the appearance of being bookish and somewhat frail. Casey, on the other hand, was an extraordinarily beautiful and outgoing girl. One year older than Ben, Casey had long curly red hair, green eyes, and a splattering of freckles across her nose. Casey played volleyball, basketball, softball, and ran track as well.

As the last second ticked off the clock, the final bell rang and students and teachers alike erupted into cheers. Summer was here; glorious, wonderful, magical summer. As the doors of the school were flung open, the summer of 2010 stretched out before all the kids, like a great sea of endless possibilities and adventures. Ben smiled, slung his empty backpack across his shoulders and headed to the parking lot where his father picked him and his sister up every afternoon. Their father, Charles, was a computer programmer for a small company that wrote software for the automotive industry. He always left work in time to pick them up from school and usually worked from his office at home after they had gone to bed. Their father was the one who always picked them up after school because their mother, Carol, had been in a coma now for almost two years. A car crash with a drunk driver had brought this tragedy upon them on a bright crisp fall afternoon - one of those autumn days where the sky seems impossibly blue, the sunshine exceptionally bright, and the fall colors deep and vibrant. The kind of day that gives you a spring in your step and all seems right with the world. The kind of day when you least expect to hear the shattering news that your mother has been involved in a car accident and will probably not make it through the night. However, their mother did make it through the night. Yet now there were no sunrises or sunsets to mark the passage of days for her, only endless hours of sleep and dreams.

When Ben got to the parking lot he saw that Casey was already in the car with their dad. He opened the rear door of their little Honda Accord and tossed his backpack across the seat as he slid in. No one was speaking.

"What's going on?" Ben asked. Casey ignored him and continued to stare out the window. Charles turned the rear view mirror down to look at Ben.

"Ben, the company has a special project they need me to do and I'm going to be away from home for a while."

"That's cool, Dad. Me and Casey can manage for a few days, we're not little kids any more."

"I'm afraid it's more than a few days Ben. We have a new chain of stores going live on our system and I'm going to be the project manager. That means I'll have to be on-site to oversee the installations." Charles turned around in the seat to look at Ben. "All of these stores are in the Chicago area. The project will take at least two months to complete so I want you and Casey to stay with Grandma and Grandpa Alderman while I'm gone."

Now Ben knew why Casey was so upset. Grandma and Grandpa Alderman (George and Louise) lived on a small farm in upstate South Carolina. The closest mall to their farm was over forty miles away. Ben, however, thought it would be cool to stay there over the summer. He always enjoyed the peace and quiet, and the slow, tranquil pace of farm life suited him just fine. Grandpa was always joking, playing pranks and telling the funniest stories. Grandma always cooked the best meals. Every morning she would fix country ham, scrambled eggs, and hot grits with a lake of butter in the middle; or stacks of pancakes smothered with maple syrup and thick slices of crispy bacon. Ben's stomach noisily rumbled as he leaned forward and snaked his arm around the front seat to poke his sister in the ribs.

"What about Mom? Who will look in on her while we're gone?" he asked.

Ben and Casey's mother was staying in a full-care nursing home called Newberry Downs. Round-the-clock nurses were on staff to look after her and the other patients who were no longer able to take care of themselves. For the past two years, Charles, Ben, and Casey faithfully visited Carol every Monday, Wednesday, and Friday. Their visits would mostly consist of Ben and Casey telling their Mom everything that happened in school and at home since their last visit, and Charles telling her about work and family. Their mother never responded, but Ben and Casey firmly believed she could hear them and understand them. They believed that one day she would wake up, ready to go home, fix them supper, tuck them into their beds and kiss them goodnight. Charles kept the kids away from the Downs on the weekends though and tried to make sure that their lives were as normal as possible.

"Aunt Joann has promised to go see her three times a week, just like we do, while we are gone. And when we get back you will have a whole bunch of adventures to tell her about."

"Cool!" Ben said, patting his sister on the shoulder. "Casey gets to milk cows and feed pigs all summer!"

The rest of the ride home was quiet. Ben thought about all of the fun he would have this summer while staying with Grandma and Grandpa Alderman, while Casey thought about her friends that she would miss and all of the fun they would be having this summer without her. Charles worried about them both. He had to leave them home alone at least twice a year while he attended a user's conference but that was only for three days, not all summer. Forty-five minutes later, after a quick stop at Wal-Mart to pick up a few things for their trip (Ben liked to call it Wally World), they pulled into the driveway of their suburban Atlanta home.

"Okay kids, let's unload, get some supper and start packing. We'll go see Mom tonight and leave out early tomorrow morning."

The next morning was overcast with puffy gray clouds that promised rain on what was already starting out as a gloomy day. Ben was quiet, still worried about being away from his mom, and Casey, sullen and pouting, was not speaking to anyone. Charles, however, tried to stay in good spirits and, by 9:30 AM, they were on the road heading north to the Alderman farm in South Carolina.

The plan was to drive to the Alderman farm, drop the kids off, then drive to the Greenville-Spartanburg Airport in time to catch a flight to Chicago. The airport was only about ninety minutes from the farm and Charles would leave his car there while he was away. His flight was at 7:00 PM, so he had plenty of time to visit with his parents before he left. They would arrive at the farm in time for lunch and, knowing his mom, there would be a huge spread laid out on the table waiting for them.

In the back seat, Ben was playing with his electronic chess set. The set was a little metal box that opened up into a game board. The tiny men had magnets in their base and each square on the game board had a little red light. When you played against the computer, the little red lights would blink and show you where to move the men. The set was old. It had belonged to his dad when he was young. When Ben had learned to play chess, and had developed a love for the game, his dad had given him the set. No one at school could beat him and, most of the time, he won the computerized games too.

Charles turned the radio down. "Hey guys, I've got something for you." Ben looked up from his chess game and Casey, who had been listening to her iPod, pulled the earphones out of her ears. "Casey, open the glove compartment and get the two boxes out. The one wrapped in red paper is yours, and the one wrapped in blue is Ben's."

Casey opened the glove compartment and retrieved the two gifts. She tossed the blue one over the seat to Ben and began opening hers.

"A cell phone?" Casey asked with disbelief as she tore off the last shred of wrapping paper. She had been begging for a cell phone all year. All of her friends had one.

"Yes, a cell phone," Charles replied with a grin. "I don't want you running up your Grandma and Grandpa's phone bill over the summer. You know how Grandpa feels about long distance phone calls. The phone is activated and ready to go, so now you can stay in touch with your friends while you're away from home. Just don't go overboard."

"Thanks, Dad!"

Casey unbuckled her seatbelt and threw her arms around her dad's neck. "I'm sorry I've been so awful about this. I'll be fine and I'll do better, I promise."

"I know you will, sweetheart. You'd better put your seatbelt back on. Ben, are you going to open yours?"

Ben tore the wrapping paper from his gift and opened the box. Inside was an Excalibur hunting knife and a leather sheath. Ben carefully lifted the knife from the box and drew it from the sheath. The blade was about six inches long with a serrated edge on the back side. The hilt was wrapped in tan leather and had a compass on the end.

"Awesome!"

"You like it?" Charles asked, grinning ear to ear.

"It's totally cool, Dad! Thanks!"

"I had a knife like that when I was your age. You'll find a lot of uses for it on the farm over the summer. Just promise me you'll be careful with it and you won't cut yourself. Or your sister either."

"I'll be careful Dad, I promise," Ben said.

"Don't run with it and remember to always cut away from your body, not toward your body. That's how people get their eyes poked out."

"Can I put it on now?" Ben asked.

"No, you'd better wait until we get to the farm. We'll be there in about an hour."

Ten minutes later, they crossed the state line. A big sign welcomed and informed them that South Carolina was a place of smiling faces and beautiful places. Shortly after crossing the state line, they left the interstate and took state highway 11 -- a long and scenic highway that wound its way through the Cherokee Foothills. Ben put his chess game away and was enjoying the scenery. Casey seemed to be entranced as well. The highway cut through rolling meadows, over hills and into valleys, with the Blue Ridge Mountains as a constant escort to their left.

"Hey look Dad! A fireworks stand!" Ben yelled. "Can we stop and get some?"

Actually, it was more then a fireworks stand. Sparky's Fireworks was housed inside a large industrial steel building and had a sign proclaiming it to be the largest fireworks dealer in the southeast.

"That's not a good idea, Ben. You know Grandpa doesn't like them. He says they scare his chickens and cows and that makes them stop laying eggs and giving milk. If you are good this summer, and do not get into any trouble, I'll buy you both a bag on the way home. How's that?"

"Can we get some roman candles?" Casey asked.

"And some M80s?" Ben chimed in.

"We'll see. You'll have to be extra good though. Mind your grandparents, clean your plates at every meal, go to bed on time, and all that other stuff."

"What if we have boiled okra for supper? Do we have to eat that?" Casey asked.

Ben wrinkled his nose. He hadn't thought of boiled okra. There could even be boiled squash too! He leaned forward to hear what his dad would say about that.

"I guess you could skip the boiled okra," Charles laughed. "Casey, find us some tunes on the radio."

Casey picked up some rock and roll on a station called B93.7 and went back to programming her cell phone. She already had her best friends on speed dial and most of her other friends phone numbers entered in the address book too.

Highway 11 seemed to go on forever but, eventually, they turned off on a secondary road that was mostly tar and gravel and just barely wide enough for two cars to pass by each other. These back roads were so small that it was pointless for the state to paint a dividing line down the center of the road. Charles slowed the Honda down to a safe speed, cut the A/C off, and rolled the windows down. The deep earthy aroma of forests and fields instantly filled the car. The clouds had burned off by now and the day was simply beautiful. Out here, the houses were few and far between. There were no subdivisions and certainly no shopping centers. They did pass a small country store located in the fork of the road. The store was a small whitewashed clapboard building. The side facing the road was painted red, with Coca-Cola written on it in big white cursive letters. There were two old gas pumps in front of the store, the kind with the crank handles you had to turn to clear the numbers of the last purchase. Several old men were passing time sitting on benches in front of the store. They threw up their hands in a friendly wave as the Honda rolled by. Charles waved back to them.

"Do you know them, Dad?" Casey asked.

"No, honey, I can't say that I do."

"Then why did they wave to you and why did you wave back?"

"That's the way people are out here in the country, Casey. Here comes a car now -- watch."

The car was an old primer-gray Camaro. As it passed by, the driver raised his finger from the steering wheel in a friendly hello and Charles reciprocated with a nod.

"See what I mean?" said Charles.

"That's weird." Casey replied.

"That's country," said Charles, "and here is Grandma and Grandpa's farm."

2 ALDERMAN'S FARM

Charles flipped on his turn signal and eased the Honda into a narrow, unpaved driveway on the right side of the road. The wheels crunched loudly on the gravel as they cruised through a stand of loblolly pines toward a small hill in the distance. When they topped the hill, the driveway continued on through several curves and crossed two old wooden bridges. The bridges were built from big logs and thick planks which were coated with tar. Beneath the bridge, a small stream bubbled merrily along as it wound its way through turkey ferns and mountain laurel. Charles stopped the car on the bridge to let the kids get out and look over the sides for crawdads along the shady banks. When his stomach started growling, he called the kids back to the car and continued down the road. Finally, a meadow emerged on the left and there, on the other side of the pasture, nestled at the foot of a hill crowned with giant oaks, beechnuts, and hickory trees, was Grandpa and Grandma Alderman's house.

The Alderman farm was the kind of farm you would expect to see on a calendar or in one of those country living magazines. The house was a typical two story white farmhouse with wrap-around porches, while the barns were painted dark red and trimmed with white. The main barn was actually bigger than the house and had a cavernous hay loft where Grandpa stored his winter hay for the cows, horses and goats. Ben and Casey had loved to play hide-and-seek there when they were little. The bottom floor of the barn contained a tack room, a feed room, and four stalls. Ben loved the smells of leather, mink oil, and saddle soap that permeated the tack room, and also the sweet smell of molasses coated oats and corn that filled the feed room. On one side of the barn was Grandpa's tool shed, and on the other side was Grandma's chicken house. Her laying hens were Rhode Island Reds and Plymouth Barred Rocks -- the kind that laid big brown eggs with dark yellow yolks. Also, Grandma had a goat house in a small pasture located behind the barn. Although she claimed that goat milk was soothing to her stomach, everyone knew they were her pets.

Charles pulled the Honda around to the side yard where some guineas were scratching in the dust beneath an ancient magnolia. The tree's dark green foliage was ablaze with huge white flowers. The smell, though cloyingly sweet, brought back a nostalgic wave of childhood memories. He eased the car under the shade of the magnolia, switched the ignition off and tooted the horn. A moment later, George and Louise came bustling out of the house to greet them. Louise was a slightly plump and bespectacled lady with a kindly face and gray hair pulled back in a bun. She was wearing an apron which meant that lunch was probably on the table. George was tall and lanky with his face, neck, and forearms tanned a leathery brown from many days in the field. He was wearing what he always wore -- blue denim Kentucky overalls and a John Deer ball cap. Charles had asked him once why he always wore a John Deere ball cap, when he did not own a John Deere tractor and George simply responded that he liked the green and yellow colors. Louise was the first one down the steps, wiping her hands on her apron, as she practically ran to meet them.

"Ben, Casey, give me a hug!" she cried.

Ben and Casey ran into their grandma's open arms while Charles unloaded the luggage from the trunk of the car. George paused to hug the kids too, then helped Charles gather up the luggage.

Inside the house, the aroma of batter fried pork chops and freshly baked biscuits filled the air. "Just leave the suitcases here in the den and we'll unpack later," Louise said. "Let's eat lunch while it's still hot."

After lunch, Louise and the kids unpacked, while Charles helped his dad hook up the mower to his tractor. Ben and Casey were put in the two bedrooms upstairs. The bedrooms faced each other from across a short, narrow hallway and each one had its own bathroom. Ben's room was a hodgepodge of mismatched furniture. There was an old brass bed in the center of the room. On one side of the bed, a small pie safe with punched tin doors served as a nightstand; on the other side, sat a huge rocking chair with thick blue velvet cushions. At the foot of the bed was a large twelve drawer dresser, made of tiger maple, where Ben stored away his clothes. Casey's room had a matching bedroom set that consisted of a sleigh bed, a night stand, a chest of drawers and a small dresser. The set was solid oak, and according to Louise, over one hundred years old.

After unpacking their luggage, the remaining time they had together was spent on the front porch enjoying quiet conversation and the relaxation that always follows a big meal with close family. Louise made a pitcher of lemonade for everyone to enjoy while they passed the time. Charles sat on the old porch swing, with Casey on one side and Ben on the other, his arms around them both. It abruptly dawned on Casey that while this summer would probably not be fun for her, her dad was not looking forward to it either. She began to feel sorry for her dad and suddenly realized how much she was going to miss him. Ben must have been thinking the same thing as they both snuggled closer to him.

George and Louise were sitting in their rocking chairs -- two old ladder back chairs, with rickety cane bottoms that had seen better days. Louise sensed what Ben and Casey were thinking and tried to take their minds off of things by rattling on and on about how much fun they would have over the summer and all of the different things they would do.

"Casey, a new family moved into the old Gibson farm a couple of years ago and they have a daughter your age. Her name is Meg. She's really sweet and I just know you two will get along so well together. We'll go visit real soon so you can meet and get acquainted. And Ben, George tells me the fish are really biting now. He caught a mess of catfish in the pond last week. Eight, wasn't it, dear?"

"Ten!" George shot back. "And I threw three back in."

The pond was a small spring fed pool of water about a hundred yards behind the house. George had built a short dock off the dam and kept it stocked with bream and catfish. Ben loved to fish, but hardly ever got the opportunity, so he was eagerly looking forward to catching a few. Casey was glad to learn of another girl her age living nearby and was eager to meet her. Who knows, maybe she would even have a handsome big brother too.

The afternoon wore on. Soon, Charles stood up and stretched.

"I hate to go guys, but it's time I hit the road. I need to be at the airport at least an hour before my flight leaves."

Everyone stood up with Charles and followed him out to the car. George and Louise hugged him and then stepped back to give the kids some privacy to say their goodbyes. As Charles leaned over, Ben and Casey threw their arms around his neck and squeezed. Charles pulled them close and hugged them tightly.

"I'm going to miss you guys."

"We're going to miss you too, Dad," Casey said.

"A bunch," Ben added, wiping his eyes.

"Listen, you guys will have so much fun here. The summer will be over before you know it. And I'll call you every Monday, Wednesday, and Friday. How's that?"

Ben and Casey nodded.

"Well, I've got to go. You kids behave and don't drive Grandpa and Grandma crazy, okay?"

Ben and Casey nodded again. Charles kissed them both, then got into the car and started the engine. He backed the car up and rolled his window down.

"I love you guys!"

"I love you too, Dad!" Ben and Casey replied in unison.

Charles put the car in drive and slowly pulled off, waving goodbye out the window, as he drove down the driveway. Ben and Casey stood in the yard and waved until the Honda, with a plume of dust behind it, was out of sight. The silence of the afternoon descended like a soft blanket and, a moment later, Louise's hands were on their shoulders.

"What would you two like to do today?" she asked.

"I'm kinda tired," Casey answered.

"Me too," Ben said.

Casey turned and looked up at her grandma. "I think we'd like to bum around in front of the TV for a while… if that's okay. Maybe even take a nap"

"That's just fine, sweet heart. You and Ben run inside and make yourselves right at home. George is getting ready to mow the front pasture and I've got a few chores I need to do out here anyway. Maybe, later, we can all run into town to pick up a few things and get some stuff to make some home-made ice cream. How does that sound?"

"Sounds great, Grandma," Casey smiled. "Come on Ben, race you."

Casey was the first to the door. She always won their races, but Ben never gave up trying to beat her. The television was located in the den, the first room in the house. The den was a comfortable room, not large, not small, but as Goldilocks would have said, "Just right". As you walked in, to the right of the front door, were two oversized leather recliners with an end table and a lamp between them. On the opposite side of the room, was a rock fireplace with a thick wooden beam for a mantle and, to the right of the fireplace, a built-in cabinet, that housed the television. Ben and Casey plopped down into the recliners and turned the TV on. Casey flipped through the channels and eventually settled on Animal Planet reruns of The Crocodile Hunter.

"I'm thirsty," Ben said. "Think Grandma has any sodas in the fridge?"

"Go look," Casey replied, "and bring me one too."

Ben got up and went into the kitchen located in the rear of the house. He opened the refrigerator and found a dozen sodas lined up on the bottom shelf in the door. He retrieved two cans of Pepsi and walked over to the kitchen sink to wash the tops off. This was a habit that annoyed Casey to no end, but Ben would not put his lips to a canned drink until he washed the top. As he reached over to turn the water on, he happened to glance out the window over the sink and saw Louise standing in front of a patch of bamboo that grew at the edge of the back yard. She was looking around as if checking to make sure that no one was watching her. Ben leaned over the sink and peered out the window. He felt as if he was spying on his grandma and a twinge of guilt passed over him. Louise, apparently satisfied that no one was watching her, turned and disappeared into the dark green foliage of the bamboo. A minute passed. Casey yelled from the den.

"Where's my soda?"

"I'll be there in a second," Ben yelled back.

"I hope you're not washing the tops of the cans! That is so lame!"

Another minute passed and Louise emerged from the bamboo patch, brushing her dress off with one hand and checking her hair with the other. She hastily looked around, then hurried off toward the goat house.

Ben watched her leave, then looked at the bamboo and tried to mark the spot where she had gone in. What was she doing in there? Ben knew by the way she was acting she did not want anyone to see her going into the bamboo, so he couldn't ask her. He figured if she did not want anyone to see her going into the bamboo, then she would not want anyone else going into the bamboo either. Curiosity was killing him. He hastily washed the Pepsi cans off and hurried back into the den.

"Did you get lost in there?" Casey asked.

"No," Ben said, "but I did see the strangest thing."

Ben told Casey what he had just witnessed in the back yard. Casey, intrigued by his story, stood up and walked to the front door. She looked through the screen, at the goat house, on the hill behind the barn. The door to the goat house was open. Grandma was probably inside feeding her goats. She'd probably be there for a while, making sure that every goat got some attention.

"Come on," Casey said, "let's check it out. We can be back in five minutes and no one will know."

Ben looked up at the goat house. Again he felt a twinge of guilt, but curiosity won out. "Alright," he said. "Let's go."

They slipped out the screen door, scampered down the front porch steps and tore around the house towards the bamboo patch. The bamboo grew to the edge of the yard and suddenly stopped, as if an invisible barrier prevented it from spreading any further. The canes grew so close together that it seemed impossible for anyone to enter.

"Where did she go in?" Casey asked.

Ben turned toward the house to look at the kitchen window to get his bearings. He moved to the left a little, looked at the bamboo and then back at the house.

"Right here. This is the spot."

"Well, what are you waiting on? Go!"

3 GRANDMA'S SECRET

Ben turned sideways and slipped in between the tall, thick canes. It seemed that the canes only grew close together around the perimeter, as if the bamboo patch were guarding some deep dark secret from prying eyes. When they finally made their way to the interior of the patch, the canes were far enough apart for them to walk around freely. The tops, however, were so dense and full of leaves that not a single ray of sunlight fell onto the thick carpet of leaves beneath their feet. In the very center of the bamboo patch, they discovered a strange looking tree with a thick, twisted trunk and two stubby limbs that looked eerily like arms. The tree had a huge crack in the trunk and appeared to be dead. Ben suspected the bamboo had choked the life from the tree by denying it sunshine and drinking up the rain before it could seep down to the tree's deeper roots.

"You check out this side," said Casey, "and I'll check out the other side. I'm not sure what we are looking for though."

"Anything that's not bamboo," Ben replied over his shoulder, "and snakes."

"Snakes?" Casey asked. "Why are we looking for snakes?"

"So we don't get snake bit, duh!"

Casey punched her brother on the shoulder and then hurried off to explore her side before he could retaliate. Ben made a mental note to punch her later and began poking around on his side of the bamboo. There was nothing obvious inside the patch, so he began walking about slowly while peering into the dimly lit canes for anything out of the ordinary. The canes closer to the outside edge of the patch were dark green in color. The further you came into the patch, the lighter in color they became until, by the time you were in the center, they were a light tan with no trace of green at all. Ben suspected it had something to do with sunlight not being able to penetrate down here. He wondered if the rain could even find its way through the dense canopy overhead. After several minutes of searching and finding nothing, Casey walked up behind him.

"I didn't find anything. How about you?" she asked.

Ben shook his head. "Not even a snake. As a matter of fact, Casey, I haven't seen any bugs. No flies, no mosquitoes, no gnats or spiders. Nothing. I even kicked some leaves around and scratched around in the dirt. There's nothing alive in here."

"This is kinda creepy. What do you think Grandma was doing in here?"

"I don't know," Ben answered. "I don't see anything in here that she could do. There's nothing in here but bamboo. And that dead tree."

"Listen," Casey whispered.

They both stood still for several seconds.

"I don't hear anything," Ben whispered back to Casey.

"That's my point," Casey said. "I don't hear Grandpa's tractor, I don't hear any birds and I don't even hear any leaves rustling in the breeze."

Grandma and Grandpa Alderman's farm was always alive with noise. During the day time, chickens were clucking, ducks were quacking, cows were mooing and goats were bleating. At night time, the frogs in the fish pond

26

would compete with the cicadas and katydids. The frogs always won on sheer volume alone. Ben strained his ears. The silence was deafening.

"You're right," he said. "I don't care what Grandma was doing in here anymore, I just want to leave. This place is giving me the heebie-jeebies."

"Wait," Casey said, "let's check out that tree before we leave. Maybe Grandma hid something in it."

"That's crazy!" Ben exclaimed. "What on earth would Grandma hide in a bamboo patch?"

"I haven't got a clue," Casey answered. "But you're the one that said she was acting suspicious and that's the only place we haven't looked."

The tree was short, the top well below the bamboo roof, but what it lacked in height, it made up for in girth. The dark twisted trunk was split down the center, forming an oddly shaped opening large enough to walk through. Ben and Casey both walked through the opening. Not finding anything out of the ordinary, they decided to leave the bamboo, resolving to keep an eye on their grandmother to see if she ever came back. They also decided to leave the bamboo on the opposite side. Maybe there was nothing in the bamboo after all; maybe their grandma was just going through the bamboo to check on something on the other side? Ben led the way through the canes. Once again, as they drew near to the outside, the canes became closer and Ben and Casey had to twist and turn to slip in between them. Finally, sunlight began to appear between the canes, and with a few more twists and turns, Casey and Ben stumbled out of the patch, into a lush green meadow. The meadow ran up a gentle slope in front of them, to a thick stand of pines on a hilltop, and seemed to encircle the bamboo patch, stretching around to the right and left.

"It seems brighter on this side," Ben remarked while shading his eyes.

"It just seems brighter because it was so dark inside the bamboo," Casey told him.

"No, it's definitely brighter. Look down at your shadow. It's shorter now and it's pointing in a different direction than it was before we went into the bamboo."

"That's crazy. You're just disoriented."

Casey was feeling edgy now. She didn't remember which way her shadow was pointing before they went into the bamboo patch, but doggone, it did seem shorter. A cold shiver ran up her spine and goose flesh prickled her arms. Suddenly, she wanted to be back inside Grandma and Grandpa's cozy little den, sitting in a recliner, sipping on a cold Pepsi and watching TV.

"There's nothing here, so let's get moving. You go that way," Casey said pointing to her left, "and I'll go this way. That way we will have covered the whole patch. See you back in the yard."

Ben nodded, turned, and began walking. Casey watched him for a few seconds before she turned and started walking in the other direction. Something just didn't feel right. The bamboo patch grew on the edge of the woods that surrounded Grandpa and Grandma's back yard. Grandpa did have a small pasture in the woods behind the bamboo and there were usually several cows grazing in the pasture. But here, there was no fence behind the bamboo to keep the cows contained and this was no small pasture. Behind her, where there should have been tall hardwood trees, the meadow stretched out to the horizon like a great sea of green and gold. In the far distance in front of her, the meadow disappeared into some rocky foothills that led to towering snow capped mountains. That should be the Blue Ridge Mountains, but Casey knew that was not the Blue Ridge in front of her. The Blue Ridge Mountains were not tall like these and there was never snow this far south in May, not even on the highest peaks. Panic began to overtake her and she started to run. She yelled over her shoulder to her brother, "Hurry, Ben!"

Ben picked up his pace and glanced over his shoulder. Casey was already turning the corner and disappearing from sight. He wasn't sure but it looked like she was running. Anyway, now that he could no longer see her he began to jog. While he was trotting along the edge of the bamboo he scanned the meadow to his right. Where were the woods? He should have come upon them by now.

A few years ago, when Ben was only six years old, he got separated from his mother when they were doing some Christmas shopping in a large mall down in Atlanta. Ben never forgot that hopeless feeling of being lost; completely and utterly lost. That feeling began to creep up on him again as he remembered the despair he felt when he realized his mother was not anywhere around. He remembered the terror he felt when he imagined, in his six year old brain, that he would never see his home again. That same terror began to come upon him now and he started running faster as he turned another corner. Still no sign of Grandpa and Grandma's woods. He should be in the yard by now. Looking over his shoulder, in the grip of a full-fledge panic, Ben was practically flying through the tall grass. And so was Casey, when they collided together and collapsed in a tangled heap in the warm noon sunshine.

"Did you find the house?" they both asked at the same time.

"No," Ben said.

Casey stared at Ben with wide eyes.

"What's going on here?" Ben asked with a trembling voice.

"I don't know. But I do know we're not on Grandpa and Grandma's farm anymore."

"Well, where are we? And how did we get here? And how do we get back?" Ben asked, his voice rising with each question.

"Shut up and let me think!" Casey yelled.

Ben stood up and, shading his eyes from the bright sunshine, began a thorough search of the meadow, while Casey remained seated on the ground, her head in her hands, thinking. Suddenly, she looked up.

"You saw Grandma go into the bamboo, right?"

Ben nodded.

"And you saw her come out, right?"

Then it dawned on Ben. The bamboo! He did not have a clue where they were, but Grandma had been here. He was sure of it. She had come here through the bamboo, and then returned to the farm through the bamboo.

"Let's go!" Ben cried, as he made a dash for the bamboo. He only made it a few steps though because Casey dashed after him, grabbing him by the legs and tackling him to the ground.

Ben struggled to loosen himself and he even tried to kick his sister to get free, but she held on tight and would not let him go.

"Wait," Casey cried, "stop fighting and listen to me. I think we should go back into the bamboo at the same place we came out. What if we go in on this side and come out in a different place altogether?"

Ben stopped struggling as Casey's words sank in and reason began to return. "Yeah, you're right. Now let me go and let's get moving."

Casey released her brother and helped him to his feet. They brushed themselves off and set out to the other side of the bamboo patch at a brisk walk, both secretly afraid that running would bring the fear and panic back upon them. Soon they rounded the corner and the tall green pines on the hilltop sprang into view, soaring up into an impossibly blue sky. Luckily for them the bamboo grew on the edge of the meadow and the pine clad hilltop offered them a point of orientation. They walked to the spot where they thought they had come out.

"Is this it?"

"Yeah, I think so."

"But what if we are wrong?"

Ben looked at his sister. "So, what if we are wrong. We can't stay here for Pete's sake!"

Then a deep voice ripped through the quietness and shattered the serenity of the meadow like the first thunder clap of a sudden spring storm. "Hey! What are you doing? Get away from that bamboo!"

Ben and Casey both jumped and spun around, their hearts pounding. At the top of the hill a huge hairy man had emerged from the pines and was running toward them. Ben's first thought was Big Foot was upon them. Then, he saw the man was draped in furs and waving a giant club over his head. Long wild hair and a beard flowed over his shoulders as he ran toward them and his eyes were so wide that Ben could see the whites, even at this distance. Ben's feet were rooted to the ground in fear. He couldn't move. Then Casey screamed and Ben's paralysis broke. He grabbed his sister by the arm and together they plunged into the bamboo. They plowed through the thick canes, into the center of the patch and, once again, darkness and silence descended upon them.

"This way," Ben yelled, still clutching Casey's arm. They crossed the center of the patch and plunged into the thick canes around the perimeter. A few seconds later, they tumbled out of the patch, back into the meadow on the other side. Grandma and Grandpa's house was no where to be found. They sat there in stunned silence and then suddenly it dawned on Ben.

"The tree," he yelled as he grabbed his sister's hand.

Both kids scrambled to their feet and wormed their way back into the patch. Once in the center they could here the giant man searching for them, bellowing like a crazed beast, pulling down canes and making his way slowly and steadily toward them.

"Hurry," Casey whimpered.

The two kids, still holding hands, raced through the opening in the dead tree. As soon as they were out the other side the sudden silence should have alerted them that they were back on the Alderman farm, but the kids were too terrified to notice. Back into the canes they dashed, scratching and clawing their way through until they burst out into Grandpa and Grandma's back yard. Casey looked up at the goat house. The door was still open and she could hear Grandpa's tractor rumbling in the distance too.

"Come on, let's get inside."

They hurried across the yard, up the steps and back into the house. Casey plopped into a recliner and grabbed her soda off of the end table, while Ben ran into the kitchen to look out the window. He wanted to make sure that the crazy man didn't come through the bamboo after them, waving his club and looking for two plump little children to eat for supper. He watched the patch closely for several minutes, then returned to the den. Casey was standing now and looking out of the screen door. Ben walked up behind her and laid his hand on her shoulder. Casey let out a squeal of fright and spun around.

"Don't sneak up on me like that!" she cried.

"Sorry," Ben said, "we need to talk though and we need to pull ourselves together before Grandpa and Grandma get back."

Casey sat back down in one of the recliners and Ben sat in the other one.

"What just happened out there?"

Ben pushed his glasses back up on his nose and cupped his chin in his hands. This is what he always did when he was thinking. After a couple of minutes he sat up and looked over at his sister. "I think we went through some kind of portal to a parallel universe."

Casey stared at him for several seconds, not believing what he had just said. "That's the craziest thing I've ever heard. There are no such things as portals and parallel universes. You've been reading too many science fiction stories and watching too much TV."

Ben stood, angry at his sister now, and planted his hands on his hips. "You asked me what I thought and I told you. If you have any better ideas, let's hear them!"

"I'm sorry," Casey apologized. "But we were in a different place, weren't we? Could it really be true? I think it would be easier for me to swallow if it was a portal to a different place here on Earth, and not some other world, in some other universe."

Ben sat back down, his anger vanishing as quickly as it arose. "I don't know. I'm just guessing, but, yeah, we were definitely in a different place. Maybe it was even a different place here on Earth, just like you said. But what I want to know is, what was Grandma doing there? Should we ask her? I mean, I think we need to say something. What if she goes back there and that crazy man gets her?"

"Yeah, you're right," Casey said, "we've got to say something. Let's wait until later though. Grandma said she would take us into town to get some stuff to make ice cream. We'll ask her then. Maybe Grandpa doesn't know about the tree inside the bamboo."

"Maybe Grandpa does know about the tree and maybe Grandma is not supposed to go in the bamboo?" Ben countered.

"Who knows? But we are going to find out. Look, here comes Grandma now."

4 THE CONFRONTATION

Ben and Casey straightened their clothes, tried to look relaxed and somewhat interested in what was on TV. They heard their Grandma come up the steps and, a moment later, she bustled through the screen door smiling.

"Tomorrow, I want you two to come up to the goat house and see my new babies. I've got two new little goats. They were born last week. These are Annabel's first kids. Usually they only have one baby the first time, but she delivered two and they are so precious."

Louise had fifteen goats and every one of them had a name. She would keep the babies until they were old enough to wean from their mothers and then take them to the flea market to sell. The flea market, or the Jockey Lot as all the locals called it, was a crazy maze of pole buildings with tin roofs located a couple of miles outside of town, on a long flat stretch of land, beside the Twelve Mile River. In the center of the market, you could find people selling pigs, chickens, turkeys, ducks, geese, goats, kittens, and puppies. The crazy thing about the Jockey Lot was that it was only open on Wednesday mornings. And, every Wednesday morning, it was jammed packed with people buying and selling. And then by lunch time, it would all be over.

"We'll have to go see them when we get back from the Jockey Lot, though. Tomorrow's Wednesday, you know," said Louise, with a wink. "Let me wash up and change clothes, then we'll head to town. You guys like strawberry ice cream?"

Ben and Casey nodded. "Strawberry is my favorite," Casey replied with a smile.

"Wonderful," said Louise. "I'll just be a minute, then we'll be on our way." As soon as their grandma disappeared into the back of the house, Ben leaned over and whispered to Casey, "Do we talk to her on the way there or on the way back?"

"Let's wait until we are on the way back," Casey said.

"Yeah, that's what I was thinking. Let's wait until we've already got the stuff to make the ice cream before we hit her up with some questions."

The 'town,' where they were going, was only five or six minutes away from the farm. The name of the town was Pickens, named after the famous revolutionary war hero, General Andrew Pickens. The town was originally located on the Keowee River, but after the Civil War, when the Pickens district was split into counties, the town was pulled down and physically moved to its current site. Main Street had four lanes lined with old two story brick buildings. Most of the oldest buildings had been renovated and were now occupied by attorneys or quaint little antique shops. Though, some of the businesses had been there for years. There was the West Main Barber Shop, that was owned and operated by Sam Carter and George Albertson, both of whom had been cutting hair for over thirty years now. And there was Burdett's Hardware, where you could still buy wood burning cook stoves and tin wash boards. Although a small town, Pickens had two supermarkets for your grocery shopping convenience. Today, however, they were not going to either of the supermarkets. As a matter of fact, Louise had told them she never went to the supermarkets. They were too big and it was hard to find what you were looking for. Since most of what they ate came from their own farm, Louise shopped at a place located on the outskirts of town called The Community Grocery. The store was established in 1911 and Louise had been buying things, like coffee and sugar, here for as long as she could remember.

When Louise arrived at the grocery, she crept to the front of the small parking lot and eased her old Galaxy 500 into an open space, near the store's entrance. The grocery store looked like a building that belonged on Main Street in some western town, like Dodge City. The store front was a tall gray clapboard structure, with a tin awning that overhung a wooden boardwalk. The double doors leading into the building were propped open on the inside, and identical screen doors, with Sunbeam Bread labels painted on the screens, kept the flies at bay. With hardwood floors beneath their feet and the punched tin ceiling over their head, Ben felt as if he had just stepped backward in time. Louise introduced Ben and Casey to Mr. Evatt, the grocer. He was a tall thin man, with balding hair and spectacles and a friendly smile. Then, she pulled a list from her purse and handed it to him and Ben and Casey set off to explore the store while he filled the order. Fifteen minutes later, they were pulling out of the parking lot with a box of Morton Rock Salt, a couple of cans of Carnation Condensed Milk, and a bag of fresh peaches and strawberries stowed safely in the back seat. All three of them were sitting in the front seat. Ben had called shotgun on the way to the store, so Casey had it on the way home. That was one of the unspoken rules of shotgun – you could never have the window seat both going and coming. Ben, sitting between his grandma and his sister, was looking forward to home made ice cream so much, that he momentarily forgot about their scary adventure earlier today. Or at least until Casey poked him in the side. Louise had been rattling on about the proper way to make home-made ice cream and about how George always had to have strawberry ice cream any time they made it. Casey wanted to ask her now, before she got off on another subject and another story.

"Grandma," Casey prompted.

"Yes, dear?" Louise replied.

Casey swallowed the lump in her throat. "Ben and I did some exploring this afternoon while you were up at the goat house. We went into the bamboo patch behind the house."

"Well, why on earth did you do that child? I've been after your Grandpa to cut that nasty old patch down for years. It's nothing but a breeding ground for snakes. George says we've got to have it for the chickens though. He says it gives them a place to hide from hawks and owls."

Ben and Casey watched her closely. She was smiling, looking straight ahead, eyes on the road.

Boy, she's good, Ben thought. Let's drop a bomb on her now and see what she does.

"Grandma," Ben said, "there's a funny looking tree in that bamboo patch; a dead tree with a big hole right through the center. The hole is big enough to walk through."

Louise's smile faltered for just a moment. "Hmmm. Do you mind telling me what you were doing in the bamboo? Of all the places on this farm to explore, I can't imagine why you would ever want to go inside of that nasty, old, bug infested bamboo patch."

"Well, I saw you go in," Ben told her, "and I wanted to find out what you were doing in there."

"Were you spying on me, Benjamin Alderman?" Louise asked.

"Oh no, I wasn't spying on you Grandma, I promise."

Whenever someone called him Benjamin that usually meant he was in trouble. Whenever someone called him Benjamin and used his last name, that meant serious trouble.

"You see," Ben explained, "I had gone into the kitchen to get me and Casey a soda and whenever I drink a soda from a can I wash the top of the can first; and that's what I was doing when I saw you go into the bamboo. I was just washing the tops of the cans at the kitchen sink… and so we were just curious, that's all."

Louise's smiled was completely gone now and her knuckles were white on the steering wheel.

"Grandma," Casey said, "there's more to the story than that. We went through the hole in the tree. We know."

Louise flipped on her turn signal and veered off into a roadside parking lot of a small Baptist church. She drove to the rear of the parking lot and parked the car under one of the sodium arc lamps that illuminated the lot at night with an eerie orange glow. The lamp had just come on, and when Louise switched the engine off, they could hear the light on the tall wooden pole humming as it slowly came to life in the gray evening twilight. Louise stared straight ahead and no one spoke for several seconds. Then, she turned in her seat to look at her grandkids.

"I am going to tell you what happened to you today and then you are going to promise me that you will never, ever go back into that bamboo. Okay?"

Ben and Casey nodded.

"The bamboo patch was there when we first moved in back in, oh… 1948. We didn't know anything about it; it was just a bamboo patch. We cut a few canes off the edge to make fishing poles and tomato stakes every summer, but we never went into the patch. Not until the summer of 1957. I remember it like it was yesterday. It was June, hot and humid. It must have been ninety-five degrees in the shade that day. I had a hen, setting on a nest of eggs, somewhere inside the bamboo patch. I wanted to catch the little dibbies when they hatched and put them in a brooder, because we had been having trouble with foxes eating them before they were old enough to fly to roost. Anyway, I worked my way into the bamboo. It took me a while to get in there. It was almost like the bamboo was trying to keep me out."

"I know what you mean," said Casey. Ben nodded in agreement.

"Well, I finally got into the center of the patch and it opened up in there enough so I could move around.   I searched for that chicken's nest all over the center of that patch, but I couldn't find it. And, I guess at some point during my search, I had walked through the Merlin Tree because when I came out of the bamboo, I was in Camelot."

"A Merlin Tree?" Casey asked, "Camelot?"

"Yes," Louise answered. "The tree is named after Merlin, a powerful wizard who conjured it. It is the opening of a pathway between Earth and Camelot, a world he discovered and named after a valley, where he lived on his home world of Zorn."

"Merlin and Camelot!" Casey exclaimed. "Like King Authur's Merlin and Camelot?"

"Wait a minute," Ben interrupted. "If Merlin's home world is Zorn, and Merlin discovered Camelot, then why is the Merlin Tree here on Earth?"

"There have been five Merlin Trees on Camelot," Louise answered. "The first tree was the original one that connected Camelot to Zorn, the wizard's home world. Later, the Earth Tree, the Faerie Tree, and the Crag Tree were created. The Zorn Tree and the Crag Tree have since been destroyed, so there are only three left."

Ben and Casey stared at Louise with puzzled expressions.

"Faerie and Crag are the home world of elves and dwarves," Louise explained.

The kids continued to stare at their grandmother, though now, as if she'd lost her mind.

"Listen, I'll explain all of this tomorrow in great detail. We'll hit the Jockey Lot early and then go to Mario's for lunch. We'll order one of their big greasy pepperoni pizzas, I'll tell you everything I know, and then we are going to lay down some ground rules for your stay here over the summer."

"Grandma, you said there are only three trees left," Ben noted, "but you've only named two. What's the third tree?"

Louise turned away from the children and stared out the window, across the empty parking lot. It was several seconds before she answered.

"That would be the Pluton Tree," she replied, turning back to the kids. "Do not ask me anything about it. Now, before we leave, tell me what happened while you were in Camelot."

Both kids began talking at once. Louise held up her hand and pointed to Casey. Ben glared at his sister, but respectfully sat back while Casey told about their brief visit and the crazy man who chased them back into the bamboo. They learned that the crazy man was named Amos and that he was not crazy at all. As a matter of fact, he happened to be very good friends with their Grandma. They also learned that he was the guardian of the Earth Tree, and that was the reason he was chasing them.

"Next time I'm there I'll tell Amos what happened. Right now let's get home and make some ice cream before your Grandpa comes looking for us. And speaking of your Grandpa, DO NOT mention any of this to George, okay?"

"What would we say anyway?" Ben asked, "Hey Grandpa, did you know that Grandma has been traveling through a wormhole, created by a wizard named Merlin, to another world called Camelot, behind your back?"

Louise stared at Ben for a few seconds, trying to look stern and serious. Then Casey, trying her best not to laugh, snickered and Louise's countenance cracked. Everyone felt the stress and tension melt away as they began to howl with laughter.

The peach ice cream was the best Ben ever had. George and Louise had finally upgraded to an electric churn and they all sat on the front porch watching the fireflies twinkle in the pasture, while the churn was freezing up a batch of strawberry. When the strawberry ice cream was ready, everyone ate a bowlful. Louise took the rest inside to put in the freezer for later. George stood and stretched.

"It's way past my bedtime. You kids going to the Jockey Lot tomorrow?"

"Yes," said Casey. "I'm really looking forward to it."

"Well, you'd better hit the hay too. Your Grandma likes to get there early."

Ben and Casey gave their Grandpa a hug and headed upstairs to their bedrooms. A few minutes later, Louise came upstairs to tuck them in and kiss them goodnight. Ben snuggled into the freshly washed, sun dried sheets. After all the excitement that happened today, with a portal to another world just a stones throw away, Ben did not think he would ever be able to go to sleep. But as he lay there in bed, with his imagination in overdrive, a cool night breeze danced with the curtains and tickled his back, and the insects in the fresh mown pastures serenaded him into a deep, peaceful sleep.

5 WEDNESDAY MORNING FLEA MARKET

It seemed to Ben that he had just laid down his head on his pillow and then his Grandma was shaking him, trying to wake him up. He opened his eyes a crack, against the light from the hallway and turned to look out the window. It was still dark. Why was Grandma waking him up in the middle of the night?

"Come on, sleepy head. If we don't hurry we'll miss all of the bargains," Louise whispered.

Ben looked at his watch and pressed the little wind-up button. The face lit up a pale greenish-blue to reveal that it was 5:30 AM.

"Grandma, do we have to go so early?" Ben groaned.

"Yes, dear. If we're not there by seven, we'll have a hard time finding a parking place and all of the good stuff will be picked over. You can stay here if you'd like, but remember, we promised to have that talk today over some pizza at lunch. Of course, Casey is going. I suppose I could just have that talk with her and then she could fill you in when we get back. George is going to be mucking out the stalls today too. You could stay here and help him; I'm sure he'd appreciate it."

Ben threw the covers off and hopped out of bed. "No, I'm fine. I think I'd rather go to the Jockey Lot instead of shoveling horse poop. Besides, I want to hear your story firsthand."

Louise smiled and patted him on the head. "Hurry and get dressed. We'll eat a bite of breakfast before we leave."

They pulled into the Jockey Lot at 6:30 AM. Ben and Casey were absolutely amazed at the size of the crowd this early in the morning. The highway ran parallel to the river and the buildings followed alongside the river, with the parking area between the buildings and the road.

Even at this early hour, the closest parking space they could find was three rows from the rear of the parking lot. The Jockey Lot itself did not have any sort of defined entrance. The buildings were just pole sheds with tin roofs, so you could walk 'into' the Jockey Lot from anywhere.

They walked the outer perimeter first and worked their way inward. Casey found a vendor selling name brand knock-offs and bought a tee shirt, while Ben found a table full of used Play Station games, five dollars per game or three games for twelve. He started to buy one, but changed his mind and put it back.

Eventually, they made it to the center of the complex, where Louise began looking at chickens and goats. Casey worried she might actually buy one and she or Ben would have to hold it in the car on the way home, but luckily, Louise did not see anything that caught her eye.

Time flew by quickly and by nine-thirty the crowd was already noticeably thinner. They had covered the main area under the buildings. Now they were making their rounds through the parking area where a lot of people sold stuff right out of the trunk of their car, or the back of their truck. Louise had been looking at jewelry all morning and finally bought two necklaces from an oriental lady, after several minutes of intense haggling. By eleven, they were back in the car and heading into town for lunch.

Mario's Pizza was located in a building that used to be a Bantam Chef restaurant on the west end of Main Street. The original building did not have any seating. You ordered your food at a window on the left side of the building, then walked over to the right side of the building to pay for it and pick it up. When you got your food, you went home to eat it.

When the Bantam Chef went out of business, Mario bought the facility and enlarged the structure, so there would be seating for his customers. To create an Italian restaurant atmosphere, Mario installed booths under arbors bearing plastic grapes and painted a country side mural on the wall that divided the kitchen from the seating area. All of that aside, Mario did have some totally awesome pizza. Louise directed them to a booth in the back corner, and as soon as they were seated, a waitress was there to get their drink orders. Everyone requested Cokes, and when the waitress returned with their drinks, Louise ordered a large pepperoni and sausage pizza.

"Okay, Grandma," said Casey, "Tell us some more about Camelot and what you are doing there?"

Louise sipped her cola and dabbed her lips with her napkin. "I'm going to start with the story of Zorn first. Zorn was the home world of wizards. It was a dying world where the polar icecaps were melting and the sea levels were rising."

"You mean they had global warming in Zorn too?" Ben asked.

"Yes, it appears so," Louise answered. "Anyhow, all of Zorn's inhabitants had some inherent magical talents and those with the most powerful magic were called wizards."

Louise paused once more to sip her cola and then continued, "Zorn was governed by a council of twelve wizards; one from each district on the last remaining continent on Zorn. On this world, wizards used magical tunnels called pathways to travel to and fro about their world. One of the wizards on the council, an eccentric old man by the name of Merlin, used an ancient and powerful magic on these tunnels to probe for worlds that existed in other planes of existence. The first world he discovered he named Camelot, and to the wizards delight, Camelot was a beautiful, uninhabited world that was strong in magic. Many of the creatures from Zorn, not native to Camelot, were brought there and a great city named New Zorn was constructed. Soon the wizards at New Zorn, eager to complete their perfect utopia, began probing with their tunnels for other worlds, searching for intelligent life. Eventually, tunnels were established to Faerie, Crag, and Earth."

"The elves and dwarves home worlds!" said Casey.

"Tell us about them too!" Ben exclaimed, sliding up to the edge of the booth and leaning across the table.

"Faerie was another beautiful world, rich in magic, and inhabited by elves. When the wizards made contact with the elves and invited them to Camelot, the elves eagerly accepted their invitation."

"What do the elves and dwarves look like, Grandma?" Casey interrupted.

"And how were the wizards able to communicate with them?" Ben added. "Did they all speak the same language? What language do they speak?"

"The elves are tall and very beautiful. Dangerous, too. They all have fair skin, black hair and piercing blue eyes. The dwarves are short, stocky, and very powerful. Their beards are their pride and usually, a dwarf's rank and importance is reflected by the length of his beard. Most dwarves have nasty tempers too, but deep down they are good creatures. As far as language goes, they speak the same language as you and I."

Ben pushed his glasses up on his nose and wrinkled his forehead. "I wonder if we brought the language to them, or if they brought it to us?"

"What about Crag?" Casey asked. "Finish your story."

"Crag was a primitive and primordial world, ruled by dragons and other fierce magical creatures. The dwarves lived there, deep under the rocky mountains, and seldom came to the surface. The wizards, however, did manage to locate the dwarves. They welcomed them to Camelot as well. The dwarves accepted their invitation and, as soon as they arrived in Camelot, sought out the nearest mountain range and started digging new homes deep into the mountain sides. And last of all, Earth. Earth was the most primitive world and had no magic what-so-ever. The wizards felt pity for the humans they found and brought many of them back to Camelot to teach and instruct. After a short time, the humans began to view the wizards as overlords. They soon rejected the wizards and began to build their own cities to govern themselves."

"It sounds like things didn't work out the way they had planned," Casey noted.

"No, they didn't. And as time passed, it became evident to the wizards their Utopia would never come to fruition. The elves, using their own magic, had conjured a magical forest they called the Twilight. Here, they withdrew from the other races of Camelot and seldom left the confines of their forest. The dwarves and humans warred with each other constantly and the humans even warred among themselves."

"What did the wizards do?"

Lousie studied her two grandchildren for a moment, a thoughtful expression on her face. "Let's stop the story about the wizards there and let me finish telling about Camelot, okay?"

"Sure," Casey replied. Ben just nodded in wide-eyed agreement, still on the edge of his seat.

"Camelot is very much like our world on the surface. The sky is blue, there is a sun, a moon, and stars - the same stars we have it seems."

"Well, it can't be another world in another part of the solar system or the stars would be different," said Ben. "It must be a parallel universe, a parallel world."

"I wouldn't know anything about that, Ben. But as I was saying, on the surface it appears to be just like Earth. There are plants and animals just like we have - roses, dandelions, pine trees, horses, cows, dogs, and people. Camelot is not a technically advanced world, though. There is no electricity there. It is more like our world was five hundred years ago. But with magic. All kinds of magic. And I'm not just talking about magic like witches and wizards, although those do exist. There are magical plants, magical animals, and magical beings. A lot of the things we have heard of in legend and folklore here in our world, exists in Camelot. There are dragons, unicorns, gnomes, ogres, trolls, fairies and more. It can be an extremely dangerous place and that's why I do not want you kids going there anymore."

"Okay," said Ben, "but if it is so dangerous, why are you going there?"

"That's a bit complicated," Louise answered. "Let's just say for now, that there are some very important things that need to be looked into. Things that may have an impact on our lives in our world."

"Does Grandpa mind you going there?"

"George doesn't know about Camelot. If he knew about it, he would think it was the Devil's work, or something silly like that, and burn the bamboo patch and the Merlin Tree down to the ground."

"How do you go there without him knowing?" Casey asked.

"It seems that when you are in Camelot, no matter how long you stay in Camelot, when you return to this world the only time that has elapsed is the amount of time you were in the bamboo on this side. Yesterday, Ben, when you saw me go into the bamboo, how long was I in there?"

"I don't know. Two or three minutes maybe."

"Well, I was in Camelot for two hours."

Ben and Casey stared at Louise with open mouths.

"Holy cow!" Ben exclaimed. "What would happen if you went into Camelot and never came back?"

"Yeah," said Casey, "What would happen if someone from our world died over there?"

Louise took another sip from her Coke and dabbed her mouth with her napkin again. "I'm not sure. I've often thought about that and it doesn't make any sense to me. The longest amount of time I've ever spent in Camelot is three weeks. I even had an accident there that produced a nasty cut on my arm. But when I came back though the Merlin Tree to our world, I returned at the same time I had left, and the cut I had on my arm had even disappeared."

"If you stay in Camelot for a year and come back, when you go back to Camelot do you go back to the age you were the last time you were there?" Ben asked.

"No, it's like starting over each time you go in."

"So the cut on your arm would not have come back, if you went back in that time you had your accident?"

"No, it seems that anything physical that happens to you while you are over there gets 'erased' when you return here. Like I said, it doesn't make any sense to me. I suppose if someone died in Camelot, they would be dead here too. What I mean is, if I died in Camelot and you brought me back through the Merlin Tree, I would still be dead here too. I don't think death can be erased."

"What do you mean by anything 'physical'," Casey asked.

"Well, your memory obviously doesn't get erased so you could very well be emotionally traumatized if something bad happened to you or someone you loved. I'm not certain, but I believe magical spells can be carried through to our world too."

"What makes you think that?"

"I can't say right now, but that's one of the important things I mentioned I am looking into."

"Grandma," Ben interrupted, "You went into Camelot yesterday. If you waited a year before you went back, how much time would have passed in Camelot since your last visit?"

"If I wait a year before I go back, the exact amount of time that has passed here since my last visit is the same amount of time that will have passed there."

Ben scratched his head. "You're right, Grandma. It doesn't make any sense at all."

At that moment, the waitress appeared with the biggest, greasiest, cheesiest pizza Ben had ever seen. The question and answer session was over. All three of them attacked the pizza with a vengeance. When they finished, Louise left the waitress a tip and the three of them walked out of the cool, dim restaurant, into the bright and hot May sunshine. As they were walking across the parking lot, Ben tugged on his Grandma's sleeve.

"Grandma, do you think you could take us to Camelot and show us around one day? I'd love to see a unicorn or a dragon."

"Unicorns are very, very rare and there is actually only one dragon in Camelot," said Louise as she rummaged in her purse for her car keys, "but that is another story."

"Well, I still want to go. Don't you, Casey?"

Casey shook her head. "No. Well, yes, but only if Grandma will take us."

Louise found her car keys, unlocked the car and slid in. The Galaxy did not have electric locks, so she had to slide across the seat to unlock the passenger door. Ben and Casey hopped in and buckled their seatbelts while Louise turned the key in the ignition. The old car protested laboriously, but finally roared to life and, with a puff of blue smoke, they pulled out of the parking lot onto Main Street.

"Well?" Ben asked.

"Well, what?" Louise replied.

"Will you take us to Camelot and show us around a little?"

Louise drove on for a few minutes in silence, then finally spoke to her grandkids in a quiet voice. "Remember how I said there were magical beings in Camelot? What would happen if you kids went there and were captured by gnomes? I'll tell you what would happen. They would take you both to the slave mines and you would spend the rest of your lives digging in the dark with dull pick axes and shovels. What would happen if an ogre caught you? He would eat you both, right on the spot. It's a very, very dangerous place."

Casey turned white, but Ben just pushed his glasses up on his nose and scrunched his brow up. "Grandma, you went in yesterday. You said that when you go back, the same amount of time will have passed in Camelot that has passed here. So what if we went in today and we stayed for ten years and then you came in right after us? How could ten years go by for us, over there, and only one day go by for you?"

Now it was Louise's turn to scrunch up her brow. She drummed her fingers on the steering wheel as she drove. "Wow, Ben. I've never even considered that."

"Well, I've got an idea," Ben said. "If it is a parallel universe then, maybe, there is more than one."

"What do you mean by that?" Casey asked.

"Here's what I think. If I went through today and stayed over there for ten years, and then you came through a couple of minutes behind me, I would be in Camelot in one universe, where ten years has elapsed, and you would be in Camelot in a different universe where one day has elapsed. In other words, we would never be in Camelot together unless we entered at the same time."

"Okay," said Louise, "but let's take this one step further. Let's say you were there ten years and then you come back and we go in together - which universe do we go into? The one you were in last, or the one I was in last?"

"My guess is we would always go to the newest. So, to answer your question, we would probably go back to the universe you came out of. Why don't we find out? Do a little experiment? Besides, I really want to see this place."

By now they were back at the farm. Louise turned into the driveway and put the car into park. "Okay. Here's the deal. George is taking some cows to the sale in Anderson this Saturday. He'll leave early and come back late. We'll do our little experiment when he leaves. Until then, I do not want to see you kids go anywhere near that bamboo. Deal?"

"Deal!" said Ben.

"Deal," said Casey.

Louise put the car in drive and proceeded up the driveway. "Now it's time for me to show you my new little babies," she said with a smile.

6 JOEY AND MEG

All of the goats came running to the gate when they heard Louise's old car, rumbling up the driveway. She parked the car under the big magnolia, beside the house, to help keep the interior cool. They did not have an attached garage, just a metal carport and George always kept his hay rake and baler parked in there. As soon as Louise got out of the car, all of the goats began bleating. They knew it was petting time and, more importantly, feeding time. Ben and Casey followed their Grandma over to the woven wire fence, where she cracked the gate open just wide enough for all of them to slip through. As they walked up the hill to the goat house, the little goats were running and prancing all around them. Some of them would shake their heads, some would sprint around in circles, and some would leap high into the air, kicking their feet out to the side. It was as if they all were saying, "Look at me! Look at me!" Louise stopped at the goat house and, paused a moment, to pet all the little goats clamoring for her attention. Then she opened the door and motioned Ben and Casey inside, while all of the goats scrambled around to the other side of the building.

"Where are they going in such a hurry?" asked Ben.

"They are going around to the stall door to wait for me to let them inside. I feed them in here."

The interior of the goat house was surprisingly cool, for such a hot day. The building was divided into two sections. The section they were in had a wooden floor made of wide, rough cut planks. There were bales of fresh green hay stacked in the corner and, beside the hay, a large metal barrel full of corn, oats, and molasses. The partition that divided the building was a half wall, about four feet high. In the center of this wall, was a narrow door that allowed access to the other side, where a low manger ran the length of the wall on the left, and a hay rack transversed the wall on the right. The floor on this side was covered with fresh wood shavings, and in the center of the floor, stood a little black goat with a swish of white hair on the top of her head. Laying in the shavings beside her, were two tiny baby goats, both coal black. Casey took one look at the baby goats and squealed with delight.

"Oh, Grandma, they are so precious! Can I hold one?"

"Me too!" Ben chimed in.

"Absolutely," said Louise, "this is what I brought you up here to see. Just be gentle with them."

Ben and Casey opened the stall door, and crept up to the little goats. They eased down into the soft shavings and, very carefully, scooped them up into their arms.

"Have you named them yet?" Casey asked.

"No, I figured I'd let you two name them."

"How can we tell them apart? They look identical."

"One of them is a billy goat and the other one is a nanny."

"So what does that mean?"

Ben looked up at his Grandma and rolled his eyes. "Great day, Casey, don't you know anything? It means that one of them is a boy and one of them is a girl."

"Oh," said Casey. "Well, I want the little girl. And I'm going to name her Tinkerbell and call her Tink."

Ben rolled his eyes again and Louise laughed.

"Well, I'm going to name my goat Arnold."

"Arnold?" Casey asked.

"Yes, Arnold. He's going to be Arnold, the goatinator - the biggest, baddest goat in town."

"That is so lame!"

"Not as lame as Tinkerbell!"

"Kids, kids!" Louise interrupted, "they are both fine names. Arnold and Tink. Now, no more arguing. Let's head back down to the house so you two can wash up. I've got some work to do in the garden first and then later on, after I've cleaned up too, we'll go visit the Langston's. They actually live within walking distance so, if you two hit it off with Joey and Meg, you can spend a lot of time with them this summer."

"Who is Joey?" Casey asked, with sudden interest.

"Joey," Louise replied, "is Meg's older brother."

"How old is he?"

"He's a couple of years older than you, dear. A very sweet young man, and handsome too."

Casey got a far away look in her eyes and Ben, knowing what she was thinking, playfully poked her in the side.

"Are we walking over there?" Ben asked, as Casey, not so playfully, punched him in the arm.

"Lord, no. I meant that it was walking distance for two children, not for an old Grandma. We'll drive over there this evening, when it's a little cooler."

Louise dug a plastic scoop out of the metal barrel and filled a bucket to the top with sweet feed. She took the feed into the stall and spread it from one end of the long manger to the other, so that all of the goats could have some. Then, she gathered up several bats of hay to place in the hay rack and added some fresh water to the pail beside the door. Satisfied that everything was in order, she opened the stall door to let the rest of the goats inside, and they all scrambled to the manger for the tasty oats and corn.

"They won't hurt the babies?" Casey asked.

"No, sweetie, the babies are fine. I keep them in here with the door closed, so that nothing else can harm them."

"Like what?"

"Wild dogs and coyotes, mostly."

"You have wild dogs and coyotes around here?" Ben asked, with wide eyes.

"Oh, yes, but you don't need to worry about it. They run away from people."

"Oh," Ben said, rather dejectedly. "I was hoping to see one."

Louise tousled Ben's hair and they petted the goats once more before leaving the barn. On the way back to the house, she stopped at the tool shed and retrieved a hoe.

"You kids run on inside and wash your hands and find something to do. I'm going to hoe out some tomatoes while the goats are eating and then I'll have to go back up and close the stall doors when they are done. I should be finished in about an hour then we'll get ready and go call on the Langstons."

Ben and Casey went inside and flopped into the recliners. An Andy Griffith marathon was playing on the 'TV Land' channel. Andy and Barney had a billy goat in the court house. The goat had eaten some old dynamite, and Barney was trying to calm it down, by playing his harmonica. They watched a couple of episodes until Louise came in, hot and sweaty, from working in the garden.

"Whew-wee, it's hot out there. Let me get a drink of water and take a quick shower and we'll head out."

An hour later, they were back in the old Galaxy cruising down the driveway. The Galaxy did not have air conditioning, so in order to stay cool, the windows had to be rolled down. There were also small triangular windows on the front doors, that acted as vents. These windows pushed open to the outside and, as you drove down the road, they directed air into the car at a surprisingly high velocity. Ben used to think this was the coolest invention ever and could not understand why all cars did not have these window vents

on the front doors. Until he found out that they also
directed bees into the car at high velocities as well. Not high
enough to kill the bees, but just high enough to really
aggravate them. Louise turned left out of the driveway,
drove for about three miles, and made another left turn onto
an old dirt and gravel road.

"Here we are kids. This is the Langston's farm."

"I thought you said it was within walking distance,"
Casey remarked.

"It is. You see, their farm adjoins ours. You walk
across the back pasture, cross the fence, follow the ditch on
the other side up the hill and through the woods, and you
come to one of their pastures. You'll be able to see their
house as soon as you come out of the woods."

At the end of the driveway was a long brick ranch-style
house with two massive water oaks in the front yard. A tire
swing hung from the tree on the left, a picnic table sat under
the tree on the right, and a field stone walkway ran between
the two trees, leading the way to the front door. Louise rang
the doorbell. Inside, soft chimes floated through the house
announcing visitors. A moment later, the front door opened
to reveal a petite and very pretty young woman, wearing an
apron. Her sandy brown hair was pulled back in a pony tail
and there was a smudge of baking powder on her cheek.

"Louise! What a pleasant surprise, come in, come in.
Are these your grandkids that I've heard so much about?"

"Yes, this is Ben and this is Casey. Ben and Casey, this
is Mrs. Langston."

"Oh, jeeze, Louise. You kids call me Rebecca."

Rebecca led them into her kitchen and motioned for
them to sit at the table, while she removed her apron and
peeked inside the oven. "I've got some cookies in here and
they should be ready in about five more minutes. What
would you guys like to drink?"

"Do you have any coffee on?" Louise asked.

"I sure do. What do you kids want? We have milk, tea,
lemonade and Coke."

"I'll have a Coke, please," said Casey.

"Lemonade," said Ben.

"Rebecca, where's the rest of the family?" Louise asked.

"Sam had to make a run to Maine. He'll be back Sunday. Joey and Meg are down at the pond fishing. Oh, my heavens, what am I thinking. You kids don't want to sit around the table with two old hens like us. Come here."

Rebecca took them out the kitchen door onto a large deck in the back yard. She put her arm around Casey and pointed to an old gate in a picket fence, at the corner of the yard. "Go through that gate and follow the path. It will take you right to the dock. Oh, wait one second before you go."

Rebecca ran inside and a couple of minutes later, popped back out with two bamboo fishing poles and a big brown paper sack. "Here are your fishing poles. I put some drinks and some fresh cookies in the sack. Just introduce yourselves, then catch some fish and have fun!"

"Thank you, Mrs. Langston," said Casey.

"Rebecca! If we are going to be friends, I want you calling me Rebecca. Okay?"

After thanking Rebecca, Ben and Casey took the sack and fishing poles and lit out for the pond. The trail wound its way down through the woods between ivy covered banks and opened up into a small glen, where sunlight glimmered on the surface of an emerald green pond. A short dock jutted out into the pond from the center of the earthen dam and, on the end of the dock, with fishing poles in their hands and feet dangling in the water, sat Joey and Meg Langston.

Joey and Meg laid their poles down and stood up when Ben and Casey walked out onto the dock. Ben spoke first. "Hi. My name is Ben. Ben Alderman. And this is my sister, Casey. We're George and Louise Alderman's grandkids."

Joey walked forward and stuck out his hand. "I'm Joey and this is my sister, Meg."

Ben shook his hand, while Casey stood back, practically drooling on her sneakers. Joey was a handsome boy with dark brown hair, brown eyes, and muscles that Ben had always dreamed of having. Meg, Ben noted, was no eyesore either. She had the same dark hair and dark complexion as her brother, but her eyes were the color of the summer sky above them.

"How long are you guys visiting?" Meg asked.

"We're here for the summer," said Casey. "Here, your mom sent these with us."

Meg took the sack and opened it. "Awesome! We were just talking about how good a nice cold Pepsi would be right now. And cookies too! Let's eat."

Ben and Casey took off their socks and shoes, rolled their pant legs up, and joined Joey and Meg on the end of the dock. The water in the small pond was rather warm, but the Pepsis were cold and refreshing and the cookies were absolutely delicious. The next half hour was spent getting to know everyone. How old are you? Where are you from? Where do you go to school? Casey and Meg were the same age, while Joey was two years older.

"Are the fish biting?" Ben asked.

"Yeah," Joey replied. "Look at this." He unhooked a small cord from the dock and pulled a stringer out of the water, with four fat bream dangling by their gills.

"Cool," Ben said. "Mind if I try?"

"Sure, we've got plenty of worms," said Joey, reaching into his tackle box. He pulled out a blue plastic container, popped the lid off and set it on the dock between them. "Night crawlers. Big, fat, juicy ones."

Casey wrinkled her nose, but wanting to impress Joey, she screwed her courage up and asked for a worm too. They spent the next hour fishing, talking, laughing and having fun. When they wound their lines up to leave, they pulled a stringer out of the water with eight bream, three bass and one catfish.

"What are we going to do with those?" Casey asked, pointing at the stringer of fish.

"Clean them and cook them," Joey answered. "Hey, why don't you guys come over tomorrow and we'll have a fish fry!"

"Yeah," Ben exclaimed, "that would be a blast. We don't have to clean the fish, do we?"

"Mom will clean them for us. She'll cook them for us, too. All we have to do is eat them."

"Well, I can do that!" said Ben. "I love fish."

"What can we bring?" Casey asked.

"Bring yourselves and your appetite." said Meg.

"No, we've got to bring something. How about a chocolate cake for dessert?"

"Mmmmm, that would be awesome," Joey said, rubbing his stomach. "I bet you make a great chocolate cake, too."

Casey smiled and tried very hard not to blush. "Chocolate cake it is then."

The sky was beginning to darken to a deep purple and a couple of stars had opened their eyes to catch a glimpse of the final minutes of this last day of May, as Ben and Casey, with their two new friends, made their way back up the trail to the Langston's back yard. New friendships had been forged this day and as the sunlight faded, so too did all thoughts of Camelot and the mysterious Merlin Tree.

7 BEN SPILLS THE BEANS

Casey awoke bright and early the next morning. She was so excited about seeing Joey again, and Grandma had promised to help her bake the cake to take to their fish fry. However, when she came running down the stairs, she was surprised to find Ben already up. He was sitting at the table with Grandpa, munching on a bowl of Captain Crunch, while Grandpa was having his coffee and toast. Grandpa had coffee and toast every morning for breakfast. Nothing weird about that. But Grandpa liked to dip his toast in his coffee. Now that was weird.

"Good morning, Casey," said George, over his saucer. George dipped his toast into his coffee cup, but he drank his coffee from the saucer.

"Good morning, Grandpa. Morning, Ben. Where's Grandma?"

"Grandma's sleeping in this morning. She's a little sore from hoeing out those tomato plants yesterday. I hear you kids are having a fish fry over at the Langston's today. That Joey Langston is a handsome little devil ain't he?" Grandpa winked at Ben and Casey began to blush.

"He's nice," Casey said, avoiding her Grandpa's eyes, "Meg's really cool too and I've never been to a fish fry."

"What time are you going over there?"

"We're going for lunch. Grandma told us how to get there by going through the back pasture. We're going to leave here about eleven-thirty. Ben, where's the Captain Crunch?"

"In the top cabinet, by the fridge," Ben replied, with milk dribbling down his chin.

After breakfast, Ben and Casey went up to the goat house to pet their goats. Grandma showed up later on and told Casey it was time to get started on the cake, because it had to cool before they could frost it. Ben, not interested in any baking, strolled down to the barn where George was greasing the fittings on his mower.

"What are you doing, Grandpa?"

"I got a little bit left to mow in the goat pasture. Want to get it done before it gets too hot. You ever drove a tractor before?"

"I'm twelve, Grandpa. I don't even know how to drive a car yet."

"Well, we are going to have to do something about that. I'll be cutting hay in a couple of weeks and I'm going to need you to drive the truck in the field for me."

"Are you serious?" Ben asked, with wide eyes.

"Dead serious. Why, I was driving when I was eight years old."

"No way. You really drove a truck when you were eight?"

"No, when I was eight we didn't have a truck, or a tractor for that matter. We used horses to do our work. I used to drive the hay wagon for my dad." George laid the grease gun down on top of a barrel, wiped his hands on the front of his overalls, then climbed up onto his tractor and motioned for Ben. Ben grabbed the handle on the fender over the big rear tires and scrambled up onto the side step, then George helped him climb into his lap where he could reach the steering wheel.

"Let's take her for a spin around the house," George said as he turned the switch and pushed the starter button. The tractor's engine turned over three times, then roared to life. George put it in low gear and pulled the throttle down a couple of notches. "Put your hands here, in the two o'clock and ten o'clock positions."

Ben grasped the steering wheel as George eased off the clutch. The tractor pulled out of the barn and Ben wrestled the steering wheel to the right. He drove the tractor around the house and back to the front of the barn, where George brought it to a stop and shut it off. Ben carefully climbed down to the ground, grinning from ear to ear.

"Thanks, Grandpa. That was awesome. When do I get to start learning how to drive the truck?"

"Maybe Saturday, when I get back from the cattle sale. You want to go with me?"

Ben remembered the little experiment they had planned with Grandma on Saturday. He felt bad doing something behind Grandpa's back, especially since Grandpa was going to take the time to teach him to drive this summer. However, he was dying to know more about the Merlin Tree and the magical place called Camelot.

"Gee Grandpa, I got plans this Saturday. Can I go with you next time?"

"Absolutely. I'll be taking some more calves in a couple of weeks. You can go with me then. We'll stop at Hardees and get us a sausage biscuit on the way." George looked at his watch. "Morning's getting away from us. I'd better get busy and you'd better skee-daddle to the house and get ready for that fish fry."

Ben took off for the house as George fired up the tractor again, to finish the mowing. In the kitchen, Louise was washing some pans at the sink while two yellow cake layers were cooling on a wire rack on the kitchen table. Ben heard the hairdryer whirring away upstairs and knew that Casey would be preening for at least another fifteen or twenty minutes. He sat down at the table and sniffed the cakes.

"What kind of icing are you putting on these, Grandma?"

"Chocolate. Isn't that what Casey said she'd bring?"

"Yeah, I guess so."

"Well, I soon as I get these pans washed up, I'm going to make some."

"You make your own frosting?"

"Ben Alderman!" Louise said, planting her hands on her hips. "You know I don't use any store bought frosting on my cakes."

Ben laughed and then realized that if Grandma was making the frosting, then there would be beaters and bowls to lick when she was finished. Louise read his thoughts.

"You can lick one beater and Casey can lick the other one. If you want any more after that, then you both can lick the bowl too. Now, why don't you go get ready while I finish up in here?"

"I am ready," Ben replied.

"Then go watch TV. I'll call you when the frosting is finished."

Ben flipped through the channels and settled on Sponge Bob Square Pants. It was a cartoon he and his dad loved to watch together. He hadn't had much time to think about his dad since he arrived here, and even though his dad had only been gone for a little while, Ben missed him already. Sponge Bob just didn't seem as funny today, so Ben turned the TV off and picked up an Outdoor Life magazine that was laying on the end table. He flipped through the pages and found a story about a grizzly bear and some very unfortunate campers. He was really getting into the story when he heard Casey come bounding down the stairs. A few minutes later, the blender began singing loudly in the kitchen and Ben hopped up and ran to the table, to wait patiently for one of the chocolate frosted beaters. After he and Casey licked both beaters and the bowl, Casey picked up the cake (which Louise had placed in a plastic carrier with a handle on top) and kissed her Grandma on the cheek.

"Thanks for the cake, Grandma. Are you sure I can't help you wash up?"

"No, no, I've got this under control. You kids run along and have a good time today. Just be home in time for supper."

"Oh, wait one second," Ben told Casey. He raced up the stairs, taking two steps at a time and when he came back down he had the knife his dad had given him hanging from his belt.

"Oh good grief," said Casey rolling her eyes.

Outside the dew had long since burned off, and the purple and white morning glories, along the edge of the yard, were curling up and hiding their faces from the warm sunshine. Ben and Casey walked to the gate leading to the back pasture and climbed over. Grandpa's cows were in the middle of the pasture grazing, and although both kids were a little afraid of walking through an open field full of cattle, the cows did not seem to mind at all. One or two of the cows raised their heads briefly to look at them, but after a long winter of eating nothing but dry hay, nothing could tear the cows from the tender green grass. In no time at all they were across the field, to the fence on the other side. Ben put his foot on one strand of the barbed wire and pushed down, while he pulled up on the next strand with his hands. This allowed Casey to slip between the strands without snagging her clothes and Casey repeated the action from the other side for Ben. Their grandpa had shown them how to cross a fence like this. Most kids just grab onto a fence post and use the strands of wire like rungs on a ladder. He told them that was not good for a fence and if a staple popped out while someone was crossing that way, they could be hurt very badly. Once they were safely through the barbed wire, they scrambled down into the ditch that Louise had told them about and followed it alongside the fence, until it veered away into the woods. Eventually, the ditch petered out, and soon after that, the woods ended too at another fence. This was the Langston's pasture, and across the field, they could make out the tops of the big water oaks in front of the Langston's home.

"You think they got any cows in here?" Casey asked, as they made their way across the field.

"It's not cows you should worry about," said Ben, with a mischievous grin. "You should worry about the bulls with all that red hair of yours. You know red makes them angry."

"That's not true," Casey said.

"Of course it is. Why do you think bull fighters use red capes?"

Casey looked around anxiously. "What do we do if a bull comes after us? We can't outrun a bull."

"I don't have to outrun the bull, Casey. I just have to outrun you!" Ben yelled, as he took off across the pasture. He knew Casey was carrying the cake and could not run fast for fear of dropping it. He won the race across the pasture, but only by a slim margin. But a win was a win, and Ben took them anytime and anyway he could get them. They entered the Langston's yard through a stile; a place where the fence splits into a V shape on one side, while the other side runs into the center of the V. The two sides never meet and this allows people to walk, in a zigzag, through the V, while cows are too large and too long to navigate the turn.

Joey and Meg were in the front yard. Meg was sitting in a tire swing that hung from one of the massive lower limbs of the oak tree and Joey was spinning her round and round. The rope was all knotted up and wound tight. Casey sat the cake down on the picnic table, where the other food had been placed, and then walked over to join Ben.

"Are you ready?" Joey yelled.

"No, you've got it wound too tight!" Meg squealed.

"Hold on then," Joey replied. He twisted the tire one more time and then gave it a fling with both hands.

As the rope began to unwind, the tire spun faster and faster while Meg screamed louder and louder. When all of the knots were out of the rope, the tire continued to spin and the rope began to knot up again. Eventually, the tire came to a stop and slowly started to spin in the other direction, as the rope began to unwind again. All of them took a turn on the tire before they ate. Ben couldn't imagine doing this after eating. Especially, after eating fried fish.

Joey's and Meg's mom had brought out a turkey fryer earlier and, by the time the kids were finished playing on the tire swing, the grease was good and hot. She had already cleaned the fish and battered them with corn meal. All that was left to do was to place them in the basket and drop them in the oil. Once the fish were sizzling, Rebecca brought out a big bowl of coleslaw, a huge platter of golden brown hush puppies and two milk jugs full of ice cold sweet tea. The fish were done in just a few minutes and everyone plowed into the food. By the time they finished eating Ben did not think he had any room left for cake, until Casey started slicing it. The cake turned out to be a big hit and, when Ben told Joey that Casey had made it just for him, Joey commented on how good it was and asked for a second slice.

After helping clear the table and putting the food away, the kids ambled down the path to the fish pond, to sit on the dock and dip their feet into the water. Meg and Casey were chattering away about school, boys and the latest fashions, when Joey interrupted them.

"Casey, what's the deal with the bamboo? Is Ben pulling my leg?"

Casey glared at Ben. "What are you talking about?"

"Ben says you have some kind of magical tree growing in a patch of bamboo at your Grandma's house. Says it's some kind of portal to another world."

"Ben watches too much TV and reads too many fantasy books," Casey replied.

"Ah, come on Casey," said Ben. "Let's let them in on it."

"Let us in on what?" Meg asked.

"Ben thinks the bamboo patch, behind Grandma and Grandpa's house, has some kind of magical doorway to some kind of magical world. How dopey can you get?"

Ben felt the heat rising in his neck and he knew that his ears were probably turning bright red. He put up with this kind of teasing at school, but dog-gone if he was going to put up with it over the summer, especially from his own stupid sister. He stood up from the dock and rolled his pants legs down, then pushed his glasses up on his nose.

"Alrighty then. Let's go to Grandma and Grandpa's house and I'll prove it."

"We're not walking all the way to Grandma and Grandpa's house for you to make a fool of yourself," Casey yelled.

"Whoa! Calm down," Joey said. "We don't mind walking over. It's not that far and besides, I want to see the baby goats Ben was telling me about."

"Well, we can go see the goats, but we can't go into the bamboo. Grandma said it's full of snakes."

"Sure," Joey said, "I don't want to go climbing around in an old itchy bamboo patch anyway."

Casey, now relieved, was suddenly excited about showing Joey and Meg their little goats. Ben, however, felt dejected and as Casey and Meg walked past him, Casey shot him a warning glance that said, "Ha-ha, I won and you'd better keep your fat mouth shut." But as soon as the girls had their backs to them, Joey punched Ben in the arm, winked at him and mouthed the word 'bamboo'.

8 SPYING ON GRANDMA

Back at the house, Joey and Meg found their mom enjoying a slice of watermelon. She was sitting at the picnic table under the shade of the big water oaks in the front yard. On the table, a long striped watermelon had been halved, then quartered. Then, each quarter had been cut into thick slices of juicy red relief from a hot summer day. The kids all piled around the table and grabbed a slice.

"Where did you get the watermelon, Mom?" asked Meg. "It's kind of early in the season isn't it?"

"I picked it up yesterday at that little road-side produce stand, beside the BP station. I needed to get some cabbage to make the cole slaw for your fish fry today; I saw these watermelons and had to have one. I figured you kids would enjoy it too."

"It's cold!" Ben remarked.

"Yes, I know. It's been in the fridge all night. They are much better cold, don't you think?"

Ben had just taken a big bite, and with his mouth now full, and juice dribbling between his fingers and down his arms, he could only nod.

"Hey, let's see how far we can spit a watermelon seed," said Joey.

Joey went first, followed by Ben and then Meg. Casey thought spitting was gross, even if it was just watermelon seeds. But once again, wanting to impress Joey, she took a big bite from her slice of watermelon and spit seeds with the rest of them. Ben saw Casey was no good at spitting watermelon seeds and jumped at the opportunity to finally beat her in something. Watermelon seed spitting may never qualify as an official sporting event of any kind but, if he could beat his sister at it, then it was a worthy activity in Ben's mind. He challenged everyone to a contest, then promptly trounced his sister. Rebecca, however, beat them all.

After finishing the watermelon, they all threw their rinds over the fence for the cows to eat. Yellow Jackets were already beginning to swarm around the watermelon juice on the table top, so Rebecca dragged out the garden hose to wash it off. While she had the garden hose out, the kids washed the sticky juice off their hands as well, then set off across the pasture to the Alderman farm to see the baby goats.

The Langston's cows were Black Angus beef cattle. Most of them were standing in the shade at the edge of the pasture, lazily chewing their cuds and swishing their tails back and forth across their sides to keep the flies from biting. Several of them did, however, brave the hot afternoon sun for a few more tasty morsels of the sweet spring grass and clover. Casey asked Joey if they had any bulls in the pasture. Joey said that they had only one, but that he was gentle and wouldn't harm them. Casey edged closer to him anyway. When they got to the Alderman's farm, Ben noticed that Grandpa had finished mowing the field. The tractor was parked back under the shed by the barn and the truck was gone. They searched the house and called for their Grandma, but they couldn't find her either. The old Galaxy was still parked in the same spot under the magnolia tree, so they assumed that she had gone with Grandpa. After each of them grabbed a soda from the fridge, and waited for Ben to wash off the top, they strolled up to the goat house. It appeared that all of the other goats only came for Louise because they never even glanced at the four kids walking through their pasture.

"Oh, they are beautiful," Meg exclaimed as they entered the stall. "What are their names?"

"I named mine Tink and Ben named his Arnold."

"Arnold?"

"Don't ask."

Casey and Meg sat down in the shavings to pet the little goats. After a couple of minutes of holding them and chatting away about everything under the sun, Casey turned to ask Joey if he was going to pet the babies too. Joey and Ben were gone.

"Where did they run off to?" Meg asked.

"Hang on one second," Casey replied. She gently put her goat down and hurried out of the barn. As she stepped outside into the bright sunshine, her eyes adjusted to the light just in time to see Ben and Joey disappearing into the bamboo patch beside the house.

"BEN!" she screamed. "STOP!" But it was too late. The bamboo swallowed them up. Casey, feeling both angry and scared at the same time, burst down the hill in a sprint to catch them. Her heart was pounding in her chest. She heard Meg yelling behind her, but she couldn't make out what she was saying. All she knew was that she had to catch them before went through the Merlin Tree. At the bottom of the hill, Casey vaulted over the fence and crossed the driveway. When she hit the loose gravel on the side of the driveway, her feet shot out from under her and she took a nasty tumble. Meg arrived at her side, just as she was scrambling to her feet.

"Casey, what in the heck is going on?"

"I can't explain now, just follow me."

The two girls arrived at the bamboo patch and Casey immediately plunged in. Meg hesitated a moment, then followed. Eventually they made it to the center of the patch and Ben and Joey were no where to be found.

"Oh no, we're too late," Casey cried.

"Too late for what?" Meg asked. "Casey, tell me what's going on! You're starting to freak me out."

"I saw Ben and Joey go in here."

"Well, they are not here now; they must have gone through to the other side."

"That's what I'm afraid of. Listen Meg, I know I'm acting crazy and this is going to seem crazy too, but I need you to humor me for just a moment. I promise this will make sense in just a few minutes, okay?"

"Sure, Casey," Meg replied with a worried look on her face.

"Come on then, follow me."

Casey took Meg by the hand and led her to the center of the patch where a fat twisted tree stood with two small gnarled limbs sticking out like arms. The center of the tree was split just below the limbs. This split ran all the way to the ground, widening along the way and forming an arch large enough to walk through. Casey started to go through this archway, but Meg halted, jerking her to a stop.

"Casey, what are you doing?"

"Meg, just humor me. We have to walk through this tree before we leave the bamboo."

"Why not?" Meg replied, rolling her eyes. "This day cannot possibly get any weirder."

As they passed through the Merlin Tree, Casey mumbled to herself, "you have no idea how weird this day is fixing to become."

Once through the tree, Casey released Meg's hand and plunged into the thick wall of canes around the outside perimeter of the patch. Meg followed close behind. The canes became closer together, barring their way, but the two girls pressed on and soon tumbled out into the lush green-gold meadows of Camelot. Casey spotted Ben and Joey climbing the hill, making their way to the pine trees on top.

She turned to look at Meg, who was staring at the snow capped mountains in the distance.

"Ben was telling the truth, wasn't he?"

"Yes, he was telling the truth. And he is in big trouble too."

"Why is he in trouble, and why did you not want us to know about this?"

"I don't have time to explain right now. Come on, we've got to get the guys to come back. This place is not safe."

Meg raised her hands and cupped them around her mouth to yell at Ben and Joey, but Casey grabbed her hands and shushed her. "Keep quiet. The last time we were here, a crazy man chased us with a club. Grandma said he was harmless, but I'd rather not meet up with him again."

"Your Grandma knows about this place?"

"Yes. Let's get the guys and, when we get back home, I'll tell you all I know."

The two girls raced up the hillside where, just inside the pines, they found Ben and Joey crouched behind a large boulder. The two boys were peering over the rock at a little log cabin nestled in the trees. Casey and Meg crept up behind them.

"Ben Alderman, you are in so much trouble!" she whispered.

"Shhh!" Ben whispered back and pointed to the cabin.

Casey peeked over the rock. The cabin was small, probably one room. A thin gray stream of smoke spiraled up through the branches of the pines from a rock chimney on the side of the cabin. Casey could smell food cooking from inside the cabin. She turned back to Ben.

"That's probably where that crazy man lives Ben; let's get out of here now."

Ben shook his head. "Grandma's in there."

"What?"

"Grandma is inside the cabin. When we came into the pines, we saw her standing in front of the cabin talking to

Amos. We slipped down here so we could hear what they were talking about, but they went inside."

"Well, now we really have to leave. And we can't let Grandma know we were here, we promised her we wouldn't come."

"I didn't promise her," said Joey. "If we get caught, you tell her I went into the bamboo and ya'll tried to stop me. I want to know more about this place."

"Me too," said Meg. "This is too cool."

"But that won't work! Grandma will want to know why you decided to go into the bamboo to begin with. Can you come up with good reason for that one?"

"I want to know more about this place too," Ben added. "Don't you, Casey? Aren't you the least bit curious? And I really want to know what Grandma is up to. So, me and Joey are going to ease down to the side of the cabin and see if we can hear anything. You two stay up here and watch the front door."

"I really don't think this is a good idea," Casey whispered. "Let's just go back now before we get into any trouble. Please."

Ben looked over the rock at the cabin and then back at Joey. Joey shook his head. Ben turned to Meg and she shook her head as well. He thought for a moment and offered his sister a compromise.

"Let us find out what Grandma is doing here and then we'll leave."

"You promise?"

"I promise."

"Well, what do we do if they come out?" Casey asked.

Joey turned to his sister. "Can you whistle if the door opens? Do some kind of bird call?"

"What kind?"

"Do a whippoorwill. Wait, no, don't do that one, they only sing at night time. How about a bobwhite?"

Meg nodded and Ben and Joey slipped out from behind the boulder and quietly made their way to the side of the cabin where a small window was located to the right of the chimney. Crouched below the open window, they could hear the conversation inside clearly.

"Amos, are you certain?"

"I'm positive. A unicorn has been spotted in Camelot and the witch is on the move. The last sighting was in the Great Oak Forest."

After several moments of uncomfortable silence, Louise spoke again. "We have to stop her. If she kills this one she wins. It's that simple."

"We'll stop her, I promise. The Blight has spread far in Faerie and the elves are abandoning their home world for Camelot, in great numbers. I'm sure they will expend all of their efforts against the witch."

"I certainly hope so. I know there is more at stake here, but her spell has caused our family so much pain and suffering. Surely with her death, the spell will be broken."

"Louise, don't cry. Here, let me fix you some hot tea."

Ben and Joey heard a chair slide across the floor and footsteps retreating to the other side of the small cabin. Apparently, Louise had gotten up from the table and had gone with Amos to fix the tea, because they could still hear conversation from within, but only faintly. Then it was quiet. Both boys pressed their ears to the log wall, straining to hear what was being said inside.

Ben whispered to Joey, "I wish that stupid bird would shut up, I can't hear a thing!"

Joey whirled around. There it was. "Bob-white, bob-white." He was so intent on listening in on the conversation that he totally missed the signal. Ben saw the color drain from Joey's face and realized that was no bird singing. Someone had come outside the cabin and Meg was trying to warn them. Ben jumped up and scrambled to the rear of the cabin with Joey right on his heels. They turned the corner and ran smack into the giant, hairy, club-wielding man that Louise called Amos. But it was more like running into a brick wall and both boys collapsed in a heap at the giant's feet.

Amos had left the cabin to draw water from the well for the tea. When he stepped outside and heard the bobwhite whistle, he knew that it was not a bird. He also knew, from the direction the signal was coming from, that whoever was being warned had probably been listening in on their conversation by the window. The only place for them to run would be to the rear of the cabin. So, he sat the bucket down and walked around the other side. When he turned the corner at the rear of the cabin, two terrified little boys ran into him and collapsed at his feet. He promptly snatched them under his arms and took them inside.

"Look what I have here!" Amos cried. "I found them sneaking around outside. Think they will make a good meal?"

Amos sat the boys down and they scrambled away from him.

"Ben Alderman, what are you doing here?" Louise hissed. "You not only disobeyed me and put yourself in danger by coming here, but you bring Joey and put his life at risk too?"

Ben could not speak. His ears were burning and he knew that his face was probably bright red too. He was not going to cry in front of Joey though so he just stared at the floor and mumbled an apology.

"Are Casey and Meg with you?" Louise asked.

Ben knew that their signal had not fooled Amos and that Amos knew someone else was still outside. He also knew that he would be in really hot water if he got caught in a lie right now. Besides, he really was feeling bad about disobeying his Grandma.

"Yes ma'am. Casey and Meg were keeping watch for us."

"Exactly what were you two doing while they were keeping watch for you?" Louise asked, raising her eyebrows.

"We were by the window listening in on your conversation," Ben replied. His ears were definitely on fire now.

"Well, I'm very disappointed in you children. Go outside and tell Casey and Meg to come here at once."

Ben walked by Amos, who was grinning from ear to ear, poked his head out the door and yelled, "Casey, Meg! Come here! Grandma wants to see us."

9 THE FAIRY GLEN

Casey and Meg watched the cabin door from behind the rock, while Ben and Joey crouched beneath the window on the side of the cabin, listening to Louise and the big hairy man called Amos. Actually, Meg watched the cabin door. Casey kept looking over her shoulder, as if someone might be sneaking up on them. Meg had no idea that Casey was looking for gnomes, ogres, and dragons. Suddenly Meg whistled. "Bob-white, bob-white." Casey spun around. The big hairy man named Amos had come outside with a bucket in his hand. Meg kept whistling. Casey looked down at Ben and Joey. Either they did not hear Meg whistling or they were so intent on trying to hear what was going inside the cabin that they forgot all about the signal. Meg whistled louder. "BOB-WHITE, BOB-WHITE." Casey looked back to the front of the cabin. The bucket was sitting on the ground in front of the door and Amos was gone. She was getting ready to sprint down the hill and get them when they suddenly realized that Meg was sounding the alarm. The two boys sprang up from their crouched positions and sprinted to the rear of the cabin. As they rounded the corner, they ran into Amos who had sneaked around the other side. Amos quickly snatched them up and took them inside.

"Oh no," Casey moaned. "We are so dead. Grandma is going to kill us."

"Joey won't tell them we are out here. We can leave now and they will never know we were here."

"Ben will tell. All Grandma has to do is give him one of her stern looks and he'll spill his guts,"

"Should we go on down then?" Meg asked.

"No, let's wait and see what happens. Maybe Ben won't talk."

A few minutes later, Ben poked his head out the door and yelled, "Casey, Meg! Come here! Grandma wants to see us."

Casey and Meg entered the small cabin, while Amos held the door open for them. The cabin was one room, as they had expected. The oak floor was aged and polished to a deep honey-amber color. To their right, a black iron kettle bubbled on the hearth of a massive stone fireplace, filling the cabin with the heavy scent of a thick and hearty beef stew. A copper bound trunk, with a padlock the size of a dinner plate, sat under the window to the right of the fireplace and in the corner, to the left of the fireplace was a bed. This bed, a king size bed for any of the kids, was just a small cot for Amos. The only other furnishings in the cabin were a hutch, a rocker, and a table with benches on each side. Louise was perched on top one of these benches, shaking her head and drumming her fingers on the table top. Casey hung her head and tears welled up in her eyes, threatening to spill down her cheeks at any moment. Ben saw his sister's grief and shame and it tore at his heart to know that he had brought this upon her. He stepped forward and cleared his throat.

"Casey had nothing to do with this, Grandma. I had told Joey about this place and we sneaked away while Casey and Meg were petting the baby goats. Casey even tried to stop us when she realized what we were doing."

Casey looked up at Ben, he saw the gratitude in her eyes and maybe even a little bit of admiration too. But Louise's eyes told a different story altogether: anger, hurt, and disappointment. Ben walked over to the table and sat down across from her.

"I'm very sorry I disobeyed you. Joey and I were just going to pop in and then pop right back out, but when we got here we saw you and we wanted to know what you were doing here."

"So, you spied on me?" Louise asked, raising her eyebrows and staring down at Ben over the rim of her glasses.

"No! Well, yes... I guess we did," Ben replied.

After a long awkward pause, it was Amos's deep rumbling voice that broke the silence. Casey and Meg both jumped and Joey edged away from the towering man.

"Louise, it appears that no harm was done here. These kids are just curious, as all children are and should be."

"Well, we have a saying where we come from," said Louise. "Curiosity killed the cat."

"And satisfaction brought him back," Ben added.

Amos threw back his head and roared with laughter. Even Louise could not hold on to her anger after that remark and she finally gave in, threw her hands up in the air and declared, "I give up."

"I will have to remember that saying," said Amos, wiping his eyes. "Let's all have some stew. Later we will take a walk and I will show the children the forest."

Ben looked up at the smiling giant; Amos winked at him and tousled his hair. He really wasn't that scary once you got over his size and appearance. He had, what Ben would have called, a merry face and twinkling eyes. Kind of what you would expect Santa Clause to look like, if he were seven feet tall with wild black hair, bulging muscles, and draped in black and brown furs instead of red. Well, maybe Santa Clause was a stretch. But Ben did sense a kind and gentle spirit in Amos. A kindred spirit. And yet, there was still something dangerous about Amos. Something Ben could not put his finger on.

The kids were surprised to discover that they were even the least bit hungry after all of the food they ate at their fish fry. But when Amos got some bowls and spoons from the hutch and began ladling out the thick brown stew, their mouths began to water. While they were eating, Ben brought up the little experiment they were supposed to do on Saturday.

"Grandma, it seems that there are not any parallel universes here. When we came through, we ended up in the same place and time that you were in. What time did you go through the Merlin Tree?"

Louise swallowed a mouthful of stew and thought for a moment. "Let's see. George went to town to get some mower belts. He left about a half hour after you and Casey left. I guess I came through about fifteen minutes after that."

"Hmmm," Ben thought. "I don't know what time it was when we came through, but it was a good while after you. How long have you been here?"

"Not long. I came straight to Amos's cabin when I got here."

"How can that be?" Ben asked. "We came in a long time after you, and yet, we saw you going into the woods when we came out of the bamboo."

Louise shrugged her shoulders. "I simply do not know. It would seem that time gets distorted when you travel here. I came back to the same time frame here - the same amount of time that passed in our world has passed here since my last visit. But when you kids came through, you came through to my time and that means more time has passed here than in our world since your last visit. Now, when I go back, I don't think it will be the same time I left, like it normally is. I bet I go back to our world in your time frame; the point in time that you left."

Ben pushed his glasses up on his nose and sat forward on the edge of the bench. "So, it's almost like the Merlin

Tree is a portal that not only connects two worlds, but two time frames as well."

"What do you mean?" Louise asked.

"Think of time as a fabric. As long as one person is using the Merlin Tree, then there is only one thread of time in the fabric and there are no time differences to account for between the two worlds. But when two people start using the Tree, then we have two threads in the mix and the Merlin Tree has to weave those threads into a single fabric."

"That's a remarkable analogy," said Louise, "and probably a correct one too."

Amos scratched his head. "I have no idea what you two are talking about. All I know is that Merlin Tree gives me the creeps and I do not like to go near it."

The kids looked up at Amos with wonder. How could this giant mountain of muscles be afraid of anything?

"Are you really going to take us for a walk?" Joey asked.

"Sure." Amos replied with a huge grin. "How would you kids like to see some real live fairies?"

"You mean like Tinkerbell?" Meg asked.

Amos scratched his head again. "Who is Tinkerbell?"

"She is a fairy in the Peter Pan movie."

Now Amos tugged on his beard. "What's a movie?"

"Yes, these are fairies like Tinkerbell in the Peter Pan movie," Louise interrupted as she rose from the bench and smoothed her skirts.

"Cool!" Ben yelled. "Let's go!"

"One moment," Louise said, rising from her seat. She reached into her pockets and pulled out two necklaces; the small emerald necklaces she had purchased at the Jockey Lot. "Put these on first. I was going to give them to you Saturday, but since you couldn't wait until Saturday to come here, you need to put them on now."

"What are they for?" Ben asked.

"The emerald is the only jewel not native to Camelot and it has some powerful magical properties here."

"Like what?"

"They are called spell catchers. If you are wearing one of these when a magical spell is cast at you, the stone will catch the spell and hold it. If you take the necklace off and lay it down, so that it is not touching you, the spell will be harmlessly released. However, if you touch someone before the Spell Catcher has released the spell, then that spell will be transferred to the person you touch."

Ben and Casey snapped the necklaces around their necks and tucked them beneath their shirts.

Louise began clearing the table. "I'll stay here and clean up while you are gone. Don't be too long though, because I'm not sure what time the Merlin Tree will put us back when we go home."

Amos ushered the kids out the door and set off down a winding shady lane thickly carpeted with pine needles. The path paralleled the hillside, looping in and out between great moss covered boulders. After a while, the trail turned and began to climb the hill. When they reached the top, which was clear of trees, they could see for miles. Behind them, the pine forest ended at the edge of the great meadow that stretched into the horizon, and they could make out the bamboo patch, a small speck of green afloat on a great sea of green and gold. The snow covered mountains, to the left of the patch, seemed even larger from the hilltop.

"There's where we are going," said Amos, pointing down the other side of the hill into the valley below. On this side of the hill, the pine forest stretched out for miles.

"Where?" Casey asked. "All I see are trees."

"Look down there." Amos said. "At the bottom of the hill there is a small clearing. See it?"

Casey shaded her eyes from the bright sunshine. "Yes, I see it. What's that twinkling down there?"

"You'll have to wait and see for yourself," Amos teased and set off down the hillside. The kids followed behind, and once again, the trail disappeared under the tall canopy of pines. The scenery, on this side of the hill, was pretty much the same. Joey was beginning to think that Camelot was a boring place where everything looked the same. Depending on where you were standing, you either saw all trees, or no trees at all. Ben was thinking the same thing. They had been here for over an hour now and had not seen a single troll, ogre, dragon, or unicorn. However, when they reached the bottom of the hill and the trail opened into a small glen, they changed their minds. The clearing was about half the size of a football field. In the center of the field, a fountain gushed skyward from a round stone basin and arced over to splash on top of a tall slab of red granite beside the basin. The mist from the artesian geyser formed a perfect little rainbow over the granite slab. Around the slab and across the clearing, wild flowers of all shapes and sizes bloomed in brilliant blues, reds, and yellows. Ben scanned the field.

"Where are the fairies?" he whispered.

"I don't see them either," Joey muttered.

"That's because you are looking for them," Amos replied. "You cannot see them if you are looking for them."

Now, it was Ben's turn to scratch his head. "Then how are we supposed to see them?"

Amos pointed to the center of the field. "Fix you eyes on either the stone basin or the granite slab. Pick a spot and stare hard at it."

The kids lined up beside Amos and began to stare at the basin and slab. After a few moments Casey grabbed Ben's arm with both hands. "I see movement!"

"Those are the fairies," said Amos.

"But when I turn my eyes toward the movement they disappear."

"I see movement too!" Meg exclaimed.

"This stinks," Joey complained. "We see something moving and as soon as we look at it - it vanishes."

"I told you," said Amos, "you cannot see them when you look at them. As soon as you see them moving, look as close to them as you can without looking directly at them."

"What do you mean?" Joey asked.

Amos held his big ham fist beside Ben's head. "Look at my fist Joey. Now don't take your eyes off of my fist. Can you see Ben?"

"Yeah," Joey replied.

"Well that is how you see the fairies. Look as close to them as possible, but do not look directly at them or you will not be able to see them."

The kids turned back to the field and began staring at the stone basin and granite slab once again. Within a few seconds, all of them were jumping up and down, shouting and pointing.

"Look at that fairy!"

"Look over here!"

"Look over there!"

It was difficult at first. Every time someone pointed to a fairy for the others to see, they would immediately look to where the person was pointing and the fairy would vanish from their sight. After a while, they got the hang of it though. The small clearing was filled with fairies; fragile little creatures two or three inches tall, all clothed in colors matching the flowers of the field. Some had on the cool blues and purples of bluets and wild irises, while others wore the warm yellows and reds of jasmine, fleabane, firepink, and dewdrops. All of them were fair skinned with silvery wings and had a golden aura about them. No one could tell what color their eyes were though, without looking directly at them. Ben tried several times with no success. A split second before his eyes would come in contact with the fairy, the woodland creature would vanish. As soon as he would look away, the creature would reappear.

"This is too cool," Ben exclaimed.

The other kids nodded in agreement and Amos cracked his hairy face with a huge grin. Then suddenly, for no apparent reason, all of the fairies disappeared. The kids turned to Amos, who was still looking down at them with that silly grin on his face.

"What happened?" Casey asked.

"What do you mean?" Amos replied.

"Where did all of the fairies go?"

Amos quickly scanned the field, his smile now gone, then turned to the children and bellowed, "RUN!"

10 SNAKERS

The kids scrambled behind Amos, as the huge giant rushed back into the forest and up the hillside. This time he did not take the path they had followed down from the top, but plunged into a dense growth of laurel and brambles. The thorns tore at their clothes and the limbs slapped at their arms and legs, as they plunged deeper and deeper into the thicket. Then, Amos abruptly turned left, parallel to the side of the mountain, and started leading them away from the clearing at an even faster pace. Casey, Joey, and Meg were right behind him, too terrified to look over their shoulder. A tremendous crash erupted from the clearing behind them and images of red-scaled fire breathing dragons arose in Casey's mind, spurring her on even faster. She had already left Joey and Meg behind and was steadily gaining ground, catching up with Amos when, suddenly, the giant man disappeared. One second he was in front of her, thrashing through the underbrush like a charging bull elephant, the next second, he was simply gone. Casey did not even have time to process this turn of events because, in the next instance, her feet shot out from under her and she found herself sliding down a steep embankment into a shallow ravine. Amos was waiting for her at the bottom. He promptly snatched her up and shoved her into a small hole in the side of the bank. Joey slid down immediately after Casey and, a couple of seconds later, Meg followed. Amos shoved them both inside the hole as well and waited for Ben. Seconds ticked by. No Ben. No sound of pursuit. Nothing. Finally, not daring to wait any longer, Amos crouched down and crawled into the hole with the children.

The hole in the side of the ravine wall was actually a small entrance to a cave. It was hidden from view by a thick veil of woody vines that grew from the top of the ravine, to the bottom. The entrance was a tight squeeze for Amos, but with a little wiggling, and with the kids tugging on his furs, he finally made it inside.

"Where's Ben?" Casey whispered frantically.

"I don't know," Amos replied.

"We shouldn't have left him like that, he can't run fast!" Casey cried, tears welling up in her eyes.

Amos put his finger to her lips to silence her. "If we all get caught, we'll be of no help to your brother. Now be quiet and listen."

They huddled together in the darkness, staring at the bright opening, straining their ears for any sound of Ben and his pursuers. A couple of times they thought they heard a twig snap, as if someone accidentally stepped on a limb while trying to move stealthily through the underbrush. Both times everyone held their breaths, but nothing else happened. An hour passed before Amos would permit them to speak or move, and even then, he would only allow them to whisper.

"What were we running from?" Meg asked, her lips trembling.

"And what made that huge crashing sound?" Joey added.

Casey was now hysterical. "What happened to Ben, Amos? We have to find him. Find Ben and take us home, please!" she cried.

87

Amos put his arms around the three children and pulled them close. "Listen to me. I'll answer all of your questions, but not now and not here. We have to get back to the cabin first. Louise needs to know about this and we are going to need her help as well. And right now, Casey, there is nothing we can do for Ben. I feel pretty certain that he is okay, for now, and we will get him back but, you are going to have to trust me that now is not the time."

Casey wiped the tears from here eyes and nodded.

"Good girl. Now, I am going to go out and have a quick look around. I want you kids to stay right here until I get back, understand?"

The kids nodded as one.

"Count slowly to one hundred," Amos continued. "If I am not back by the time you get to one hundred, I want you to count to one hundred again and then head back to the cabin on your own. When you get to the cabin, Louise will want to know what's happened. All you need to say to her is snakers."

"Snakers?" Meg asked. "What does that mean?"

"I don't have time to explain now," said Amos. "Louise will know what it means."

"Which way is the cabin?" Joey asked.

"Follow the ravine to your left, until it runs out into a field. From there, go uphill to the top of the mountain. When you start back down the other side of the mountain, you will come across the trail that leads to the fairy glen. Go left on that trail to get back to my cabin."

Amos crawled from the cave and, with all of his furs, looked very much like an old grizzly bear awakening from a long winter sleep. Casey began counting. It seemed as though she was counting to one thousand instead of one hundred but, by the time she reached eighty-seven, Amos reappeared at the cave opening.

"Come on out," he whispered. "Follow along behind me and move as quietly as possible. And absolutely no talking until we are back at the cabin. Can you do that?"

Once again, all three nodded as one.

"Good. Follow me now and remember, keep quiet."

The three children scrambled out after him and together they trudged up the ravine as it wound its way up the hillside. The ravine was really nothing more than a large ditch, carved into the earth over the centuries by some nameless river, long dead and silent now for many years. In some places this ditch, or river bed, was twelve to fifteen feet deep. In other places, it was only three to four feet deep. In the shallow stretches, Amos and the children would pause and listen for several minutes, then crouch down and hurry through to the deeper parts that could shield them from unfriendly eyes. Soon, they came to a shallow stretch that widened out into a field strewn with small boulders and dotted with small twisted scrub pines and broom sage. Amos led them out of the field and into the tall pines, taking them straight up the hillside. When they reached the top, they paused to listen and catch their breath. The woods were eerily quiet. No birds were singing, no squirrels were chattering. Even the wind was silent. Amos motioned for the children to follow and started down the other side of the hill. In a few minutes, they came upon the path that led back to the cabin and, there, they broke into a brisk jog. Casey, however, truly terrified for her brother, could not hold back any longer. She sprinted ahead, with a sudden burst of speed that surprised everyone and even Amos, with his long legs, could not keep pace with her.

Louise was sweeping the ashes off the hearth when Amos and the kids burst through the door screaming. They surrounded her and began talking wildly, all at once. It took a few seconds for Louise's heart to slow back down to a fast gallop and, as soon as she gathered her wits about her, she realized that Ben was missing. Her heart leapt into her throat and then slammed against her chest like a jack hammer.

"SILENCE!" she screamed.

Amos and the children froze.

"Kids - sit down at the table and zip your lips," Louise ordered, pointing to the benches. Then she turned an icy glare on Amos and planted her hands on her hips. "Where is Ben?"

"Snakers," Amos whispered.

The color drained from her face. Her mouth was moving, but no words were coming out, then her eyes rolled back into her head as she fainted and collapsed into Amos's arms.

"Joey, get the pail and fetch some water from the well," Amos instructed, while he gently laid Louise on the cot and arranged the pillow behind her head. Joey brought the bucket in and set it on the floor by the cot. Amos pulled a rag from beneath his furs, dipped it into the icy water, and began to dab Louise on her forehead. She moaned, then slowly opened her eyes and looked around, as if she did not know where she was. When her memory returned, she bolted upright in bed and grabbed Amos by his beard with both of her hands.

"Tell me everything that happened. Do not leave out even the tiniest detail."

Amos recounted the story of their visit to the fairy glen, occasionally glancing over at the children, who would verify his account with a nod of their heads. When he finished, Casey spoke up.

"Grandma, what are snakers?"

Louise stared at the children for several seconds, then rose from the bed and walked over to sit with them at the table.

"Snake people," Louise whispered. "They are all very, very wicked creatures." She placed her face in her hands and began to sob.

"What's going to happen to Ben?" Casey asked, her eyes brimming once more with tears. "Is he going to be okay? Are they going to eat him?"

Amos walked over and patted Louise on the shoulder. "Nothing is going to happen to Ben if we hurry. Louise, if we are to get the child back, we must leave now."

Louise stood. "You're right. We've no time to lose. But first, you children are going back to our own world. If what Ben said about the Merlin Tree is true, and I believe it is, then no matter how long it takes me to get back with him we should arrive home shortly after you do."

Now, Casey stood. "I'm not going back."

"Oh yes you are, dear."

"No, I'm not. You cannot make me leave and even if you could, I would just turn around and come right back. I feel responsible for Ben. I shouldn't have run off and left him, and I am going to help find him and bring him back."

"I'm not going back either," Joey declared. Casey smiled at him with teary, but thankful, eyes.

Then, Meg piped up. "Well, if Joey is not going back, then neither am I."

Louise tried to stare the children down, but they stood their ground with their chins defiantly up in the air. "Oh well," she sighed. "If you are determined to go, I guess I cannot truly stop you and I'd rather have you with me where I can keep an eye on you, than have you sneaking about on your own. Amos, get my cloak and staff please."

Amos retrieved a brown hooded cloak from a peg on the wall and slim wooden staff from beside the fireplace. He helped Louise into the cloak and handed the staff to her, then went over to rummage in the trunk under the window. Louise urged him to hurry and, frantically, he picked the trunk up and turned it over, spilling its contents all over the floor. Scrambling around on his hands and knees, feeling through the pile of things scattered around him, he finally found what he was seeking.

"Ah-ha! There you are!" he cried, pulling out a wicked looking double bladed axe. The handle was as thick as a man's arm and as long as any of the kids were tall. Amos stood and hefted the axe. He twirled it over his head with one hand and then stuffed it into the belt around his furs. Louise and the children were already across the small yard and were entering the trail at the edge of the pines. Amos shut the door of his cabin and loped after them. Once again he looked like a big grizzly bear, only this time he did not appear as a bear still groggy from a long winters nap. This time he looked like an angry sow bear, charging down on some unsuspecting creature for venturing too close to her cubs.

11 ESCAPE

When Amos bellowed for the children to run, everyone went into action, except Ben. Ben simply froze. At first, it was fear that rooted his feet to the ground, but as he watched Meg disappear into the thick laurel behind Joey, he realized that if any kind of horrible monster gave pursuit, he would be the one to get caught. He also realized that if he followed the others into the thicket, he might also endanger them by putting the monster (or whatever it was they were running from) onto their trail. So, Ben, without even knowing it, did the bravest and most unselfish act of his entire life. He stayed behind in the fairy glen while the others escaped, hoping to find a place to hide and hoping to catch up with the others when the danger had passed.

After the others disappeared from sight, Ben overcame his fear and frantically began looking for a hiding place. Nearby, on the edge of the clearing, to his right, he noticed a thick clump of hedge with dark green shiny leaves that looked very much like the boxwoods bordering the fence by his grandparent's front yard. He remembered playing hide-and-go-seek once and hiding inside one of the boxwoods. No one ever found him there. Not seeing any other suitable places to hide, he made a dash for the shrub and clawed his way inside. The center of the shrub was, in fact, hollow and Ben was able to sit on top of the root ball with the plant's thick woody stems curving out around him. The leaves were too dense to allow him to see what was going on, so he sat as still as possible, straining his ears for any noise. A loud crash broke the silence. Startled, Ben almost fell from his hiding place. After recovering his composure, he slowly parted the branches to see what was happening.

In the center of the clearing, the large red granite slab had toppled over and the fountain of water was now gouging a big muddy hole into the earth where the rock had once stood. Movement caught Ben's eyes. At first he thought it was a fairy, but when he looked toward the movement, the creature did not disappear. Ben sucked in his breath. The creature was dark brown in color and the sunlight glinted on its skin when it walked. Actually, the creature appeared to glide across the ground. No, that did not quite describe how it moved either. The creature seemed to slither as it walked. Like a snake. More of them entered the clearing and began to fan out, as if searching for something. Ben let the branches close and very slowly sat back down on top of the root ball. Fear clasped an iron hand around his lungs and began to squeeze. Panicking, he began to dig around in his pockets for his inhaler, and a dry rustling sound made him freeze. His hand closed on the inhaler as the rustling sound came closer. Movement at the top of the shrub made Ben look up just in time to see two big luminous serpentine eyes staring down at him. Without thinking, Ben raised his inhaler and fired two quick bursts into the creature's eyes. The snake man (this was the name that popped into Ben's head) reeled backwards, clawing at its face while Ben tumbled out the other side of the shrub and landed on his back. Not waiting to see what was going to happen next, Ben rolled over and sprang to his feet. Attempting to flee, he only managed a single step before a searing white, hot bolt of pain shot through his shoulder and sent him stumbling back to the ground. His limbs were instantly heavy and, in just moments, the world around him began a slow and steady descent into darkness. The last thing he heard before the darkness completely engulfed him was that strange rustling sound.

When Ben awoke, to his horror, he found himself captive and dangling from a long pole by his hands and feet. He had some kind of crudely woven sack over his head, but he found that if he squinted his eyes just right, he could see through the loosely woven threads. Two snake men, with the pole on their shoulders, were carrying him. Every muscle in Ben's body ached and, once again, he felt his lungs closing up in the icy grip of fear. Mercifully, he passed out.

The next time he opened his eyes, he was laying on the ground. His hands and feet were untied and the sack was gone from his head. Lying as still as possible, he cracked his eyes open and took in his surroundings. Three of the snake men were sitting not far from him. They seemed to be communicating with each other - hissing and clicking as they waved their hands. One of them turned to look at Ben. Satisfied that Ben was still unconscious, he turned back to the others and the clicking and hissing started up again. Ben could not see any other snake men, but he was certain there were more. Maybe, they were scouting ahead. Or maybe, they were looking for the others. Slowly, Ben flexed the muscles in his legs. They were stiff and a little sore, but he knew he had to make a break for it. Whatever these creatures had in store for him could not be good. After taking two deep breaths and counting to three, Ben sprang to life, rolling over and digging in his heels, he took off like a race horse out of the starting gate. He had gone no more than ten or fifteen yards when his foot caught on a rock and sent him sprawling to the ground. On his way down, he heard a whistling noise and felt the air stir as something whizzed over his head. Quickly, he scrambled to his feet and began running in a zigzag pattern. The snake men were shooting at him. Probably darts. It was coming back to him now. Rolling out of the shrub in the fairy glen. The searing hot pain in his shoulder. The darkness. More darts whizzed past him and a surge of adrenaline sped him on even faster. Ben ran and ran. Tree limbs slapped at his face, brambles tore at his legs. He ran until he thought his lungs would burst and then, he ran some more. Finally, unable to go any further, he collapsed in a patch of reeds and grasses that were growing beside a rushing stream.

After a brief rest, Ben stood up and listened for his pursuers. There was no sign of them. The only sounds were the sounds of the forest; wind in the trees, an occasional bird, and water babbling over the stones behind him. Everything seemed so eerily normal that it was hard to believe he was fleeing from creatures that should only exist in dark fantasies and bad nightmares. Several minutes passed. Finally satisfied that he had eluded his captors, and aware that the afternoon was wearing on, he turned his attention to getting back home. The others, if they hadn't been captured, were probably worried to death about him and were, more than likely, out looking for him right now. However, the first thing he had to do was find some cover where he could think. He followed the stream into the forest and found a suitable place beneath an old cedar where he could hide and sort out his dilemma. Parting the limbs, he crawled underneath the ancient shaggy branches and leaned back against the trunk. Pushing his glasses up on his nose, he began to count on his fingers:

1: The snake men were carrying him downhill.
2: It would be logical to assume they were carrying him away from the fairy glen.
3: When he fled the snake men, he fled downhill.
4: That would mean at least three of the snake men were between him and the fairy glen.
5: That would mean that the remaining snake men were either scouting ahead, and could be anywhere around him, or they were pursuing the others and he would run into them later.

6: If he did not act quickly, he might end up having to spend the night in Camelot, alone.

That last point spurred him into action. Ben crawled out from under the cedar and brushed the needles off his pants. He would have to make a wide circle to get back to the top of the hill, so he decided to follow the stream. Maybe the stream originated from the fountain of water in the fairy glen. He walked as quietly as possible, following what seemed to be a well worn path that meandered alongside the twisting stream bed. Minutes stretched into hours and the evening sun began to cast a rosy glow on the western sky.

"Red sky at night, sailor's delight," Ben mumbled to himself. "Should be a pretty day here tomorrow. With any luck, I won't be here to see it."

As the western sky turned rosy, the eastern sky began to darken and the first star of the evening twinkled faintly above. Much to Ben's dismay, it occurred to him that he was not going to make it back before nightfall. He must have been unconscious longer than he realized and, that meant, he was probably further away from the fairy glen than he had hoped. He had been traveling in a westerly direction and assumed that it would now be safe to turn back towards the north to begin his long trek to the top of whatever hill he was skirting. He did not want to spend the night out in the open, so he decided to follow the stream a little further to look for a safe place where he could hole up for the night.

He followed the path for a while longer; eventually, the path began to diverge from the stream and slowly wound its way up the hillside. Soon the path ended at the base of a towering rock wall that jutted out from the side of the hill. After a brief search, Ben found small steps carved into the rock and followed them up to a ledge about twenty feet above the ground. The ledge was no more than three or four feet wide and at the back of the ledge there was a crevice in the rock wall that offered protection from the wind, or any dew that might fall during the night. Ben crawled into the crevice and, after exploring every nook and cranny to make sure there were no spiders or snakes present, lay down on the hard stone, instantly falling into an exhausted sleep.

Ben had no idea how long he had been asleep, but the sound of footsteps roused him instantly and he scrambled as far back into the crevice as he could. In here there was total blackness, but just outside, the moon cast a silvery sheen on the ledge that lit the night up just enough for him to make out the huge gnarled trunks of the pine trees, that were growing just beyond the ledge. The footsteps were coming from the stone staircase. Had the snake men been able to track him this far? How many were there? It sounded like at least three.

"Hurry up, Hob. I'm done in for."

"Yes, Hob, get up here. I can hardly keep my eyes open."

"I'm coming, I'm coming. You're not the only ones tired tonight. I have twice as much in my sack as the two of you together, so quit your grumbling and give me a hand up."

Ben listened intently to the commotion outside. He was relieved it was not the snake men, but still very wary about whom it might be. For all he knew, it could be three big ugly trolls, ten feet tall with warts, fangs and claws, ready to pounce and devour him at once. Whoever they were, or whatever they were, bedded down to the left of the crevice, just out of his sight. Once they settled down, it was just a matter of minutes before the night sounds of forest insects were drowned out by the sound of their snoring.

After they had been snoring soundly for about half an hour, Ben crept to the opening in the rock wall. He could not pass the night here. The creatures might have passed him by in the dark, but in the light of morning they would see him clearly in the shallow crevice. Fortunately, the moon was bright enough for Ben to see and when he poked his head out of the shadows, he saw three short, but very powerfully built men lying on their backs, side by side, with their large hands folded across the long flowing beards on their chests.

"Dwarves!" Ben thought in amazement. However, he did not know if dwarves were good creatures or evil creatures. In all of the stories he had ever read, they were basically good. But those were stories and this was real, so he decided not to take any chances. He couldn't go back down the stairs because the dwarves had the way blocked, so he crawled out onto the ledge, slowly got to his feet, and began carefully inching his way to the right. The ledge ran on for about thirty feet and gradually began to disappear. Ben felt along the rock face for stairs that might lead up. When he found none, he lay down on his stomach and felt along the wall below the ledge. Dismayed, he realized that this was a dead end and the only way down was the way he came up. Tip-toeing back towards the stairs, he came within three feet of the sleeping dwarves. Their heads were touching the rock wall, their feet stuck out over the ledge, and they were sleeping shoulder to shoulder. The only place Ben could step was between their heads. Maybe he should just go back into the crevice and pass the night there anyways. Maybe the dwarves knew this was a dead end, and maybe, they were just spending the night up here like he was. The steps leading up here were small steps after all. These three dwarves may have even carved them. Then again, if they did carve those steps, that meant that this ledge belonged to them and they might not take kindly to Ben's trespassing. So, taking a deep breath, he hugged the rock wall and stepped over the first dwarf's head with his right foot and stood there for several seconds, waiting for his heart to quit hammering in his chest. For a moment, he was afraid that the dwarves would actually hear his heart beating and wake up to find him straddled over them. When his pulse finally calmed down, he lifted his left foot and placed it beside his right foot. So far so good. All three of the dwarves were still snoring loudly. Ben then raised his right foot to step over the next dwarf's head and froze. The next dwarf's eyes were wide open. Ben teetered, and tried to bring his right foot back down, but lost his balance. As he began to fall, he frantically tried to find purchase with his hands on the rock wall. At the last second, he hopped back over the first dwarf and landed with a loud thud on his backside.

12 HOB, GOB, AND NOB

Ben hit the ground with a loud plop and the three dwarves awoke in a flurry of arms and legs. They were on their feet in an instant and their axes seemed to materialize out of thin air into their hands. One of the dwarves had his axe raised, ready to bring it down on top of Ben's head, when another dwarf yelled out to him.

"Hob! Stop!"

The dwarf froze, his axe still poised over his head, his beard quivering.

"Put your axe down, you lummox, it's a man child."

Hob slowly lowered his axe and bent over to peer at Ben.

"So it is a man child. Come over here Gob and take a look at this."

The three dwarves gathered around Ben, poking him with their fingers and firing questions at him without giving him time to respond.

"What's your name, man child?"

"Where are your parents? Is anyone else with you?"

"Where are you coming from and where are you going?"

"What are you doing in our woods, trespassing on our ledge no less?"

Ben sat up and adjusted his glasses. The dwarves, although rough in manner, did not appear to mean him any harm. He had just startled them.

"Hold up guys! I can't answer all of your questions at once." Slowly, Ben rose to his feet. He recalled reading something, somewhere, about dwarves bowing upon introductions. Placing one arm behind his back and one arm across his stomach, Ben bowed low and introduced himself. "My name is Ben. Ben Alderman. I am from Atlanta Georgia and I am trying to go back there. Who may I ask are you?"

The dwarves seemed quite impressed with this display of formality and cordiality.

"Oh, forgive us please," said the dwarf on the left, who bowed low in return. "My name is Gob, this is Nob, and the gentleman who was about to split your noggin open a few moments ago is Hob."

Nob and Hob bowed as well, their beards brushing the tops of their boots.

"I did not know this was your ledge," said Ben, "and I apologize for trespassing. I just needed a safe place to sleep tonight."

"Safe place indeed. How do we know you are telling us the truth?" asked Hob. "For all we know, you might be looking for our treasure!"

Gob and Nob immediately kicked Hob in the shins to silence any talk of treasure. Hob swore loudly as he fell to the ground, clutching at his shins.

"The woods are safe enough," Gob stated, turning his attention back to Ben. "There are no dragons in these parts. No ogres or trolls. Not even any gnomes."

"As a matter of fact, the wildest creature you may find in these woods would be a fox," Nob added. "So, what were you afraid of?"

"Snake men," Ben replied. "I was on your ledge, hiding from the snake men."

Hob jumped up, his poor bruised shins now forgotten, and grabbed Ben by the shoulders. "Snake men? What do you mean snake men? Speak, man child!"

"Okay, okay, let me go," Ben cried, pulling away from Hob's grasp. "And quit calling me man child. I told you that my name is Ben."

"Okay, Ben," said Gob, "forgive Hob, he hasn't any manners. We have many questions to ask you, but first of all you must tell us about the snake men. Please."

The three dwarves sat cross-legged on the ground in front of Ben, with their axes across their laps. Ben took a deep breath and started his tale with the visit to the fairy glen. The dwarves actually knew of the fairy glen and were very distraught to learn that the beautiful fountain had been destroyed. They promised Ben that they would return to the fairy glen and repair the fountain the first chance they got. Ben thanked them and continued on with his story. When he got to the part about escaping the three snake men, the dwarves stood up and hurriedly began packing their sacks.

"What's going on?" Ben asked. "I haven't finished my story."

Gob looked up while stuffing his sack, "You may finish your tale later. If snakers are about, then the woods are indeed not safe. It is not even safe to pass the night upon this ledge."

Hob had finished packing his sack and slung it across his shoulders. "If they are tracking you, and I'm sure they are, they must be near by now. We are going inside."

"Inside where?" Ben asked, looking around.

Gob and Nob hoisted their sacks over their shoulder as well and motioned for Ben to follow them. Hob led the way and entered the crevice Ben was hiding in earlier. Nob followed Hob, then Gob, and Ben brought up the rear. Ben wondered how they would all fit inside and how cramming into the small cave could possibly offer them any protection from the snake men, or snakers as the dwarves called them. When Gob disappeared into the dark opening, Ben shrugged his shoulders and followed. Once he was inside, where it was darker, he held his hands out in front of him, expecting to bump into Gob at any moment. Then, suddenly, a bright light flared in front of him and he saw Gob disappear into a tunnel that had opened up in the rear of the cave. Intrigued by the discovery of this secret passage, Ben followed Gob into the tunnel where Hob was holding up a torch so that everyone could see.

The torch cast an eerie orange glow around them and made their shadows flicker and dance across the stone walls of the tunnel. The floor was smooth and disappeared straight into the hillside. Once they were all in the tunnel, Nob pushed the stone door shut and the three dwarves set off down the passageway, at a brisk pace.

"Wait," Ben cried. "Where are you going? Aren't we safe here?"

The dwarves didn't stop, but Gob motioned for Ben to catch up.

"We can't sleep close to the door. The snakers would detect our body heat. There's a chamber up ahead. We'll bed down there and pass the remainder of the night."

A few minutes later, Hob stopped in front of a massive iron bound wooden door and Nob pushed it open on groaning hinges. When everyone was in the room, Nob pushed the door shut and Gob dropped a thick wooden beam across the door, while Hob lit an old oil lamp with the torch.

"This is an old treasure room," said Hob as he extinguished the torch and placed it into a rusty sconce on the wall by the entrance. "That's why the door is so thick and strong."

"Now that the treasure is gone," said Nob, emphasizing the word gone and looking temptingly at Hob's shins, "this has become a junk room."

"But, it's also a handy place to sleep when we are late getting home and have need to be inside," Gob added.

The room was about the size of Ben's bedroom. Against the back wall, a small table was laden with an assortment of oil lamps and clay jugs filled with oil. In the corner of the room was a pile of rusty and broken shovels and pick axes. The three dwarves pulled blankets out of their sacks and rolled them out on the floor in the center of the room. Hob pulled an extra blanket out of his sack and tossed it to Ben. "Let's get some shut-eye. In the morning, you can tell us your whole story and then we'll decide what to do."

Ben didn't argue. He could hardly keep his eyes open. Stretching out on the thick woolen blanket, he was asleep before Hob could even trim the lantern.

The next morning, Gob had to shake Ben to wake him. Ben opened his eyes to find Gob staring at him, just inches from his face. "Good morning, Ben. You sleep like a dwarf. Are you sure you're a man child?"

Ben sat up and rubbed the sleep from his eyes. "I'm starving," he moaned.

"Well, get up and let's get moving. We've nothing to eat here, but we can be at our home in a couple of hours and there, we'll have a grand feast."

"And after we are done with our breakfast," Hob added, "you may finish your story and regale us with tales of your grand adventures."

The march through the rest of the tunnel seemed to take much longer than a couple of hours. Along the way, they passed several more doors, all of which were shut. Finally, the tunnel ended at another door, beyond which they found themselves in a round chamber. In this chamber were thirteen doors, just like the one they had just passed through, evenly spaced around the walls.

"This door," said Hob, pointing to the door they had just entered, "opens into the tunnel that leads to the ledge. These other doors open to tunnels that lead nowhere. These tunnels are long and winding with many twists and turns, but no way out. All except one. And that door opens into our home. Can you tell which one?"

Ben slowly walked around the room and examined each door. All of the doors looked exactly the same. He looked closely at the door handles to see if one might be shiny with use, but they all were polished to a shiny gleam. Lastly, he examined the floor, but could find no clues there either. "May I see the torch?" he asked, turning to Hob.

Hob handed Ben the torch. Ben walked around the room once more, holding the torch to the edge of each door to see if some small current of air might cause the flame to flicker and reveal to him which door to choose. Still no luck.

Then he smiled. He'd just open every door! Handing the torch back to Hob, Ben opened the door to the right of the one they had just come through. Then, he went to the next door. But as soon as his hand touched the handle, the door he had just opened slammed shut and the floor began to move. The three dwarves roared with laughter, as the floor spun in circles. Poor Ben turned green, as the doors flipped by in rapid succession. When the floor finally came to a halt, Ben put his hand against the wall to steady himself.

"Okay, I give up," he said, holding his stomach and thanking his lucky stars that he had not eaten breakfast yet. "Which one is it?"

Hob smiled. "We work very hard to keep our home and our mines secret. As you just found out, you cannot open all of the doors at once. The ledge door and the home door may stay open at all times. But, only one dead-end tunnel door may be opened at any one time. As soon as you open a second dead-end tunnel door, all of the doors will close and the floor will spin to disorient you. Do you even know which door we came through now?"

Ben shook his head. He certainly did not want to try and find out either.

Hob smiled again and continued. "The hinges on the doors that open into the dead end tunnels are ever so slightly tilted so that if someone enters one, the door will eventually close while they are exploring the tunnel. When they discover the tunnel is a dead end, and if they ever manage to find the door again, they will discover that it is not only closed, but locked as well. You see, the doors to these dead end tunnels can only be opened from inside this chamber."

Ben looked around the room, a new worry forming in his mind. "I am sure that my Grandma and Amos are looking for me by now. What if they find this tunnel and they get caught in one of these traps?"

"That would be a problem," said Hob. "We wouldn't really be able to even know if they had stumbled into one."

"I wouldn't worry about it, Ben," said Gob. "Even if they manage to track you to the ledge, I doubt very seriously they will be able to find the tunnel entrance."

Nob was pulling nervously on his beard. "They could find it you know. Remember that cave troll that found it a couple of years ago?"

Hob and Gob shivered. The cave troll never even explored the tunnel, he just took up residence right inside the ledge entrance. It took them days to drive him out. But Nob was right, there was a slim chance they could find the tunnel entrance and if they did, the odds of them getting lost in one of the dead end tunnels were pretty good.

"Drat," said Hob. "What are we to do? We can't very well hang a sign on the door that says 'Dwarves Live Here.' What if the snakers find the tunnel? Do you want them slithering into our home while we are asleep and pricking us with their poison darts? Do you want to be hauled off to who-knows-where to meet their queen and play with her?"

"Which door leads to your home?" Ben asked.

"That one," said Gob, pointing to a door across the room.

"I have an idea," Ben said. "I need something to write with though."

Hob raised a questioning eyebrow.

"Trust me," said Ben, "I don't want the snakers to find us either. I'm going to write something and only my Grandma and my sister will know what it means."

"A secret code?" asked Nob, rubbing his hands together. Dwarves liked secret codes, almost as much as treasure. Some have even said that dwarves only mined the precious metals and gems, so that they could have a reason for dreaming up secret codes with which to hide them.

Ben thought for a moment. "Yes. It is a secret code that only my Grandmother and my sister will be able to solve."

Hob nodded to Gob who disappeared into the door leading to their home and returned a few minutes later with a lump of coal. Ben took the coal and made his way around the room, writing on each and every door. When he finished, he gave the lump of coal back to Gob and wiped his hands on his pants. Hob then walked around the room and studied the numbers that Ben had written on each door. Every door had a different number. Gob and Nob studied the numbers as well. Finally, unable to crack the code, they admitted they were stumped. Hob was also satisfied that no one could determine which door led to their home, without knowing Ben's secret code. He nodded in satisfaction.

"Very good," he said. "Let's get some breakfast now and then you may finish your tale."

"And later, you will have to teach us this code too," Nob added, still staring at the strange numbers.

13 GOING FOR HELP

The dwarves lived in a cozy three room house, built into the side of a hill. The house was constructed of stone and timbers and each one of the rooms was warm and inviting. The door leading from the round chamber was hidden inside of a closet that opened up into the center room of the house. The center room was the largest room in the house and appeared to be the den. There, three rocking chairs sat in front of a beautiful fireplace made of field and river rocks. The jagged field rocks, with their glittering surfaces, provided a striking contrast with the smooth and multi-colored surfaces of the river rocks. On each side of the fireplace, thick columns of driftwood supported a great mantle made from a large log that had been split in half. The room to their left was the sleeping quarters. There, three iron beds were lined up side by side, along the far wall. Beside each bed, stood a small wardrobe of cedar, and at the foot of each bed, a trunk of cedar as well. The remaining room, to their right, was the kitchen. On the far wall of this room, a baker cabinet with multiple shelves and racks was filled with jars, jugs, pots, and pans. A table, with benches on either side, sat in the middle of the room.

"Have a seat, Ben, while we get breakfast started," said Hob pointing to the rocking chairs. Ben sat down in one of the chairs and began rocking, while the dwarves set about preparing breakfast. Nob raked some coals out of the fireplace, onto the hearth and sat a skillet full of meat down on top of the hot coals. Then he placed another pan, one with a lid on it, on top of the glowing embers and used a small shovel to scoop up more coals to put on top of the lid.

"What's in that pan?" Ben asked.

"Biscuits," said Nob.

Half an hour later, they were seated at the table. The breakfast fare consisted of meat that looked like fried steak patties to Ben, hot biscuits, cheese, and some baked apples. Ben took a biscuit, pulled it apart and placed the meat, with a thick slice of cheese, inside it. The dwarves watched in fascination as he prepared his biscuit.

"What are you doing?" Gob asked.

"What do you mean?" Ben replied.

"Why did you put your meat and cheese inside of your biscuit?"

"That is the way we eat them where I come from. Try it."

The dwarves pulled their biscuits apart and inserted the meat and cheese.

"Not bad!" said Gob. "Not bad at all. Why didn't we ever think of this?"

"You know," said Nob, "the next time we bake a loaf of bread, we could slice it and use the slices to hold meats and cheeses for other meals too. I think ham and cheese would be quite delicious prepared that way."

Ben laughed. "That would be called a sandwich, guys, and you're right Nob. A ham and cheese sandwich is delicious."

"Sandwich," the dwarves repeated, nodding in satisfaction.

After breakfast, Ben helped the dwarves clean up and then they retired to the center room. Hob brought in another chair, from the front porch, for Ben to sit in and the dwarves arranged their rocking chairs in front of him.

"Now," said Hob, "this business with the snakers troubles me greatly. They haven't been in these parts for many, many years and I fear their presence is an ill omen of worse things to come. So, tell us your tale, Ben, from Atlanta Georgia. Start at the beginning, please, and tell us everything you remember."

Ben did not know if he could explain where he was really from or how he got here. He decided to start his tale with their trip to the fairy glen. When he got to the part about squirting his inhaler into the eyes of one of the snakers, the dwarves were very interested and wanted to see his inhaler. He spent the next half hour trying to explain to them what an inhaler was, how it was made, how it worked, what was asthma, how do you get it, and is it contagious.

"Why didn't you just stick him with your knife?" Hob asked.

"What knife?"

"That is a knife on your belt, is it not?" said Hob, pointing to Ben's side.

Ben felt along his belt. The knife his Dad gave him. He had forgotten all about it. "I forgot I had it with me," he said. He could feel the heat rising in his neck and he knew that his ears were turning a fiery red.

"Don't give it a second thought," said Nob, leaning over and patting him on the knee. "It was quite a brave thing you did, squirting him in the eyes with your inhaler. Do go on with your story."

Ben told them about his capture, his escape, his attempt to sneak past the dwarves as they were sleeping on the ledge, and finally about his need to get back to his sister and Grandma so they could all go home.

Hob rose from his chair and began pacing back and forth across the room, while Nob and Gob continued to rock. Finally, he came back to his chair and pulled it right up to Ben's chair, before sitting back down. "I don't think that's the best thing to do just yet. When snakers are on the move, they travel about in many small groups that make up one large group called a hive. The Queen stays with the main thrust of the hive which is called the nest. The snakers in the nest are larger and more powerful than the kind you encountered and their only purpose is to protect the Queen. The smaller groups, that move ahead of the nest, are hunters. Their sole purpose is to provide food to the nest. They are smaller than the nesters, but faster and still very strong. It was a group of hunters that captured you."

Hob got up and began pacing again, while Gob took over. "We don't know how large this hive is. It could be as few as fifty snakers, or as many as five hundred. It's just not safe to go back the way we came. If we did, we'd probably all be captured."

"But what about my Grandma and sister?" Ben pleaded. "And Amos and Joey and Meg?"

"If they are captured what could we do? We are only three dwarves and one man-child. The best thing we can do is go to our home in the mountains as quickly as possible and return with help. A full regiment of battle-hardened warriors should be sufficient to exterminate this hive. Besides, now that your family and friends know about the snakers, they may avoid capture altogether. Look, if they are out searching for you, and if they do avoid capture, and if they do manage to track you here to our dwelling, then we shall leave a letter with instructions for them to wait here for our return."

"That's a lot of ifs," said Ben.

"Well, I'm sorry to say I have but one more. If they are captured, then the sooner we return with reinforcements, the more likely we are to find them alive. But, we need to leave soon."

Ben pushed his glasses up on his nose and tried to find fault with Gob's logic. He knew everything that Gob said made sense. What could they do? Three dwarves and a kid? Unable to think of any better plan and unable to find fault with Gob's, he sighed wearily and conceded. "How soon do we need to leave?"

Hob came back to his rocker and plopped down. "We need to leave now. If it is a large hive, then the longer we wait, the more dangerous it will be for us to get out. Also, if your friends are captured, the longer we wait, the less likely they are to survive."

Ben jumped up from his chair. "Do you have something I can write a letter on?"

Nob hopped up and went into the small bedroom and returned a moment later with parchment, a feather quill, and a small jar of ink. He went into the kitchen and called over his shoulder to Ben, "Come in here and sit at the table to write your letter."

Ben followed Nob into the kitchen and sat down at the table with the parchment before him. He had used a calligraphy pen before and had no trouble using the feather quill. When the letter was finished, he blew on the ink until it dried and then folded the parchment in half. Across the back of the letter, he wrote:

TO: Grandma, Casey, Joey, Meg, and Amos
FROM: Ben

Satisfied with the completed message, he positioned the parchment in the center of the table and placed a small jar from the baker's cabinet on top of it. The dwarves were busy packing in the bedroom, so he decided to see if he could help them pack.

"There's your sack," said Gob, pointing to a dark blue sack on the end of the bed. From the looks of the bulging sack, they had already packed it for him.

"What's in there?" Ben asked.

"Blankets, an oil skin to keep you dry if it rains, a heavy fur cloak for the mountains, flint and steel, tinder, a bit of rope, and a few odds and ends we may need on our journey," Gob replied as he rummaged through his wardrobe. "Here, try this on. You will need a light traveling cloak to help you blend in with the surroundings." Gob tossed a dark brown hooded cloak to Ben. Although Ben was about the same height as the dwarves, if not taller, the dwarves were stocky and broader in the shoulders and Ben had to roll the sleeves up to get his hands out.

"Not bad," said Gob. "Not bad at all. If you only had a beard, you would make a fine looking dwarf."

Ben smiled. In spite of the dangers that lay before him, he felt like Bilbo Baggins getting ready to leave the Shire in search of dragon gold. "Do you think we'll see any elves?"

"Not if we're lucky," said Hob, as he slung his sack over his shoulder. "Let's get moving. I want to get some miles behind us before nightfall."

On the front porch, the group paused for just a moment to admire the morning. The sun was shining brightly and glimmered on the surface of a lake, visible through the pines in the valley below. Hob was the first one off the porch and he led the way down the hillside, toward the lake.

"That stream you followed yesterday, flows to the lake below," said Hob in a whisper. "There are many small streams, such as that one, that feed this lake, but there is one great river that empties it. We will take a boat across the lake and down the river as far as the Twilight. From there, we will have to walk."

"Tell me about the Twilight," Ben asked. "Grandma told me it's a magical forest where all of the elves live."

"Yes, the Twilight is a magical elfin forest. You can walk around the perimeter of it in one day, but everyone claims it would take you a couple of months to walk through the center of it. The funny thing is, I don't know of anyone who has actually been in the Twilight. Anyone living that is. You see, whoever enters the Twilight without permission, is never heard from again."

Ben chewed on that bit of information for a little while and then dismissed it. Elves could not be evil. There must be more to the story. "Why do the elves not come out anymore?"

"The way I understand it, Ben, is the Twilight is a place of healing for them. It is their refuge and their fortress. After the last battle with the witch, the elves retreated to the Twilight and have been there ever since."

"How long has that been?"

"I don't know. No one really remembers."

"Does the river go through the Twilight?"

"Straight through the middle. There is a town a few miles north of the Twilight. We will try to make it there by nightfall. It may be our last chance to eat a hot meal, and sleep in a soft bed, for several days."

"I also heard my Grandma talking to Amos about the witch. Something about her leaving her castle and being on the move again."

Hob stopped and turned to Ben. Gob and Nob gathered around him too. "Really?" Hob asked. "What else do you remember?"

Ben scratched his neck and tried to think. This cloak was hot and it was making him itch too. "Not much," he replied, slapping at a mosquito buzzing around his ear. "There was something about a unicorn and a big oak forest."

"A unicorn?" Gob asked.

"Yes," Ben answered. "I think the witch means to kill it."

"We will have to worry about the witch later," said Nob. "Right now, snakers are our only concern."

"Yes, and I'll bet my last gold nugget the witch is behind these blasted snakers being here too," said Gob.

"Well, there's nothing we can do about it now, so hush up with all the talk and be on your guard."

A couple of hours later, they emerged from the forest onto the rocky banks of a vast blue lake. A canoe, partially out of the water, rested on a crescent shaped sandy beach between the rocks. Ben and the dwarves carefully made their way over the rocks to the canoe; a long and narrow craft made from birch bark with an oil skin stretched tightly across the top, to keep the rain out. Nob pulled the oil skin off, rolled it up and packed it away in the rear, along with everyone's gear. Once everyone was aboard and seated, Hob pushed the canoe out into the water and hopped in. Gob and Nob took the oars and began paddling to the center of the lake.

"Once we get to the middle," said Nob, "the current will pick us up and take us to the river. There are a few rapids, but if we hug the shoreline our ride should be smooth."

"Look!" cried Ben, pointing to the other side of the lake.

Slithering in and out among the shadows of the pines were fifteen, maybe twenty snakers. They had spotted the boat and were running up and down the banks, pointing and waving their arms. More snakers poured out of the forest and soon there were hundreds of them running about on the shore.

"Oh no," Hob whispered. "Faster guys. Paddle faster!"

14 A BEAR IN THE NIGHT

When Amos, Louise, and the kids arrived at the fairy glen, they were dismayed at the wreckage they found. The beautiful fountain was destroyed and all of the colorful flowers lay broken and trampled upon the ground. The fairies were out now too, flitting back and forth in quick jerky motions. All of the movement almost made Casey queasy.

"The snakers are gone," Amos said. "The fairies are upset, but they would not be out if the snakers were anywhere close by. You kids stay here with Louise and let me scout the area to see if I can figure out what happened."

Louise and the kids sat down at the edge of the glen and watched as Amos began to circle the area. The big man moved slowly, carefully scanning the ground to his left and to his right. When he came to what appeared to be a large boxwood shrub, he circled the bush three times and left the glen. Fifteen minutes later, he returned.

"The snakers have him."

Louise gasped and Casey began to cry. Amos put his hand on Casey's shoulder and gently squeezedy.

"All is not lost, child. They're gone, but I've picked up their trail. And if we hurry, I think that we will catch them

117

before they reach the queen. If we can do that, then there is hope for Ben yet. Okay?"

Casey, unable to speak because of the huge lump rising in her throat, wiped her eyes and nodded. Amos smiled and patted her on the back. "Good. Now let's get moving."

Hot on the trail, Amos sped along at a pace the others could barely keep up with. Even though they were traveling downhill, they were beginning to tire. Especially Louise. When Amos finally threw up his hand to signal the others to stop, they all collapsed beneath the shade of an old sycamore tree. Once again, he began examining the ground. As he did at the fairy glen, he circled the area until he spotted some clue and then set off down the hill, leaving Louise and the kids to rest and catch their breath. When he returned, he was smiling.

"It looks like Ben has escaped."

"Thank goodness," Louise exclaimed. "Are you certain? What about the snakers?"

"Yes, I am positive that he has escaped. There were only three snakers taking him back to the queen, but they are on his trail so we need to keep moving."

"Do you think he's okay?" Casey asked.

"I think so. But even if he evades the snakers, by nightfall he will be cold, scared, and hungry."

"Let's get moving then," said Joey. "It's already late and I don't want to be out here at night."

"Me either!" Meg added, as she looked up and saw a star glimmering faintly in the east.

Once again, Amos took the lead. The party walked down the hill and followed Ben's trail to the small winding stream with a path along side it. Amos left the path and found a spot where a hemlock had recently fallen across a large boulder. The rock and the limbs from the fallen tree offered a crude shelter, if not from the weather, then at least from any snakers that might be lurking about.

"Let's camp here for the night," said Amos.

"We can't stop, we've got to keep going," Casey cried.

"We can't see in the dark, Casey. Snakers can," said Louise. "Besides, we need our rest. Ben is a smart kid. I'm sure he has found a safe place to hide and pass the night."

"Our mom is going to be worried sick about us," said Meg.

"No she's not," Joey answered. "Remember, when we go back through the Merlin Tree it will be the same time as when we left. Even if we stay here for several days."

Amos rummaged under his furs and pulled out a sack with a leather drawstring. He opened the sack and pulled out several strips of dried beef and passed them out. "Eat this. It's meat from a white prairie stag. A small amount will fill your stomach and give you strength. I'll fetch us some water from the stream."

After eating the meager fare of dried beef and water, Louise and the kids bedded down for the night. When they were all fast asleep, Amos rose silently and disappeared into the forest. Though the night had been quietly slipping by, it seemed like they had just closed their eyes when the roar of an angry beast shattered the stillness and ripped them from their slumber. Scrambling to their feet, they rushed out from beneath the shelter just as a huge black bear burst out of the darkness, full of rage and fury. Louise and the kids jumped aside and pressed up against the bolder as the angry bear bore down on them. Now there was no where to run, no way to escape. Casey and Meg screamed and the big bear passed by them and exploded into the fallen tree that was their shelter. Shattered tree limbs flew everywhere and an ear piercing shriek made everyone cover their ears.

Although it was night, the moon was very bright and every one could see what was happening. The great bear had crashed into the tree and bowled over three snakers. The first snaker took the brunt of the bear's charge and lay lifeless on the ground. The second snaker was ripped open by one swipe of the bear's paw and the bear had the third snaker in its jaws, shaking it like a rag doll. Finally, satisfied that the snaker was dead, the bear dropped the mangled creature to the ground and ambled off into the darkness. As soon the bear was gone, Louise set about straightening the camp as if nothing had happened, while Casey, Meg, and Joey stood by with mouths agape.

"Close your mouths kids, before a bug flies in there, get over here and help me straighten up."

"Grandma, did you not just see what happened? What if that bear comes back? And where is Amos?"

"That was Amos, sweetheart."

"What did you say?" Casey asked, bewildered.

"That bear," Louise replied, "was Amos. Amos is a shape shifter dear."

Right at that time, the big man walked into camp with a sheepish look upon his face. The children backed away from him, half expecting him to turn into an angry bear at any moment. Amos saw the fear in their eyes and sat down upon the ground before them, so that he would not look so large and menacing. Louise came up and took a seat beside him, facing the children.

"Amos is a shape shifter," Louise began. "He can turn into a bear at a moments notice. The angrier he is, the larger and more powerful bear he becomes. But listen to me. You kids need not fear him. Amos is the kindest man, with the gentlest spirit, of anyone I've ever met. As long as you are with him, you are safe."

"We weren't safe in the fairy glen this afternoon," Joey remarked.

"No, we weren't," said Casey, her fear slowly giving way to anger. "Why didn't you turn into a bear then and save Ben?"

Louise started to speak, but Amos laid a giant hand on her arm which quieted her. "If I had changed into a bear at the fairy glen what would you have done?"

Casey didn't answer.

"Well, I'll tell you what you would have done. You all would have been terrified of me and you probably would have all run in different directions. How could I have protected you then? So, I kept you together by fleeing with you and got you out of harms way. When Ben was captured, I could not go back for him and leave you all alone, I had to get you to safety first. Do you understand?"

Casey nodded as the tears slid down her cheek. Joey put his arm around her and pulled her close to him. "Don't worry, we'll find Ben."

"You bet we will," Amos said as he rose to his feet. "You guys get some rest. I'm going to clean up my mess and then I'll keep watch over you the rest of the night."

"Don't you need some rest too?" Meg asked.

"I'll rest when Ben is safe and back with us," Amos replied.

Casey walked over to Amos and threw her arms around him. "Thanks. I'm sorry I was angry with you."

"That's okay, child. Now get some sleep. Nothing will bother you tonight."

The rest of the night passed uneventfully and morning dawned with the promise of another beautiful day. There was no sign anywhere around camp about what had transpired last night and though everyone was somewhat stiff from sleeping on the hard ground, they were all well rested and ready to go. Amos passed out some more beef from his sack and they all drank from the stream, before setting off down the path. As the sun rose and began to paint the gray canvas of the early morning sky with warm oranges, the forest came to life with songbirds and the chatter of squirrels. Amos seemed to be in fine spirits and struck up a conversation as they walked.

"Those snakers I disposed of last night were the ones that had Ben captive. They were the ones he escaped from too."

"So, where is Ben?" Joey asked.

"Exactly!" said Amos. "Where is Ben? Those snakers were on Ben's trail yesterday, but last night they were coming back down the path without him."

"So, do you think Ben hid somewhere and they couldn't find him or do you think he just kept running and they gave up chasing him?" Meg asked.

"I'm not sure," Amos replied. "Snakers are excellent trackers and they do not give up on their prey easily. But I believe it is a good sign that he is well."

Eventually, the group came to the point where the path began to pull away from the stream. Amos studied the ground for some time, then led them up the path to the rock wall on the hillside. They soon found the stone steps (which were almost too small for Amos' large feet) and climbed up to the ledge. On top of the rock ledge, there were no tracks to be found and the trail went dead, for there did not seem to be any exit from the ledge, other than the way they had some up.

"Trickery," Amos muttered.

"What's wrong?" Louise asked.

"Dwarves," said Amos. "Back where the path left the stream, three more sets of prints joined Ben's."

"How can you tell it's dwarves and not snakers?" Joey asked.

"Snakers don't wear boots, for one," Amos answered. "And besides, I can smell them. My guess is that Ben came up on this ledge to pass the night. There is a crevice, there, that he probably hid in. Then, sometime later in the night, the three dwarves came up here too. Since there are no tracks on the ground going away from here and since there doesn't seem to be any other way down from this place, it can only mean one thing. The dwarves found him and he has gone with them."

"Gone where?" Joey asked, looking around for an exit.

"There's probably a hidden tunnel on this ledge somewhere," Amos replied. "Maybe even in that crevice somewhere."

"Dwarves are good guys though," said Casey, "aren't they?"

"Yes," said Louise, "They are good guys. That's probably why the snakers turned back. Dwarves hate snakers and given the opportunity, will hew them down without a moment's hesitation. However, this is going to make it more difficult to locate Ben."

"Why is that?" Meg asked.

"Dwarves are pretty much like the characters you read about in fairy tales back home. They love gold, silver, and precious gems and they are forever mining them. They are always in fear of someone looting their treasure, so they spend as much time hiding the trails to their mines and to their homes, as they do mining the metals and gems they love so dearly."

"How do we find the tunnel then? If there even is a tunnel."

"There has to be a door up here somewhere," said Amos. "You won't be able to see it clearly. Look for a crack in the wall, a loose stone, or a depression in the stone. Be careful though and don't get too close to the edge."

The group spread out across the ledge and began running their hands over the rock wall. After an hour of searching with no luck, they sat down to take a break and stare at the wall. Joey was only able to sit for a couple of minutes though, and soon got up to explore the crevice once more. The opening was high enough that he only had to stoop a little to enter, and it was deep enough to lie down yet still be inside. However, it was a narrow fit and the walls converged in the rear, forming a triangular shaped room. Joey squeezed as far back into the room as he could and stared into the corner where the two walls met. Was that a crack? He tried to squeeze further into the corner and the wall to his left moved. That was definitely a crack back there in the corner and it was wider now than it was just a moment ago. He put his back to the wall on the right, and pushed against the wall on the left, with all of his strength. The wall slowly swung inward, revealing a dark tunnel leading into the hillside.

"Hey everyone, I found it!"

The crevice was too small for all of them to fit inside at once so Amos had Joey come out and then he went in first. The big man had to crawl on his hands and knees to enter the crevice, yet it was still a tight fit. Though once inside the tunnel, the ceiling was high enough so that Amos could stand, but he still had to stoop just a little, as he felt along the wall for a torch. After he found a torch and lit it, he called for the others to join him and when everyone was inside the tunnel, he pushed the stone door shut. The door closed with an ominous boom that echoed off the bare stone walls and down the long dark corridor before them.

"Why did you do that?" Meg cried. "What if we can't get back out now?"

"I closed the door to keep any other snakers from picking up our trail. Those dwarves were probably on the way home from their mines last night and, I'll bet, this tunnel leads to their home. With any luck, we'll find Ben at the end of this tunnel and maybe the dwarves can provide us with a safer route back to my cabin."

15 LAYING A TRAP

It took everyone a while to reach the round chamber because they had to open every door and explore every room in the tunnel. Most of the doors opened up into small rooms that required nothing more than a cursory glance. Some of the doors, however, opened up into large rooms. These large rooms required a few minutes of exploration in order to make sure that Ben, and the three dwarves, did not pass through them to get to another passageway. When they finally made it to the end of the tunnel, and entered the round chamber, they all groaned in dismay for all around the walls of the round room were thirteen doors.

"We'll never find him," Joey moaned.

"Not standing around complaining we won't," Louise snapped. Everyone's nerves were frayed by now, especially Louise's. "I'm sorry, Joey, I didn't mean to snap at you. Let's leave this door open and we'll work our way around the room in clockwise fashion."

"Hey, there are numbers on these doors," said Meg. "They look like phone numbers."

"What's a phone number?" Amos asked, as everyone walked over to look at the doors more closely.

"Amos, I'll have to explain that to you some other time," said Louise as she walked from door to door. "Ah! Here it is."

Casey came over to look at the door her grandma had stopped in front of. "That's our phone number. Way to go Ben." Once inside the dwarves' home, they found the letter almost immediately. Louise read it aloud.

Dear Grandma and Casey (and Joey and Meg and Amos),

I hope that everyone is Okay. I am fine. Horrible creatures called snakers had captured me but I managed to escape and I am now with three dwarfs named Hob, Nob, and Gob. If you get this letter please do not come looking for me, but stay here until we return. We are going to their home in the mountains to get some help to fight the snakers. There is enough food here to keep you for a couple of weeks. We should be back before then. I love you and miss you all.

Love,

-Ben.

P.S.

Do not go into any of the other doors in the round chamber. The doors will not stay open - they are fixed to close slowly. When they close, they lock and cannot be opened from the inside. All of them are dead ends. Do not even open those doors. If you try to open more than one of them at the same time, the doors will close and the floor will spin.

Louise dabbed at the corner of her eyes with her sleeve. "If any harm comes to him I'll skin those fool dwarves alive. What were they thinking, taking him off like that? He's just a child."

"The dwarves will protect him, Louise. He is much better off with them than he is on his own."

"I suppose you are right. I just wish they would have waited here a little longer."

Amos patted her on the shoulder. "He's going to be fine now, so don't fret. You kids help Louise take stock of the supplies, while I have a look around outside."

Amos walked out onto the porch and down the steps. He circled the yard once and found the trail Ben and the three dwarves traveled down earlier. The path led down the hill into the forest. The earth was well worn and packed hard from much use. Through the trees, Amos could see a lake in the valley below. Feeling a sense of urgency that he could not explain, Amos shape shifted into a bear and followed the trail to the lake as fast as his four legs would carry him. He found the place where Ben and the dwarves had boarded a boat. But there was still something bothering him. Something he could not quite put his finger on. Then it hit him. It was an odor. Very, very faint but an odor nonetheless. It was an odor that made the hair along his grizzly back bristle and stand on end.

Back at the dwarves' cabin, Louise, Casey and Meg were going through the pantry in the kitchen, while Joey plundered through the trunks and wardrobes in the small bedroom. The pantry was well stocked. There were two salt cured hams in burlap sacks hanging from the rafters, along with dozens of strings of dried beans and herbs. Two large barrels and two wooden crates were tucked away in the corner. One barrel was filled with dried fish and the other was half full of bright red apples. The two crates contained potatoes and onions. Louise left the pantry and began rummaging through the shelves in the baker's cabinet, where she found an assortment of pots, pans, mugs and dishes. Selecting an iron skillet and a sharp knife, she instructed Casey to bring her one of the hams and Meg to bring several potatoes and an onion to the table.

"We may as well fix something to eat, while we wait on Amos to get back," said Louise, as she began peeling the potatoes. "Casey, grab another knife from that cabinet and

help me peel these potatoes. Meg, see if you can find
enough plates, cups, and utensils for the five of us."

Within a few minutes, Louise had the skillet full of
potato wedges, onion rings, and thick slices of ham. While
she raked some coals onto the hearth, Meg and Casey set the
table.

"Where did Joey get to?" Casey asked.

"He's still in the bedroom," said Meg.

Casey walked over and peeked into the bedroom. Joey
was sound asleep on one of the beds. Louise came up
behind Casey and laid her hand on her shoulder. "That's not
a bad idea. You and Meg should grab a quick nap too, while
you can. I'll wake you as soon as Amos gets back, then we'll
eat and figure out what to do next."

"I think I will," said Casey.

"I think I will too," Meg added, when she walked up
and saw Joey stretched out and sleeping peacefully. Both
girls picked a bed and laid down on the soft, straw-stuffed
mattresses. In just a matter of minutes, they too, were
sleeping soundly. Louise decided to watch over their meal
and pass the time away rocking, while waiting for Amos to
return. The rocking chair, even though it did not have any
cushions, was surprisingly comfortable.

"Louise? Louise? Wake up."

Someone was shaking her and calling her name. Slowly,
she floated up from the depths of slumber and as the chains
of unconsciousness fell away, she opened her eyes to find
Amos leaning over her, gently shaking her and calling her
name. The smell of onions, potatoes, and ham filled the air.

"Oh no, our meal," Louise cried, jumping up from the
rocker. "I hope it didn't burn!"

"The meal is fine. I checked it and removed it from the
hearth. Let's wake the children and eat. We need to discuss
where we go from here and I fear we haven't much time to
decide."

The food was delicious. Everyone devoured their
portion and washed it down with ice cold water, drawn from

the well in front of the house. Poor Amos could not fit his knees under the dwarves' table and had to sit on the floor to eat. He would have looked comical, if the news he had were not so grim.

"I followed Ben's trail to a lake at the bottom of the hill. The trail ends there, at the lake, on a small sandy beach."

"What do you mean by that?" Louise asked.

"It looks like they boarded a small boat and paddled out into the lake. If I am not mistaken, this lake is the one called Long Lake. It is fed by many mountain streams, but empties into one very large river."

"The West River?"

"Yes, the West River. The one that runs straight through the middle of the Twilight."

"You don't think those fool dwarves will try to ride the river through the Twilight, do you?" Louise asked.

"No, dwarves stay away from the Twilight. They think it's cursed. And it is cursed for anyone who enters without permission.

"What's the Twilight? Joey asked.

"It's a forest where the elves live," Amos replied, "a magical forest. Anyway, I think they will ditch the boat before they get to the Twilight and set off on foot from there."

"I don't want to sit around here and wait for them to return," Louise interrupted. "I want to go after them."

"We will," said Amos. "But we can't leave just yet. There is a very, very large group of snakers heading our way. I don't think they know the house is here, but I'm certain they will find it when they get to this side of the lake and pick up Ben's trail. They are ruthless trackers, Louise. I don't want to set out chasing Ben, with them chasing us."

"Well, what are we going to do then?" asked Louise.

"We'll make a stand here. I've got a plan that just might work. If it doesn't, then we'll have to back track toward home and take the long way around."

"What do we need to do?" Casey asked.

"You and Louise pack up some food and look for anything else we might need. Meg, pull a chair over to the window and be our lookout. If you see anything move, yell. Joey, drop the deadbolt on the front door and come with me."

Amos arose from the floor and headed to the closet which lead to the round chamber. Joey bolted the front door shut and followed Amos into the chamber.

"I'm going to open this door and I want you to count and see how long it takes to close."

"That's one of the dead end doors," said Joey.

"I know," Amos replied, with a smile.

Amos opened the door and Joey began counting. The door moved so slowly that you could not tell it was moving unless you stared at it. While Joey was counting, Amos opened the door to the tunnel that led to the ledge and disappeared inside. Several minutes later, he was back. Joey had counted to three hundred and seventy five and the door had only moved a few inches.

"Keep counting," Amos said, "and come let me know what number the door closes and locks on." Amos went back into the house and got the supplies Casey and Louise had put together and moved them into the tunnel. Then, he went back into the house and relieved Meg at the window.

"What exactly are you planning?" Louise asked.

"When the snakers come, you and the kids will go into the tunnel that leads to the ledge. Leave the door open for me. I'll come behind you and leave the closet door open so they will be sure to find the chamber. I'll also open one of the dead end doors before I come into the tunnel with you. Once we are in the tunnel, we will bolt the door shut and wait. Joey's timing the dead end door now to see how long it takes to close."

"You think the snakers will fall for that?" Meg asked. "I thought you said they were excellent trackers."

"They are. But there are stone walls and stone floors in there so there will be no tracks to follow."

At that time, Joey came back into the house. "Eight hundred and fifty seven! Or nine minutes, if I go by my Timex. The door only moves slowly for the first five minutes and then it starts closing faster."

"What's a Timex?" Amos asked.

"It's a watch," said Joey, pulling up his sleeve to show Amos. "It let's you know what time it is."

After Joey showed Amos his watch and explained how it worked, Amos sat on the floor by the window and began his vigil. The minutes crawled by and as the afternoon wore on, the silence and waiting had everyone on edge. After what seemed like hours, Amos finally spoke in a soft whisper. "They're here. Let's get moving, quickly now."

Louise and the children scrambled to their feet and darted into the chamber with Amos following close behind. Amos opened the dead end door that Joey had timed and then ran into the tunnel with the others. He swung the door shut, dropped the deadbolt, and made everyone retreat down the tunnel, about a hundred feet.

"They should be in the house by now. Let's wait awhile and give them time to find the chamber." They waited for about fifteen minutes before Amos told Joey to start timing the door on his watch. After nine minutes elapsed, they waited another ten minutes for good measure before approaching the door to the chamber. Amos made everyone stand back.

"I'm going to go through and check things out. Lock the door behind me and wait until I get back. If I don't return, go back the way we came and head back to my house. From there, strike out across the plains and head to the castle at Overlook to seek help." With that said, he slipped through the door and Joey dropped the deadbolt back into place. In just a few minutes, he was back and banging on the door. Joey slid the deadbolt back and cracked the door to peep out.

"Come on," Amos said. "It worked."

"How can you be sure?" Meg asked. "There are no tracks in here, remember?"

"No, but there are many tracks in the dirt leading to the front porch steps and there are no tracks leading away. Let's get our supplies together and get moving. I want to get as close as possible to the Twilight before dark. Snakers are terrified of elves and will not come anywhere near their forest."

The group divided the sacks they had stuffed with supplies, and before leaving the cabin, they each, with the exception of Amos, found a cloak from the dwarves' bedroom to wear. Amos found a broad axe under one of the beds. The dwarf's axe was like a hatchet in his hand and when they went outside, he cut each one of the children a staff from a small grove of young poplar saplings, growing near the cabin.

"Everyone needs a staff for walking. A good stout staff for long journeys is invaluable," he said as he passed them out. He glanced over at Louise who was quietly watching him. Her expression was grave and somewhat sad and resigned. Staffs really were great for walking, but she knew why they were really needed. As they set off down the trail to the lake, with the children behind them, Amos and Louise both prayed that the only thing they would use these staffs for, would indeed be just walking.

16 TWILIGHT

Ben watched the snakers on the shoreline fade into the distance as the dwarves paddled the boat into the center of the lake, where the current picked them up and sped them along even faster. The dwarves put their oars down and began making sure everything was secure, before they hit the rapids. Ben had gone white water rafting with his church youth group last summer. He was a little scared and at the same time, a little excited too.

"How long before we hit the rapids?"

"Not long," Hob replied. "Less than half an hour. Here, take this piece of rope and secure yourself around the waist."

While Ben was knotting his rope, he noticed that each one of the dwarves had a rope around their waist as well. "What are these for?"

"If anyone falls out of the boat, we can haul them back in."

"Won't that be dangerous?"

"How so?"

"Could that not cause the boat to tip over?"

Hob laughed. "Not this boat. This is an elfin boat. This boat does two things other boats will not do. One, it will not tip over. Two, this boat will travel upstream without anyone having to paddle."

"Wow," Ben exclaimed. "Then why did we have to paddle out to the center of the lake?"

"Because we were not paddling upstream!" Hob replied, as if the answer was as obvious as the beard on his chin.

Ben scratched his head and then Gob laughed. "Hob is not very good at explanations. The elves built these boats specifically to travel from the Twilight to the shores of Long Lake; the lake below our cabin. Many years ago, there was a trading post and a small settlement on the lake. Elves, dwarves, and men all traded there. Now, the trading post and settlement are gone and this one boat is all that remains."

"What happened?" Ben asked.

"The battle with the witch happened," said Hob. "She came down from the north, during one of the coldest winters I can remember."

"She brought tens of thousands of snow golems with her," Gob added. "She sent half of them to our home at Nimrodell and she led the other half in a direct assault on the Twilight."

"Snow golems?" Ben asked, with wide eyes.

"Yes, snow golems. Creatures animated by magic. Black magic. Nothing would stop them at first. Swords, axes, spears, even clubs, were used against them. You could chop one's head off with a sword and the head would explode into a flurry of snow flakes. Those flakes would whirl around in the air and stick to that headless body and a new head would sprout up right before your eyes."

"How did you beat them?"

"Flaming arrows. That was the only thing that would stop them. A flaming arrow through the chest, where the heart should be, would break the spell. Anyway, to answer you question, many lives were lost on both sides in that battle. After that, the elves withdrew from the world of man and retreated to the Twilight. They have been there ever since. The dwarves, that were not at Nimrodell, returned home as well."

"Then why are you guys not living in Nimrodell?"

"Enough questions," exclaimed Hob, yanking on his beard with one hand and rubbing his shins with the other.

The trip through the rapids was short and uneventful. The river widened out into a deep and slow moving thing that lazily wound its way through the forested hills. Eventually, the curves and bends fell behind and the river straightened out as it left the pines and spilled out onto a large rolling meadow. In the distance, the river disappeared into a dark haze, that looked like a smudge on the horizon.

"What's that?" Ben asked, pointing at the smoky gray blot at the end of the river.

"That's the Twilight," Nob answered.

In a couple of hours, the hazy smudge came into focus and revealed a small forest with a gaping black maw into which the river disappeared. Ben was a little disappointed. He was expecting some giant magical forest, where gold and silver leaves adorned each and every tree. He was expecting white embattlements around the forest, with spiraling towers and bright pennants snapping in the breeze. This was no different than any other forest he had ever seen. It was small too. There could not be more than fifty or so elves living in there.

"Looks small," he muttered.

"It is small," Nob replied, "on the outside."

"What do you mean?" Ben asked.

"No time now," said Gob standing up and untying his rope, "we dock up ahead."

"Duck," said Ben.

"No, dock," said Gob.

"DUCK!" Ben, Hob, and Nob all yelled at once.

Gob planted his fists on his hips and fixed them with an angry glare. He opened his mouth to retort and the low

lying tree limb whacked him soundly on the head and
tumbled him overboard into the water.

"He's not tied!" Hob yelled. "Ben, keep your eyes on
him. Nob, bring the boat around."

Ben saw that they were not going to make it. Gob was
fighting furiously to keep his head above the water, but the
current was sucking him down as it pulled him further away
from the canoe. Without thinking, Ben untied the rope from
his waist and dove into the icy water. When he surfaced he
spotted Gob, no longer thrashing, just bobbing along, face
down in the water. Ben swam toward him and, with the
current pushing him along, he reached him quickly.
Grabbing the dwarf by the hood of his cloak, Ben began
swimming across the river, fighting the current and pulling
Gob along behind him. He spotted Hob and Nob upstream,
paddling madly on an intersect course. They reached him,
about twenty feet from the bank.

"I've got him," yelled Hob. "Grab Ben!"

Nob reached over the edge, grabbed Ben by his wrist
and pulled him into the boat. It took all three of them to
pull the cold and lifeless dwarf back into the boat. Once
they had him in, Hob scooped him up and cradled his head
in his arms and sobbed while Nob held his hands and wept
bitterly. Ben had to yell to get their attention.

"Guys! Lay him down flat on his back; it may not be
too late to save him."

The two dwarves laid their friend down on the bottom
of the boat and Ben began CPR. Soon, to Hob's and Nob's
amazement, Gob was sputtering, spitting, and flailing about
in the boat.

"You're no man child, you're a wizard!" said Hob,
narrowing his eyes and clenching his fists.

"Hob, wizard or not, he just saved Gobs' life. Show
some gratitude. If he is a wizard, he may just turn you into a
toad."

Hob thought this over for a moment then relaxed his fists. "Nob is right. Thank you, Ben. Thank you for saving Gobs' life. We are deeply indebted to you."

Ben started to reply when suddenly, everything around them darkened and Gob jumped up and cried in a loud whisper, "We're entering the Twilight!"

Hob and Nob whirled around to see the entrance slowly retreating away from them, as the boat glided deeper into the dark and forbidden forest. They promptly fainted. Ben turned to Gob. "What do we do now?"

"Steer the boat to shore. We need to get everyone out of the boat and pull it up on the beach. Then we'll push it back into the water and climb back inside. That should cause it to begin the return trip upstream to Long Lake."

Ben picked up an oar and began paddling, while Gob set about reviving Hob and Nob. When the boat bumped the shoreline and slid to a stop, everyone on board scrambled off, pushed the boat back into the river and climbed back on board. The boat floated gently back to the shore. They tried again with no luck. They tried a third time and a fourth time and each time the boat would float back to the shore. They even tried paddling the boat, but the best they could do was to maintain their position in the river.

"What's wrong?" Hob asked. "It's never done this before."

"We've never taken it into the Twilight before," Nob answered.

"I can still see the entrance," said Gob. "Let's carry the stupid boat and hike out of here."

"I don't think we can do that, guys," said Ben.

"And why not?" asked Hob.

"Look," said Ben, pointing down the river.

Coming up the river toward them was a beautiful black boat, shaped in the form of a swan. The swan boat steadily approached them, neatly cleaving the water below the graceful neck that was the prow. Like a ghost ship, it passed by them and softly beached on the shore they had just left. There was no one on board.

"We're dead, we're dead, oh no, we're dead," Nob wailed.

"Shut up, Nob!" cried Gob. "That boat is empty."

"I think we're supposed to get in that boat," said Ben.

"Nonsense!' Gob answered. "If we get in that boat, we'll never see the outside world again."

"Gob's right, Ben," said Hob. "Let's get our boat out of the water and leave at once."

The dwarves put the oars down and their boat drifted back to shore and beached beside the swan boat. Once everyone was out, Hob tried to pull the small boat out of the water. This time the boat would not budge. Hob dug his heels into the sand and pulled harder and Gob wrapped his arms around Hob's waist and pulled too. Nothing.

"Leave the blasted boat," said Hob. "Let's get our gear and go."

Ben and the dwarves got their sacks from the boat and set off across the beach. They had gone no more than a few yards when their feet began sinking into the soft white sand. With every step they took to leave the forest, their feet sank deeper into the sand and the harder they fought, the more the sand pulled them down. Soon sand was over everyone's knees and no one had the strength to fight it any longer.

"It's been nice knowing you, Ben," Hob panted. "I hope things turn out better for your family and friends. Goodbye, Gob. Goodbye, Nob."

"Goodbye, Hob," Gob and Nob cried in unison. "Goodbye, Ben."

With their goodbyes said, the three dwarves managed to form a small huddle where they threw their arms around each other and began to sob.

"Hey guys, knock it off. I really think we are supposed to get in the swan boat. Look, if you move back toward the boat, the sand releases its hold."

Ben took a step toward the boat and his foot did not sink in quite as deep. Another step, then another. Now the sand was only up to his ankles. The three dwarves scrambled for the boat. Soon all of them were once again, on firm footing.

"Wait!" said Hob, as Ben moved nearer the swan boat. "I still think it is a bad idea to get on that boat. We can't leave the way we came in and we can't hike out of here on the beach. That leaves us with only one last option for escape."

Hob and Nob looked at the menacing forest, their hands moving slowly to their axes. Ben thought it over for a moment, then decided that Hob was right - not because he feared meeting the elves, but because any delays could prove perilous for his Grandma, sister and three new friends.

"Okay, let's try it."

Everyone shouldered their packs and advanced on the trees with axes in hand. As they approached, the trees appeared to draw closer to each other, while their limbs drooped down and began to knit together to form a barrier. Gob raised his axe to clear a path. Abruptly, the axe flew from his hands and disappeared into the thick tangle of branches. Hob and Nob rushed the trees and their axes were effortlessly plucked from their hands as well. Ben laid his axe down on the beach and tried to walk into the forest, but the trees would not permit it. The dwarves tried too. They tried assaulting the forest together, at one spot, and were beaten back by the long whipping limbs. They tried splitting up and charging the forest from four different spots at the same time, to no avail.

Finally, Nob relented. "I agree with Ben. I don't think we have a choice. What do you think, Hob?"

Hob pulled angrily at his beard while he glared at the trees. "All right. Let's all get into the stupid swan boat."

Everyone loaded their gear onto the swan boat and, as soon as the last person stepped off the shore, the boat slid back into the water, swung around, and headed downstream into the heart of the Twilight. The three dwarves sat down in the boat and covered their faces, resigned to their fate, while Ben eagerly watched the shoreline, hoping to catch a glimpse of an elf. The river meandered through the forest for at least half an hour, before it emerged from beneath the canopy of leaves into bright sunshine.

"We're coming out," said Ben with a hint of disappointment in his voice.

"No, we're not," said Hob.

"Sure we are. Is this the village where we are supposed to stay tonight? I've never seen a town like this," Ben remarked. "It looks more like a campground. Like a deserted gypsy campground."

Hob and his two companions rose to their feet and peered at the structures in the village. Tents. Tents of all shapes, sizes and colors dotted the hillside, along the river bank. There were round tents, square tents, triangular tents and octagon shaped tents. Some tents were small, just large enough to stand upright in, while others were as big as circus tents. There were solid color tents, mostly blues and greens, and many colored tents with vertical stripes, in all the colors of the rainbow. However, no one was out and about and the city of tents was eerily quiet. No laughter of children, no dogs barking, nothing.

"Where are we, and where is everyone?" Ben asked, turning to the dwarves.

The swan boat passed under a great wooden bridge that spanned the river and turned toward a pier on the starboard side. Slowing and pivoting as it neared the pier, the boat glided into the wooden structure with a gentle bump and came to rest. The only noise in the still air was the sound of the river lapping at the sides of the boat.

"We are inside the forbidden city," said Hob. "All is lost."

17 THE KEEPER

Everyone waited in the boat for something to happen. After sitting in the hot sun for several minutes, Ben finally stood and pitched his gear onto the pier. The dwarves watched in astonishment as he proceeded to climb out of the boat.

"What in heaven's name are you doing?" Hob whispered loudly. "Get back in this boat!"

"We can't sit in the boat all day, guys. We still have a mission to complete, remember?"

Hob, Gob, and Nob looked around nervously.

"What are your plans?" Nob whispered.

"Well, there is no one here," said Ben. "So, I am going to take my stuff and start hiking down the river. You guys can stay here and wait for the elves to return if you wish, or you can come with me."

The three dwarves grabbed their gear and scrambled madly onto the pier with Ben. They stood for a moment, contemplating the empty city, and then hoisted their sacks across their shoulders. A sudden voice, on the pier behind them, made them all jump.

"The penalty for trespassing here is death."

Ben and the dwarves spun around. On the end of the dock, stood a tall fierce looking man, with chiseled features and piercing blue eyes. His long black hair was braided into one thick cord that hung down across his shoulders and looped around his neck. Ben noticed the man's ears were pointed.

"However, I am quite curious to find out how you managed to enter our forest."

"How did he get behind us?" Gob whispered.

"He's an elf!" Nob replied. "It's devilry."

"Hold your tongues," said Hob through clenched teeth, "and bridle your temper. I am rather fond of my head and would dearly love to keep it on my shoulders."

Suddenly, Ben pushed past the dwarves and strode right up to the elf.

"Hello. My name is Ben. Ben Alderman. And these three dwarves," said Ben, pointing behind him, "are my friends. They are called Hob, Gob, and Nob."

The three dwarves bowed low, their long beards brushing the tops of their dusty boots.

"It's an accident that we came here at all," Ben continued. "My friend Gob fell from our boat and, as we were rescuing him, the river took us into the Twilight. We tried to leave at once, but we were unable to. It is important that we leave and continue our journey. I have family and friends whose lives may very well depend on our mission."

"What exactly is your mission, young Ben Alderman?" asked the elf, with an amused look on his face.

"There are snakers near by," Ben replied, "and we are trying to go to Nimrodell to bring back an army of dwarves, to drive them away."

"Snakers?" a voice from the other end of the pier replied.

Once again, Ben and the three dwarves spun around. On the other end of the pier were two more elves. Both were tall and fair-skinned with eyes the color of an autumn sky and both had their long black hair braided and looped across their shoulders, like the first elf. On the shore, by every tent, on every street, and up and down the shoreline were more elves - men, women and children. All were standing silently, watching and waiting. Ben felt a hand lightly grasp his shoulder.

"Come with me. You and your friends have much to tell us."

The two elves, at the end of the dock, stepped aside to allow the first elf to pass with Ben and the three dwarves in tow. All of the other elves were about their business now and the city was at once alive and noisy. The elf escorted them down twisting streets of grass leading into the heart of the strange city, where a small, plain, unadorned tent of brown canvas stood alone on a barren field. The elf led them to this tent and pulled the flap back, motioning for them to enter. Ben entered first, followed by the dwarves and then the elf. Inside the tent, Ben and the dwarves stood rooted to the ground, staring skyward. Ben swayed on his feet and the elf caught him by the arm and steadied him. From the outside, the tent appeared no bigger than the six-man tent he had once camped in when he was a cub scout. On the inside, however, he could not see the far walls of the tent nor the ceiling. The tent wall behind him, where he had just entered, stretched to the horizon on both sides and disappeared into the darkness above. It was more like being inside of a giant underground cavern, rather than a tent. The elf led them over a hill, to a place where a ring of logs circled a stone pit with a dimly burning fire.

"Please be seated," the elf politely requested, nodding at the logs. "The Keeper will be here shortly."

Ben and the dwarves sat down upon the logs, on one side of the pit, and the elf sat down across from them.

"My name is Gabriel. Do you have need for a refreshment?"

Ben looked at the dwarves and all three of them shook their heads. Hob narrowed his eyes and furrowed his brow, making it very clear to Ben that he should decline.

"No thanks," Ben replied. "But it is kind of you to ask. What is this place, and who is the Keeper?"

Gabriel spread his arms. "This tent. This is the heart of the Twilight. The forest outside of these walls is part of it. The larger the forest on the outside, the smaller this tent on the inside. The smaller the forest on the outside, the larger this tent on the inside. The Twilight enlarges or diminishes as our needs demand."

"You must be talking about the inside of the forest because the forest looked very tiny from the outside," Ben remarked. "But, apparently, that is part of the magic. It is bigger on the inside, too. Like this tent."

"That is the way of it, Ben Alderman," said Gabriel smiling. "And as for the Keeper, here he comes now."

As Gabriel stood, Ben and the dwarves stood with him. A black robed figure was coming over the hill, from the opposite direction of the tent entrance, his hood was pulled down low and the dim firelight did nothing to reveal his face.

"Who are the intruders?" the Keeper asked.

Gabriel stepped forward. "Ben Alderman and his three companions."

Then, Gob leapt forward, red-faced with his chin thrust defiantly in the air. "It is Hob, Gob, and Nob of the great dwarven kingdom Nimrodell," he shouted, "and their companion!" Hob quickly grabbed his companion by the hood of his cloak and yanked him back, while Nob set about beating him on top of his head.

Gabriel's lips twitched, beginning the formation of something that might have been a smile. Nevertheless, he swiftly recovered his composure and addressed the Keeper. "It appears they have entered the Twilight quite by accident. However, they do bear news of our old enemy."

The Keeper pulled the hood of his robe back, revealing his face. Ben was shocked to discover that the Keeper was a very, very old elf. In all of the stories he had ever read elves could be killed, but they never got sick and certainly never grew old. This elf was not stooped in any way, but his face was lined and care-worn and his long braid was white as snow.

"How did these travelers enter our homeland at all?" he asked Gabriel. "The forest will not permit it and the river should have turned them away."

"They were traveling in one of our boats."

The Keeper bowed his head for a moment, deep in thought, then turned to Ben and the dwarves. "I am Marcus. Tell me how you and your friends came here, by one of our very own boats no less."

Marcus and Gabriel sat down upon the logs, while Ben and the Dwarves remained standing. Hob, Gob, and Nob moved close together, ready to flee if possible - to fight, if not. Ben swallowed the lump in his throat, then proceeded with his story. Once he finished, there was a long silence while everyone sat still as statues. Finally, Marcus stood and approached the fire to warm his hands.

"We must investigate this further. If what you say is true, we will take care of the snakers. There will be no need for an army of dwarves."

"Marcus," Gabriel interjected, "if their story is true, then I think we should allow the dwarves to continue on with their mission. Their armies can take out the advance scouts and hunting parties, while our armies go in search of the hive. We also need to consider the witch and her mission. She is truly the greater enemy."

The Keeper raised an eyebrow at Gabriel and then turned to study Ben and the three dwarves.

"Very well. But what are we to do with the trespassers?" he asked. "The penalty stands, unless perhaps the trespassers can make restitution."

The dwarves bristled at this comment, fearing that the elves were plotting for their treasure. Ben however remained calm. He thought for a moment and then slowly pulled out the chain with the emerald, from beneath his shirt. Upon seeing the jewel, Gabriel quickly stood and moved to Marcus's side.

"That is a spell-catcher," Gabriel whispered. "Is he the one?"

Marcus nodded. "Where did you get this necklace, Ben Alderman?"

"My Grandmother gave it to me. She wears one and she gave me and my sister one too and made us promise to wear them. It is called an emerald where I come from."

"Your grandmother and your sister are in Camelot looking for you and they are wearing spell-catchers?"

"Yes," Ben replied.

Marcus and Gabriel huddled together and spoke rapidly, in hushed voices. Gabriel then hurried from the tent and the Keeper turned to speak to Ben.

"Keep your spell-catcher Ben Alderman. The snakers would not know a spell-catcher, nor how to use one, but the witch must never get her hands on one. You and your friends are in no danger here. Gabriel is assembling a scouting party to find your grandmother and sister. He will bring them back to the Twilight safely."

"What about my friends? Joey, Meg, and Amos?" Ben asked.

"They will be brought back as well. When everyone is here, we will make our plans together. Until then, you will be our guests."

Another elf put his hand on Ben's shoulder. "I am Jonah. Come with me and I will provide you with food and drink, and a place to rest in private."

"How long will it take Gabriel to find them?" Ben asked.

"We have not been outside the Twilight for many years, but our memories are long and the lay of the land does not change much over time. With what you have told us, they should be able to find them quickly."

Jonah led them to another tent, this one bright red with blue stripes. "This dwelling shall be yours while you are within our city. Go inside and make yourselves comfortable. I will be back with your food and drink before I leave. Also, do not stray from this tent unaccompanied. Your safety depends on it"

Inside the tent Ben, Hob, Gob, and Nob collapsed onto a thick pile of furs in the center of the floor. Within minutes the dwarves were snoring noisily, but when Jonah came back with trays of meats, cheeses, and fruits, the aroma quickly roused them. The food was spread on top of a small table to one side of the tent and all four of the hungry guests dug into their meals. Jonah sat down upon the furs, while they ate, and Ben began to ply him with questions.

"Jonah, how old is the Keeper? I mean, is he real old? He looks old, but at the same time he looks... I don't know. Powerful maybe?"

"You are very perceptive," Jonah remarked. "We are all old by your reckoning, but the Keeper is indeed old. He is the oldest and most powerful elf in Camelot. But that is not why his hair is white, nor is that the cause for the lines in his face. He is the weaver of the magic that is here within the Twilight. It is a very, very great magic and, over time, it has taxed his life energy."

"Will it kill him?" Ben asked.

"Eventually," Jonah answered. "But not for many hundreds of years."

Ben pushed his glasses up on his nose. "What about the Merlin Tree? Is it here in the Twilight? And what is Faerie like?"

"You ask many questions! Yes, the Merlin Tree is here within the Twilight. It grows in the center tent. As for Faerie, there are no words to describe it, but perhaps you will have the opportunity to visit it one day."

The three dwarves momentarily paused from eating, to see where this conversation was going. Being in the Twilight was bad enough. Going to Faerie was out of the question.

"So, we will be allowed to leave?" Hob asked, wiping his mouth on the sleeve of his cloak.

"It appears so. You have young Ben Alderman to thank for that."

The three dwarves looked at Ben with respect and admiration. Gob patted him lovingly on the arm, while Nob leaned over the table and refilled his drink.

"Any more questions?" Jonah asked.

Ben pulled the emerald from beneath his tee shirt and rolled it between his fingers. The fading light of the day, slanting in through the tent door, caused the gem to sparkle.

"Can you tell me more about a spell-catcher?"

Jonah studied the gem as it skipped across Ben's knuckles, while he framed an answer within his mind. "All things great and small have some magical properties. Usually, the rarer the object the greater the power within it. Jewels are a particularly potent catalyst for magic and the spell-catcher, or emerald as you call it, is the rarest of all gems here in Camelot. That gem you possess has the power to maintain a magical spell indefinitely. For that reason, some people call them spell-carriers."

"So a magical spell does not last forever?" Ben asked.

Jonah shook his head. "Someone has to maintain the spell or it will fade over time."

"Well what about our boat?" Nob inquired. "It will not tip over and it still travels up the river without use of oars. It is hundreds of years old."

"Yes, it is a powerful spell bound within the old trading boats of Long Lake, but it is a magic that weakens with the passing of every season. And that is going to have to be the last question for today." Jonah rose from the furs and began collecting the trays. "It will be dark soon, so I must take your leave now. If all goes well, you should be reunited with your family and friends by morning. Sleep now and rest well. Tomorrow will be a day of decisions."

18 AMBUSH

Amos led Louise and the kids down to the lake, where the trail of Ben and the three dwarves ended at the shoreline.

"They took a boat from here," said Amos, pointing to the skid marks in the sand.

"Where would they be going from here?" Casey asked.

"This is Long Lake. It empties into a river that runs through the Twilight. There's a small town near the Twilight, called River Town. They will probably spend the night there and leave for Nimrodell in the morning."

"Nimrodell? Is that the dwarven kingdom?" Joey asked.

Amos nodded.

"We will never catch them now," said Louise, staring out across the vast lake.

Amos picked up a smooth round stone and skipped it across the still waters. "Actually, Louise, we can."

"How? We don't have a boat."

"We don't need a boat. The river makes a great curving sweep westward and then swings back to the east before entering the Twilight. There are also many twists and turns along its path. If we travel overland, as the crow flies, we can make it to River Town before morning and catch them before they leave. It will mean a long night of travel, with no sleep and very little rest."

"Look!" Meg cried, pointing up the shoreline.

In the distance, heading in their direction, was another band of snakers.

"Quickly," Amos whispered, "go into the trees, they haven't seen us yet."

The group quickly scrambled back into the forest and followed Amos, as he plunged through the pines. Soon, however, they had to stop for Louise to catch her breath.

"That was a lot of snakers," said Joey.

"How did they escape from the tunnels?" Meg asked.

"Those were not the ones from the tunnels," Amos answered. "That group coming down the shoreline was even larger than the one we trapped. I've never seen so many this far north and I've never seen this many traveling together, even down south where they dwell. We'll have to really hump it to stay ahead of them. I am certain they will pick up our trail."

"Oh Amos," Louise wept. "I am old and cannot possibly run all night. My legs ache now. Take the children and flee. I'll go in a different direction and maybe I can draw some of them off your trail."

"No Grandma!" Casey cried. "We are not leaving without you!"

"Yes you are!" Louise shouted. "You have Ben, Joey and Meg to think of now."

"Casey is right Louise," said Amos. "We are not leaving without you. But you shall not walk on this night."

The air about Amos shimmered faintly and a ripple ran through his body. The big man dropped down on his hands and knees and his wild hair and beard began to grow and meld together with the furs upon his back. In the twinkling of an eye, a monstrous bear, the size of a horse, was before them where Amos had just stood. The bear ambled over to Louise and crouched down beside her.

"Get on, Grandma," said Casey. "I told you, we were not leaving without you."

The kids helped Louise up onto the bear and handed her the pack Amos had been wearing. They could not find his axe and Amos did not wait for them to locate it. The bear set off through the trees at a brisk, but gentle pace that made it easy for Louise to stay mounted, and easy for the kids to keep up. They traveled this way for a couple of hours. When the sun began to set, they stopped to rest for a few minutes and to ate some of the food they had brought from the dwarve's house. Amos changed back into a man and, while everyone was resting, he fashioned a saddle for Louise to use while riding. The saddle was a rope harness that wound around his chest and back, with loops under his arms and across his shoulders. Louise could sit up on his back and hold onto the ropes, or she could lie down on his back and twine her hands in the loops that would be on his side.

"Okay, everyone. We'll do two hour marches and ten minute breaks all night. That should allow us to reach River Town with plenty of time to spare. Joey, do you still have your watch?"

Joey held up his arm and pushed the button to illuminate his indigo Timex.

"Great. You will be the time keeper on our march tonight. Let's go."

Amos transformed and Joey and Meg secured the rope saddle, while Casey helped Louise mount. Once again, Amos led the strange procession, guiding them safely across the dark terrain, an old woman riding a giant bear with three children running at its side.

It was on the fourth march when the ogre attacked. Everyone was exhausted, their senses dulled from endless hours of running, with no sleep and little rest. Even Amos was caught off guard when the ogre exploded from a thicket of gooseberry and prickly ash, in which it had been sleeping. The hideous monster lowered its shoulder and charged the bear, hitting it broadside and sending it sprawling down a short hill. Louise was thrown from Amos's back and lay unconscious on the hillside. Meg and Casey screamed as Joey grabbed them and yanked them backwards, away from the ogre.

The ogre regarded them for a second. The three kids were unharmed, but they posed no threat. It would deal with them later. The old woman was probably dead, but she didn't matter either - what harm could she do anyway. The bear was a different story. The bear had to be dealt with swiftly. The ogre started down the hillside to finish the bear when a thunderous roar ripped through the night air and shook loose stones from their perch on the hillside. The ogre paused, now uncertain, as fear crept up its spine and caused the course black hairs on the back of its neck to stand on end. After hearing the angry roar, it decided to leave the bear alone and snatch at least one of the children. It had turned around to go back to the kids, when the bear came hurtling up the hillside. The bear was massive now, the rage within the beast fueling its fury, strength, and size. But before the bear could reach the ogre, the monster grabbed its throat and toppled backwards into a lifeless heap, with a feathered shaft protruding from its neck. The bear slowed its charge and, with each step, shrank in size. By the time the bear reached the ogre, its transformation was complete.

Amos took one look at the ogre and knew it was dead. The arrow that killed the beast looked to be elfin, but right now all he could think of was Louise and the children.

"Louise," he yelled. "Casey! Joey, Meg, where are you?"

"Amos!" Casey cried, running to the big man. "Where's Grandma?"

"Over here," Meg called. "We found her."

Amos and Casey ran over to the spot on the hillside where Meg and Joey were crouched over a silent and still figure, lying upon the ground.

"Oh Grandma," Casey sobbed, falling to her knees and snatching up her Grandma's hand. "Is she okay? Is she okay, Joey? Please tell me she's okay."

Joey reached over and put his arm around Casey and squeezed her tight. "She's alive. I think she is just unconscious."

Amos checked Louise over. She did not have any broken bones, but she did have a nasty cut on her forehead. "Joey's right, she was just knocked unconscious when the ogre attacked. Find one of our packs and get me some water. No, stay here. Let me do it. Whatever killed that ogre is still out there."

"You didn't kill it?" Casey asked.

"No. The ogre was slain with an arrow. It looked to be an elfin arrow, but I'm not positive."

"It was indeed an elfin arrow," a strange voice replied.

Amos whirled around and the kids eased behind him. The strange voice belonged to a man who was coming down the hill toward them. In the darkness, they could only tell that the man was tall.

"I am looking for Amos, Louise, Casey, Meg, and Joey. And unless my eyes deceive me, I believe I have found them. Young Ben Alderman described you all very well."

"You've seen Ben?" Casey asked, stepping out from behind Amos. The news of her brother emboldened her and drove away some of her fears.

"He is our guest along with Hob, Gob, and Nob of Nimrodell. We have been sent to find you and bring you back safely. We must hurry though - there is evil afoot tonight."

"Yes, we must hurry," Amos agreed, "but first, you know our names and we do not know yours. Nor do we know how you came to find us and that puzzles me greatly."

"I am called Gabriel," said the elf with a bow of his head. "I sent one hunting party up the river, in case you came that way, and I led this party across land. We've been working a zig-zag pattern, hoping to pick up your tracks should you come this way. It is mostly luck that we stumbled upon you at all."

"What party are you talking about?" Joey asked peering around in the darkness.

Gabriel turned and whistled and twelve more tall and silent figures materialized out of the darkness.

"So you are an elf," Amos marveled.

"And you are a shape shifter," Gabriel replied smiling. "These are strange times indeed."

"Are you taking us to Ben?" Meg asked.

"Yes, we are going to the Twilight. It's a two hour march from here. Are you able to travel?"

"We're all okay, except Louise," said Amos. "She is hurt and cannot travel."

"Then we shall carry her," said Gabriel motioning for some of the other elves to come forward and assist.

A stretcher was quickly fashioned from two long staffs and a cloak. Louise had regained consciousness, but did not object to being carried in the stretcher. One of the elves gave everyone a drink from a flask he was carrying at his side. Joey noticed that all of the elves carried a similar flask. The liquid was warm and tingled going down. Within a few minutes of drinking it, everyone felt their strength returning and their hopes rising.

The next two hours went by quickly. The moon had set long ago, but a faint light in the eastern sky signaled dawn was near. When they arrived at the Twilight, the trees of the forest seemed to part for the elves and their guests, raising their branches and pulling back their roots to reveal a smooth and well traveled path. They soon emerged onto a sandy shoal and Amos, Louise, and the children were placed aboard a strange boat in the shape of a swan. Gabriel boarded the boat as well, but the other elves remained on shore and disappeared back into the forest. As soon as Gabriel was on board, the swan boat slowly backed into the dark river, moving on its own accord, and turned down stream, taking the party deeper into the Twilight.

"You are safe now," said Gabriel. "Be at ease and rest. You will see Ben shortly."

By the time the boat had reached the city of tents, dawn had broke. The sun had not peeked over the horizon yet, but the blackness of night had been chased away by the grays of early morning. The party aboard the boat marveled at the strange city. Louise was somewhat back to her old self and able to walk on her own. Amos was relieved to see her spirits and strength returning. After the boat docked at a pier, the party followed Gabriel through the city to the tent where Ben was staying. Gabriel pulled the flaps back and motioned for everyone to enter. Casey went in first and saw Ben sitting at a table with three dwarves. They were eating breakfast and engaged in an animate conversation. Ben looked completely relaxed and at home, as if this was just another normal day in the life of any seventh grader.

"Ben!" Casey cried, running over to the table.

Ben jumped up and ran to meet his sister. Casey threw her arms around him and began to sob.

"I thought I'd never see you again. Thank God you are okay. You are okay aren't you?"

"Yes, I'm fine, Casey. I'm glad to see that all of you are fine too. I was worried to death that the snakers would get you."

Louise came over and gave Ben a big bear hug, then proceeded to give him a thorough inspection, while Amos stood behind her and grinned. When Louise had finished and was satisfied that Ben did not have any broken bones, scrapes, or bruises, Ben introduced everyone to Hob, Nob, and Gob. The three dwarves bowed low each time they were introduced and responded with "at your service" after every bow. As they were going through the introductions, Gabriel had another table and more food brought in. When they were finished with their greetings, everyone sat down to a tasty breakfast. While they were eating, Gabriel made to depart, but before he left the tent, he turned to address the guests.

"Ben, your friends are weary from a long night of travel and must rest here until I return for them. I will wake them for the noon day meal and after that we will have much to discuss and many decisions to make. However, you and your dwarven friends may come with me if you wish. I know you have slept all night and if you feel you have rested enough, I will find a guide to show you around our city while the others rest."

Ben looked at the three dwarves. Gob and Nob nodded vigorously, indicating they did not want to spend the morning inside the tent. Hob, however, while trying not to seem rude to Gabriel, was once again scrunching up his eyebrows and shaking his head. He wiggled his finger to motion Ben over.

"What has gotten into you?" Ben whispered.

"I don't think we should split up," Hob whispered back. Or so he tried. His voice carried all over the tent and everyone heard him clearly. Gabriel smiled and waited patiently.

"That's silly, Hob, we are their guests."

"I just don't trust them, Ben!"

"Well, you sure didn't mind eating their food," Ben shot back.

Hob reddened at the accusation but knew that it was true. "All right, I'll go. But I still don't like it."

Ben turned to his Grandma.

"Go on, Ben. We are all safe here and I am going to sleep like a log for the next several hours."

"Cool beans," said Ben, turning back to Gabriel. "We'll go."

19 DECISIONS

Ben and the dwarves followed Gabriel back to the bridge by the pier. Earlier, when they had arrived in the swan boat, the pier was deserted. The whole city had appeared deserted. Now, however, the pier was bustling with activity. Several boats were docked at the pier and more were coming in. Hob noticed that their boat was now docked there as well.

"Are you planning to keep that boat we came in?" Hob asked. "We have grown rather fond of it and I would be most happy to purchase it from you."

"I thought dwarves could not swim and feared the water," said Gabriel, raising his eyebrows.

"Yes, it's true; we dwarves are not good swimmers. We tend to sink. However, it is not water we fear, but the crossing of water," Hob replied, eyeing the boat and stroking his beard. "Having a boat that will not tip over is the only reason we travel on the river at all."

Halfway across the bridge, Gabriel stopped and leaned over the railing to look at the boat Ben and the three dwarves had arrived in. "Once there were hundreds of boats, such as this, that traveled up and down the river to Long Lake. It is very old, even by our standards. Actually, I am surprised that the magic bound within it still lives. How did you come by this boat?"

"We found it in a cave," said Gob. "In one of the many caverns we have explored around Long Lake, since leaving Nimrodell."

"A cave?" Gabriel asked with a puzzled expression. "That is very strange indeed. But these are strange times, I am sure."

"What do you mean by that?" asked Hob. "Is there a story behind the boat?"

"I am not sure," Gabriel answered. "But I do know that boat is the last of its kind. With your leave, I should like to see this cave one day."

"By all means," said Gob. "We'd be delighted to show you."

"As for the boat," said Gabriel, nodding toward the pier. "You may have it. Consider it a gift and may it bring you many years of good service."

"Why, that it most kind of you!" Hob exclaimed. "Most kind indeed. It seems that what they say about elves is not true after all."

"And what is it they say about elves?" Gabriel asked, straightening up to his full height and planting his hands upon his hips.

Hob reddened and began to stutter and stammer. Gob finally jumped in to rescue him. "Never mind him Gabriel. One thing that is true about dwarves though, is that we have very large feet and are quite often cramming them into our mouths."

"Yes," said Hob, sheepishly, "begging your pardon sir, that was very rude of me."

Gabriel laughed. It was a long merry laugh and soon everyone joined him.

"Ah, too long I have been in the Twilight. My heart aches to travel the country again, seeking new friends and new adventures. Perhaps you will join me when all of this is over?"

"That would be most fun," Nob answered. "There are rumors of a dragon in the Black Hills. The rumors say this dragon has been guarding his treasure for so long, that he has turned to stone. If we can but locate his lair, we might find his treasure as well."

"Those rumors are partly true," Gabriel answered, "and that dragon's name is Zoltan. He is a black dragon, from Crag."

The three dwarves shivered. The Merlin Tree that linked Camelot to Crag had been destroyed ages ago and no dwarf living today had ever seen the home world from where their race sprang. But the stories of the terrible dragons of Crag lived on.

"Tell us what you know of this dragon," said Hob.

"Zoltan came through the Merlin tree as a young infant and stole away to the northern lands, where he grew into a giant and terrible beast. Eventually, he returned to New Zorn and destroyed the city. This occurred after Mordred's treachery and, fortunately for Camelot, before Merlin had left. When Merlin saw the destruction Zoltan had brought upon New Zorn, he sought out the dragon and found him near his lair in the Black Hills."

"So he turned him to stone?" asked Gob.

"Unintentionally, yes."

"How so?"

"Merlin cast a sleep spell upon Zoltan. He was going to slay the dragon after it was under the spell, but what Merlin did not know, is that dragons turn to stone when they sleep and blend in with their surroundings. It's part of their natural defense mechanism, to protect them from other dragons."

"So he couldn't kill it and he couldn't wake it up or it would kill him!" Nob marvelled.

"Yes," Gabriel answered. "You are correct. With his fellow wizards exiled, and the beautiful city of New Zorn destroyed, Merlin left Camelot, never to be heard from again. Most believe he went to Earth. Some believe the dragon destroyed him. We will probably never know what really happened to him."

The party crossed the bridge over the river in silence. Gabriel was thinking of the vast and far away Black Hills and how wonderful it would be to behold a magnificent black dragon, the oldest magical creature known to still exist in any world. Hob, with a strange gleam in his eyes, was dreaming of dragon's gold. After crossing the bridge, they followed a path along the bank that led them to a bright green tent near the edge of the river, where another elf was waiting for them.

"Jonah!" Ben cried.

Jonah bowed to the dwarves, then clasped Ben's hand. "Greetings."

"More guests have arrived," said Gabriel, "and they are now recovering from their journey. Entertain these while the others rest, but make certain they are at the center tent for noon day meal. You come as well. There is much to discuss and much to decide."

Jonah nodded and leaned in toward Gabriel and whispered, "Have you heard tidings from our scouts?"

"Yes," Gabriel replied in a hushed voice. "It is not good."

Jonah nodded again and clapped Gabriel on the shoulder. "Then I will see you at noon day." He then turned to the others with a smile, "Come, and follow me. We are going to the kitchen tents for some sweets!"

The morning passed swiftly for everyone and soon it was time for lunch, or as Gabriel called it - noon day meal. Jonah led them to the center tent that also happened to be the small brown tent where the Keeper dwelt. They entered the tent and followed Jonah over the hill to the fire pit, where a fire was burning brightly. Gabriel and Marcus were there along with Amos, Louise, Casey, Joey, and Meg. Once everyone was present and seated, Marcus stood to address the crowd.

"As you all know, our enemy from the south has returned and they have come against us with numbers so large they no longer fear us. We have sent out scouts to assess the situation and the news is grave on all fronts. Our forest is under attack, at this very moment, by a band of several hundred snakers and several thousand are marching this way."

"Will our forest hold?" asked Jonah.

"The forest will hold," Marcus answered, "against several hundred. But against several thousand? I do not know."

"When will they get here?" asked Amos, "And how many do you have to defend this place?"

"They will be here in three days," Marcus continued. "Four days if you count today. There are less than a thousand elves in the Twilight right now. Messengers have been sent through the Merlin Tree to Faerie for reinforcements, but we do not expect them to make it back here in time. It is two days march from the Merlin Tree in Faerie to our capital city and it will take at least one day to marshal forces. Now it seems that we must indeed accept the offer of aid from Nimrodell if any of us are to survive this attack."

"Then we must leave at once," said Hob, rising out of his seat. "It is two days march to Nimrodell from here. One day, if we can take the river half-way. If we leave now we can be back with an army to greet them when they arrive."

"I am afraid you must wait until dark," said Gabriel. "Remember, we are under attack right now, from all sides. Yet if you leave by boat under the cover of darkness, the cool waters of the river will mask your heat from the snakers and you should be able to slip by undetected. How large of an army can you raise on such short notice?"

"No less than two thousand," Hob replied. "Will it be enough?"

"It will have to be," Gabriel answered, taking a seat and prodding the embers on the edge of the fire with a stick.

Marcus watched Gabriel poking in the ashes for a moment, then cleared his throat. "The next order of business is the witch. A unicorn has appeared in Camelot for the first time in many years. It is currently in the Great Oak Forest and we are certain the witch is on her way there now to slay it."

"Why is she killing unicorns?" Casey asked.

"Forgive me; it had not occurred to me that someone here had not heard of Mordred's treachery. This world we call Camelot was discovered by a wizard named Merlin. He and his fellow wizards left their home world to settle Camelot. They also discovered Faerie, Crag, and Earth, and invited citizens from all worlds to live here. Unfortunately, these wizards were unable to create the peaceful utopia they desired. At first, robbers, thieves, and murderers sprang up from amongst the populations. Then it became gangs and mobs and from there it was just a short leap to armies and wars. The twelve wizards from Zorn despaired and made plans to return to their home world to hold council and decide the fate of Camelot. Except for one."

"Mordred," Louise whispered.

"Yes, Louise. Mordred. It is a name that strikes fear in the hearts of all who are wise. Mordred believed the wizards should be ruling Camelot, governing all races through fear and dominance, and he expressed these thoughts often, yet no one agreed with him. Over time, his heart grew black and in secret he built a tower within a fortress that he named Stone Dog. There he began to devise how he might rule Camelot himself and, when the wizards decided to return to Zorn, he saw his chance.

The Merlin Tree on Zorn stands on a desolate mountain far from any habitable place. Once back on Zorn, they would have to use pathways to get to their city. These pathways are magical portals they used to travel about their world. Merlin had mastered this art of travel and was the only wizard that could open a portal without his staff, and keep it open so that other people could use it too. Mordred went through the Merlin Tree, without his staff, so that he would have an excuse to come back to Camelot. The others thought nothing of it and opened their portals to their old city and departed. Once Mordred was back on Camelot, he conjured a spell to destroy the Merlin Tree and he was able to destroy it in such a manner, that the other wizards would never be able to reestablish a connection with Camelot. That left him as the only wizard in Camelot, free to answer to no one, but himself. Or so he thought. You see, Mordred's fatal mistake was not counting the wizards. If he had, he would have counted only ten others, besides himself. Merlin, the only wizard we truly trusted, had been visiting with us in the Twilight and as we came to understand over time, he was habitually late for any appointments. This time, it saved him from the fate of the council and, when he discovered Mordred's betrayal and treachery, his wrath was fierce to behold. To shorten this story, Merlin was unable to locate his home world, thus he was unable to establish another connection. He did, however, create another pathway, a new Merlin Tree that connected Camelot to a place called Pluton. There was where he banished Mordred then destroyed the Pluton Tree, in the same manner that Mordred had destroyed the Tree to Zorn. When satisfied the pathway was destroyed, he cast a spell that would prevent Mordred from returning to Camelot, should he ever find it and create a pathway back. And here we shall stop and eat our noon day meal."

Several elves entered the tent carrying tables laden with trays of food and pitchers of sweet drinks. After a quick bite, Marcus continued his story.

"Years later, Merlin left Camelot and, when it became apparent to us that he was not returning, we began to experiment with the magic he had taught us, trying to create our own pathways to discover other worlds, as he had done. The very first pathway we created, back on Faerie, connected our world to Pluton where Mordred had been banished. Had we known this would have happened we would have never attempted this feat of magic, for Mordred had somehow survived his exile and had grown stronger than ever. He sensed our pathway immediately and wrested it from us. Not fully understanding the magic behind creating one of these pathways saved Faerie from immediate destruction because the pathway, though connected, was not traversable. Even so, Mordred was able to detect the magical signature of the pathway that connected Faerie to Camelot, and was somehow able to triangulate Camelot's location. He immediately opened a pathway to Stone Dog, but thanks to Merlin's foresight, was unable to enter the pathway because Merlin's spell blocked him. On Pluton, where Mordred was banished, there are unnamable evils, and sicknesses, diseases, and pestilences of every fashion. Mordred was unable to enter these pathways, but a vile sickness from Pluton began to seep through to both Faerie and Camelot. This sickness, we elves call, the Blight. To all living plants, it is deadly. Strangely enough, it is deadly to us and to the dwarves as well."

"We have not heard of this Blight," Hob interrupted. "How do you know it is deadly to us?"

"How long has it been since you have been to your home in Nimrodell?" Marcus replied. "The Eastern Gates to your city have been sealed to keep the Blight at bay. We are lucky that you will be embarking to the Western Gates tonight." Marcus paused for a moment while the three dwarves huddled together and conversed rapidly in hushed voices. Finally, Hob looked up.

"Please continue your tale."

This time, Marcus smiled and nodded to the three dwarves.

"Now that you have a brief history of Camelot and the wizard Mordred, I must bring the witch into the story and explain how she and Mordred are linked together. When Mordred created the pathway to Stone Dog and the Blight began to spread, the witch found the Merlin Tree and traveled to Pluton. Mordred captured her of course and, once he realized her nature and powers, he struck a deal with her; that if she would break Merlin's spell so that he could return to Camelot, he would help her overthrow this world and she would rule with him. She agreed and he released her with instructions to return to Camelot and to begin preparations by killing thirteen unicorns. Four were slain before we realized she was behind the killings. Since then, we have tried to intervene, but she has always managed to elude us. Seven more were slain before we realized her purpose in the killings. The twelfth was butchered one hundred and seventy two years ago and now the thirteenth unicorn is here in Camelot and the witch is on her way to kill it, even as we speak. She needs thirteen horns to break the spell. If she gets the horn of this last unicorn, all is lost. No one will be able to stand against their combined might."

"This is grim news indeed," Amos muttered. "If she is able to elude the elves of the Twilight then what hope is there? No one else has the strength to face her."

"There is one," said Marcus. "Ben Alderman."

"WHAT?" cried Lousie, "Ben is a child!"

Marcus nodded, "Yes, Louise. By your reckoning, Ben is still a child. But there is steel in Ben Alderman, raw and unforged, but steel none the less."

"That doesn't matter," Louise responded, pulling Ben to her and wrapping her arms protectively around him. "He is just a child and he is NOT getting involved in any of this."

"Louise," Marcus continued, "as the Keeper I see the ends of all paths, but not always the paths that lead to those ends. And there are occasions when I am able to see the paths but not the endings that those paths lead to. Ben Alderman has been present in every path and in every ending I have foreseen in the destruction of the witch. But I could not compel him to go. I would not compel him to go. He must go of his own free will."

"It's not his choice," Louise cried, clutching him tighter. "He is my grandson!"

"And my brother," Casey added, stepping in between Ben and Marcus.

Marcus did not respond. All eyes remained on Ben.

"I won't have to go alone, will I?" Ben asked, in a trembling voice.

"I will accompany you, " said Gabriel, who was now standing by his side, "and I pledge my life, for yours."

"I, too, will go with Ben," Hob cried, "and I'll cleave the witch's head in half if she comes near him. Gob and Nob can return to Nimrodell to fetch the army."

"And if I don't go?" Ben asked.

"Then Camelot shall fall. And Faerie soon after. Your world supports no magic, so you have nothing to fear from Mordred or the witch. You shall be safe when you return home."

"Then I have to go," Ben said, pulling away from Louise. "I have to."

Louise began to sob and Casey tried to grab Ben, but Amos pulled them both aside and spoke to them for several long minutes. When he was finished, Casey ran from the tent crying and Meg and Joey chased after her. Louise and Amos rejoined the group and Louise nodded to the Keeper. Her eyes were red and teary and Ben could not look at her. He was afraid that if he did, he would lose all of the courage he had somehow managed to muster up. He was afraid that if he backed out now that he would never go. He was afraid that… well, he was just afraid.

20 DEPARTURES

"I will go with Gob and Nob," said Amos. "If their mission fails, all is lost."

"That completes two parties," Marcus responded, "but we need yet a third. Someone must go to Stone Dog and retrieve the unicorn horns that the witch has already collected. This will be our safeguard, should she escape this final time."

"But no one can go to Stone Dog," said Louise. "You said yourself that the Blight is death to all elves and dwarves." Then understanding dawned in her eyes and Marcus nodded slowly.

"Yes, Louise, because of the Blight, you and your companions are the only ones that can enter Stone Dog."

Feeling very much defeated and resigned to her fate, Louise asked, "How will we get there and how will we get in?"

"You will have to ride. If you leave tonight and ride all night, you can make it to the witch's castle by noon tomorrow."

"Ride? Ride what, horses? I'm sixty-eight years old! I can't ride a horse all night!"

Marcus smiled. "You and your companions will not go alone. Jonah and three other elves will accompany you as close to the castle as they are able. They will ride with you and make sure that you do not fall. When you get to the castle, you will find the gates open. In the center of the castle stands a lone tower and the unicorn horns will probably be located in the top room of this tower. If the tower is locked, one of the children may be able to climb the walls and enter through a window. We will send ropes along with you. If there is no access to a window, then you will have to use your wits and figure out another way in."

"That's it? Just use our wits and figure out another way in?"

"I'm afraid so. But we know you are a resourceful person. It is rumored among the elves in the Twilight that you have faced the witch before and lived. Is this true?"

Louise nervously glanced at Ben, but he was speaking with Hob and Gabriel and had not heard. She turned back to Marcus. "I'll go get the children and let them know what's happening."

Marcus nodded, then addressed everyone in a loud voice. "When darkness falls, Amos, Gob, and Nob will board one of the swan boats. Once they are out of the Twilight, they are beyond our help and must choose their own path to return to Nimrodell. Gabriel, Hob, and Ben will use the trading boat that Gabriel has given to the dwarves. The river will take them all the way to the Great Oak Forest. Louise, Casey, Joey and Meg will also depart at dusk on horseback for the witch's castle. I am sending four of our best horses and riders to accompany them and aid them on their mission."

After all of the plans had been finalized, the elves provisioned two boats with supplies for each mission. The boat that Hob, Gabriel, and Ben were taking had been painted blackl. It was now the same color as the swan boat that Amos, Nob, and Gob were going to use. Hob understood the necessity of painting the boat black. They needed to leave the Twilight under the cover of darkness, in order to get out undetected. Still, he did not like his boat being painted without his permission and he made a mental note to have it re-painted as soon as these campaigns were over. Maybe red. Ruby red. He liked rubies. He revealed his plans to Gob and Nob and before long the three dwarves were in a heated discussion over what color to paint the boat. They finally called a truce and agreed to put the boat back to it's original color.

Gabriel and Amos spent the day roaming through the woods. While deep in the heart of the Twilight, it was hard to imagine that the place was under attack. Two squirrels playfully chased each other round and round the smooth grey trunk of one of those strange trees that grew here. A rabbit nibbled at the tender green clover growing in one of the many little glades found within the forest. Overhead, a mocking bird noisily scolded them for getting too close to her nest, while nearby, tiny yellow butterflies flitted from flower to flower in a field of blue chicory. Amos breathed it all in. The peace. The serenity.

Louise and the kids gathered inside their tent to spend their remaining hours with one another. For the most part, everyone was quiet, content just to be together. The only time that someone spoke was when the silence finally became unbearable and then, it was only idle chatter. Meg stated that their mom was probably worried sick about them and Joey had to point out that when they went back home, they would be going back to the same time they left. Louise commented that she was glad she had watered and fed the goats before she left. Then, she remembered what Joey had pointed out to Meg earlier. It was kind of like going though the house during a power outage and trying to turn on the lights. You know the power is out and that the lights won't work, but you just automatically hit that light switch as soon as you walk into a dark room.

Night came swiftly and it was soon time to go. Ben stood on the pier and watched as Amos, Gob, and Nob drifted out into the current and disappeared down the river, into the darkness. Louise and Casey hugged Ben tightly. Joey shook his hand and then Meg kissed him very quickly upon his lips. With the heat rising in his cheeks, Ben stammered out a goodbye and stepped into the boat where Hob and Gabriel were waiting. Jonah pushed the boat off the shore and Gabriel, sitting at the prow with an oar in his hands, paddled them out into the center of the river where the current picked them up and ushered them out of the city of tents.

Once Ben was out of sight, Jonah and three other elves appeared with horses in tow. The horses were identical, each one black as midnight, tall and graceful with broad chests, long legs, and powerful hips that promised speed. After brief introductions, Louise was placed behind Jonah and each one of the children behind one of the other elves. The plan was simple. They would ride to the edge of the forest that was under the least amount of attack; then an advance guard of elves would pour out of the forest from two points and engage the snakers in hand-to-hand combat. Once the battle was under way, the riders would peal out of the forest, between the two skirmishes, and ride like the wind across the open plain. If things went as planned, they would escape unnoticed.

As they rode deeper into the forest, Louise marveled at how the trees raised their limbs and pulled their roots back to provide a clear and smooth trail for the riders to travel upon. They rode in silence for an hour and when they finally reached the perimeter of the forest, they found it eerily calm and quiet, the attacks having temporarily ceased. However, within a few short minutes, the battle cries of two-hundred elves rang forth from points both north and south of their position.

"Hold on tightly," Jonah commanded. "On three. One."

The horses began to prance, chomping at the bits. "Two."

The tree limbs about them began to tremble.
"Three!"

In an explosion of leaves, an opening appeared in the trees before them. The riders blasted forth from the forest, into the night and as the hoof beats of the horses faded into the distance, the trees began to shift and entwine their limbs, closing the opening in the forest wall.

Back on the river, Ben and his party had left the tent city and had entered the trees again. With the black and gnarled branches overhead, the darkness was complete. However, the river carried them unerringly through the forest and, the closer they came to the end of the Twilight, the more menacing the forest appeared. A thick tension and a sense of foreboding hung heavily in the air and caused the hairs on the back of Ben's neck to stand on end. A faint light up ahead signaled the river's exit from the forest and the sound of fighting, though muffled, filled the air. Gabriel motioned for everyone to get down as low as possible in the boat and then pulled a large, thick woolen blanket over on top of them. The elves mounted attacks upon the snakers on both sides of the river, thus drawing their attention away from the river and allowing the boats to slide past unnoticed. Still, everyone lay silent under the blanket for the next hour, letting the river carry them further and further away from danger. Finally, Gabriel threw the blanket off.

"You two get some sleep. We will travel the rest of the night upon the river and we will not see the Great Oak Forest until early morning."

"What about Amos, Gob, and Nob?" Ben asked.

"They are safely ahead of us," Gabriel answered turning and staring forward into the darkness. "I can see them now. I do not know where they will leave the river, but they will have to leave it in the next hour or so to make for Nimrodell."

Ben and Hob peered into the darkness ahead, trying to catch a glimpse of their companions, but the night sky was clouded and, the starlight that did manage to seep through, lit nothing more than a few feet past the prow of the boat. Finally, the two gave up trying to espy their companions and lay down upon the thick blanket they had hid under earlier. The rocking of the boat and the lullaby song of the river, soon put them soundly to sleep.

When dawn broke, the new day welcomed the party to the Great Oak Forest with a cold and steady drizzle. Fortunately, the elves had equipped everyone with light cloaks that kept out the wind and rain and were surprisingly warm as well. Not long after entering the forest, Gabriel found a sandy beach in the bend of the river to put ashore.

"Luck is with us - I feel the unicorn is near. We must go on foot from here."

"Can you sense the witch?" asked Hob.

"I cannot," Gabriel answered. "We must be on our guard at all times and go forward as quietly as possible. The witch travels with her shadow cat and that will have to be dealt with first. Help me pull the boat out of the water."

Ben and Hob jumped out of the boat and helped Gabriel pull it up onto the beach. After unloading their packs, they carried the boat into the forest and placed it in a shallow depression between two trees. Hob began to scavenge dead tree limbs, while Ben raked up leaves from the forest floor. While they were busy disguising the boat, Gabriel returned to the river bank to erase their tracks. He used a fistful of cattails to brush out the tracks and when he was finished, there was no longer any sign of their passing, not even to the eye of an experienced tracker. Satisfied that their tracks were well covered, he returned to find Ben and Hob putting the finishing touches on concealing the boat.

"An excellent job!" Gabriel remarked. The boat was practically invisible now. "I don't think I could have done it any better."

Hob beamed. "We dwarves are rather talented at hiding things, you know," he crowed.

"So I see. I just hope we can find it when we return."

"Don't worry about that. Finding things is another one of our many talents."

"Very well then. Are we ready to leave?"

"I have one quick question," Ben asked as he shook his last fistful of leaves over the sticks, which covered the top of the boat. "What is a shadow cat?"

"A shadow cat," Gabriel answered, "is not like any cat you have ever seen or imagined. It is a creature from the Dark Lands."

"Pluton?"

"No, not Pluton. The Dark Lands are the realm of the evil dead. Let us not speak of that place now."

Hob shivered and quickly looked around, half expecting to see the dead cat's shadow slinking between trees.

"What makes this shadow cat so dangerous?" Ben asked, eyeing Hob and checking the forest around him. Now, he was feeling jumpy.

"The shadow cat travels in our world as a shadow, even on the darkest of nights. However, it is very real and a scratch or bite from the creature is usually fatal."

"How do we fight it? Can we even see it?"

"You can see it when it moves," said Hob, still searching the trees around him. "A shadow across the ground or upon a tree or shrub. It's almost like the shadow of a great bird flying over on a sunny day or a small, fast moving cloud. You can also see it's eyes when it is looking at you. The eyes of a shadow cat burn red with the fires of the Dark Lands."

"The shadow cat must take on a solid form to attack you though," Gabriel continued. "It is then when it is most vulnerable and may be killed by any one of our weapons. So, I repeat, be on your guard at all times. Are we ready?"

"One more question," asked Ben, looking down and fingering the knife at his side. "How am I to defeat the witch? I cannot even defend myself against kids my own age, so how am I supposed to beat some powerful witch?"

Gabriel studied Ben for a moment, then smiled. "The Keeper did not say that you had to defeat the witch, Ben. He only said that you are there when the witch is defeated. The three of us will defeat the witch together."

Ben felt a great weight lift from his shoulders. "Then I'm ready."

"So am I," Hob nodded, smacking the axe handle in his thick hands.

"Follow me then," said Gabriel, "and stay alert."

The Great Oak Forest was filled with all kinds of oaks. There were white oaks, red oaks, live oaks, and water oaks. The strangest thing, however, was that there were no young trees. All the trees in the forest were giants, with trunks so large that Gabriel, Ben, and Hob could not join hands and reach around any of them. Although there was one continuous canopy of leaves high above their heads, the trunks of these giant trees were not crowded together, but rather spaced thirty to forty feet apart.

"This rain is a blessing," said Gabriel. "It dampens the leaves on the ground and helps mask our movements."

"It will also make it difficult for the shadow cat to smell us," Hob added.

The land inside the forest was mostly flat, with a only a few rolling hills. Ben and Hob were able to follow Gabriel quietly and with ease. They walked in silence for most of the day, not speaking, straining their ears for any sound and searching every tree for any shadows. As evening approached, Ben was getting ready to ask Gabriel exactly what he meant when he said the unicorn was near. Gabriel, however, held up his hand and motioned for them to stop, and then pointed ahead to something moving between the trees. In the distance, through the thick grey trunks of the forest, Ben spotted a glimpse of white and then it was gone.

"Was that the unicorn?" Ben mouthed.

Gabriel nodded and motioned for Ben and Hob to follow once again. This time the elf moved slowly and ever so quietly. Take a step and pause. Look. Listen. Take two steps. Pause. Look. Listen. They moved like this for what seemed like hours, when Gabriel finally raised his hand again and directed everyone behind a tree. Holding his finger to his lips, he pointed around the tree and then the three of them crept silently around the massive trunk. Ben spotted the unicorn immediately. It was no more than a hundred yards away, pawing the ground in search of some unknown delicacy among the leaves. The unicorn was just like Ben imagined it would be. The horse was tall and powerful with a broad chest and proud neck that sported a flowing mane of the purest white. The horn was spiraled and had a faint shimmer about it. As a matter of fact, the entire creature had a faint shimmer about it.

"It's beautiful," Ben whispered.

"Indeed," Gabriel replied quietly.

"Is the witch near?" Hob asked. The dwarf's attempt at a whisper made Ben and Gabriel cringe.

"I do not know," Gabriel answered, his eyes intent upon the unicorn.

"Well what are we to do now?" Hob asked.

The unicorn threw up its head, it's ears at sudden attention, and snorted. Ben, Hob, and Gabriel froze. The unicorn looked in their direction for several minutes, and snorted a couple of more times, before returning its attention to whatever lay beneath the leaves. Gabriel turned to Hob.

"Dear friend, you must remain quiet. Your whisper is almost a shout. We are going to guard the unicorn. We know the witch is coming for it. We need to get closer though so please, be quiet as possible. Once we leave this position we must not talk anymore, okay?"

Hob nodded. Ben, however, had been watching the unicorn and from the corner of his eye had seen a flash of movement to the right. There it was again. A shadow flitted across a tree trunk and was gone. Ben tugged on Gabriel's cloak and pointed.

"I saw a shadow moving over there," he whispered, pointing to the right of the unicorn.

Gabriel drew an arrow and nocked it. "Are you certain?"

"Yes, positive. I saw it twice."

"Draw your weapon. Let's move forward now."

Ben drew the knife from his sheath. Hob had both hands upon his axe and Gabriel had his arrow ready to fly. Gabriel took one step and the unicorn's head shot up. Once again everyone froze. However, this time the unicorn was not looking at them, but was looking into the forest away from them. Ben saw the shadow first. It was just as Hob described it, like the shadow of a huge bird racing across the ground. It was heading straight for the unicorn. Gabriel and Hob spotted it at the same time and began running toward the unicorn, trying to get there before the shadow cat. Ben tried to keep up, but quickly fell behind. He paused a moment and bent over to catch his breath, fumbling for the inhaler in his pocket. Gabriel was halfway to the unicorn, drawing his bow back as he ran. Hob was several yards behind him with his axe poised over his head. Ben stood and brought the inhaler to his lips, but a clawed hand grabbed him by the hair on his head and yanked him backwards into an embrace of long thin arms, that were strong as steel and cold as a dark December night. As his lungs began to tighten, Ben mustered all of the strength within his body and screamed. Then, drowning him out with a roar that reverberated through the forest and shook the mighty trees all around them, the unicorn screamed too.

21 MOUNTAIN REST

Amos, Nob, and Gob were all rather surprised at how easy it was for them to slip out of the Twilight, undetected by any snakers. After throwing off their blanket, Amos spotted Ben, Hob, and Gabriel in the boat behind them, but the two dwarves could not see their companions in the darkness no matter how hard they tried and this frustrated them to no end.

"How is it that you can see, what we cannot?" Nob asked, tugging on his beard and peering over the stern.

"Yes," said Gob, turning to Amos and planting his fists upon his hips. "We dwarves have exceptional night vision, yet we cannot even make out the boat in this darkness. I believe there is more to you, Amos, than meets the eye."

Amos chuckled. "That would be true, my friends. And I guess you must know the truth about me, if we are to journey on this perilous mission together."

Amos told the dwarves he was a shape shifter and answered all of their questions (which were not few). This took the better part of an hour. When the dwarve's curiosity seemed to be satisfied, everyone began looking for a place to put ashore. They found a reedy place, near the shoreline, where the water was shallow and still. Amos paddled into the reeds and stepped out of the boat into the cattails. He could not get the swan boat close to the land, and he did not want to take a chance searching for a better landing area, so he carried the dwarves upon his back, one at a time, to dry ground. After depositing them safely on the shore, he returned for their gear and bundled it together in the large blanket they had hid under from the snakers. Pulling the corners together and tossing the bulging sack across his shoulder, he gave the swan boat a gentle push, sending it out of the reeds and back into the open river. The swan boat drifted lazily out toward the center, until the current caught it and spun it around. Then, instead of floating downstream with the current, the boat neatly parted the oncoming water and began its return trip home. Amos shook his head in wonder and waded ashore with the gear, where he found Gob and Nob in some kind of quiet, yet heated debate.

"I tell you, North is that way," said Gob, pointing ahead and diagonally away from the river.

"And I tell you, the river has been curving to our left and North is that way," Nob replied, pointing back and diagonally away from the river. "If these blasted clouds would only lift for a moment!"

"You are both wrong," said Amos, unpacking the blanket. "The river has been curving to our left, but not as much as you suspect. North is that way." Amos pointed straight out, away from the river.

"Are you positive?" Gob asked.

"I am positive," Amos replied.

"Then we had best get moving," Nob added. "We somehow have to cram four days marching into three. And that's not allowing for any time to raise an army."

The three shouldered their packs and set off across the field at a brisk trot. Fortunately, they were out of the trees and on flat terrain because the night was indeed dark. However, they did make excellent time and by dawn they had covered many miles.

As day broke, the heavy clouds began depositing their load in the form of a dreary mist. Amos, Gob, and Nob wore the same elfin cloaks as Ben, Hob, and Gabriel, but the cloaks did nothing to prevent the weather from dampening their spirits. In addition to the low clouds, a thick mist hung over the ground and prevented them from seeing the mountains. Amos seemed sure of their direction though and plodded on tirelessly. Finally, Nob stopped and threw his pack on the ground.

"I can't go any further," he panted. "I can march all day and all night, but not on an empty stomach."

"Me either," Gob added, plopping his pack down beside Nob's. "Right now I am hungry enough to eat dirt."

"What about rocks?" Nob asked.

"What about them?" Gob shot back.

"Are you hungry enough to eat rocks?"

"Hmmm. What kind of rocks?"

"Shale stone. No, slate. No, no, I got it. Granite! Are you hungry enough to eat granite?"

"Well now that you mention it, if someone gave me a big plate of dirt and a big granite rock, the first thing I would do is take the granite rock and beat you in the head with it for asking stupid questions. Then I'd eat the dirt."

Amos chuckled at the two dwarves, while he rummaged around in his pack. "We will not have to eat dirt tonight. Or rocks either." He pulled out some white stag jerky and apples and tossed them to the dwarves. "Eat this. Shoulder your packs too. We can eat while we walk."

"Hey, what's that?" asked Nob.

"What's what?" Gob mumbled, around a mouthful of apple.

"That noise," said Amos. "Shhh."

In the distance, although they could not tell how far away it was, for this mist did play tricks with the sounds, they could hear what sounded like the steady ring of a hammer on steel.

"Ah yes, I hear it now," said Gob. "Probably a farm house nearby."

"Come," said Amos. "It sounds like it's in the direction we're traveling. Let's find it and see if they have any horses."

"We are not riding horses!" Gob and Nob exclaimed at the same time.

"Well, maybe the farmer has a wagon," Amos replied curtly.

Shouldering their packs, munching apples and chewing jerky, they made their way through the thick mists until they came to a cedar rail fence. The fence surrounded a small stone house with a thatch roof. Across the front yard from the house, stood a large barn made of logs and split wood shingles. The tall double doors to the barn were open wide and the warm yellow light of a lantern sliced through the gray morning mist, spilling out into the barn yard. The hammering noise came from within. Amos motioned for the two dwarves to follow him and they crept silently down to the barn and peered inside.

The barn had two stalls on the right side and a loft up above them. The loft was overflowing with sweet smelling timothy and alfalfa hay. All kinds of farming tools were hanging from the rafters and a crude table stood against the rear wall of the barn, where an old man was beating a plowshare with a hammer upon an anvil. Amos stepped into the barn and called out to him.

"Hello there."

The man spun around, plowshare in one hand, hammer in the other. Amos could see right away that he had frightened him.

"Who are you? What do you want?" The old man wheezed, his voice high with fright. "What are you doing trespassing on my property?"

Amos held his arms out to his side, his palms open. "We mean you no harm, sir. We only wish to borrow your horse and wagon. We'd gladly pay you."

"We?" the old man croaked. "How many more are out there?"

"Just a couple of my friends," Amos answered. "I asked them to wait outside so that we would not startle you."

"Come out where I can see you," the old man cried. "You've got no business sneaking about on my property!"

Gob and Nob walked into the barn, materializing out of the mists like two grim specters. The old man saw the dwarves and the blood drained from his face. He dropped the hammer and plowshare and fell to his knees with his hands and face upon the ground.

"Take what you want, but I beg you leave me be. I am an old man, too old to work the mines. I wouldn't even survive the trip. Please, take anything, but have mercy on me."

"What's he talking about?" Gob asked, bewildered.

"He thinks we are bloody gnomes!" said Nob indignantly.

"Gnomes!" Gob steamed. "He'll wish we were gnomes when I finish with him."

Amos snagged Gob by the hood of his cloak and held him back. The old man was truly terrified now, as the dwarf struggled to get at him. Amos dragged Gob back outside and Nob followed.

"You two wait here. There's a wagon in the back corner of that barn, if you haven't noticed, and the loft is full of fresh hay. That means there is a horse, or a mule, or an ox on this farm. Let him think you are gnomes for now. This may work for our benefit."

Amos went back into the barn and closed the doors behind him. Gob was still fuming over being mistaken for a gnome.

"Can you believe he thought we were gnomes?"

"It must be these blasted elfin cloaks. We sure don't look like proper dwarves with these on."

"They do keep us dry and rather warm, though. Maybe it's the light."

"Or it could be this infernal mist."

The two dwarves were going on like this when the barn doors flew open and Amos came out driving a small buckboard wagon that was pulled by a draft horse whose head was as long as the dwarves were tall. The dwarves gave the horse a wide berth as they approached the buckboard and they boarded the wagon with trepidation.

"Where did the horse come from?" Gob asked. "I did not see a horse inside the barn! You didn't shape-shift that old man into a horse did you?"

"Good heavens no, I can't do that!"

"Well it would serve him right if you could! Thinking we were gnomes and all!"

"So where did the horse come from?" Nob asked, repeating Gobs question. "And what manner of horse is this? He looks like a monster!"

"Both of the stalls opened up into a paddock on the other side of the barn. The horse was outside in the paddock."

"Is he an obedient creature?" asked Gob. "We can make it on foot if we really hurry."

"He is a fine horse," Amos responded. "He is young and powerful and, although he may not win any races with his speed, he can maintain a brisk trot for several hours and have us to Mountain Rest by late afternoon. But before we depart, I need to leave payment for the animal and the wagon."

"Ah, so he is selling this horse and wagon then. Have you settled on a price?" asked Gob, raising his bushy eyebrows and stroking his beard. Dwarves, by their very nature, love to haggle. Gob was now looking at the horse with an appraising eye. He wanted to crawl down from the buckboard and kick the wagon wheels too.

"No, he is not selling," Amos answered. "The old man is convinced you are gnomes and he was quite happy for me to take the horse and wagon and not him."

"Then why do you need to make payment?"

"Because this horse and wagon are that poor man's lively-hood. I intend that he gets them back too, but if he does not then he needs to be able to replace them."

Nob pulled a small pouch from beneath his cloak and handed it to Amos. Amos weighed the sack in his hand then tossed it over the wagon, onto the ground, in front of the barn doors. He then clucked to the big horse and they were off, with Gob and Nob staring wistfully at the small sack of gold lying in the dirt.

Finally, the dwarves turned around to see where Amos was taking them.

"Where are we going?" Nob ventured. "We cannot go overland and across country on this wagon. Not all the way to the mountains."

"This lane we travel on," said Amos, "will soon join the North Road, which goes by Mountain Rest. The farmer said the horse knows the way to Mountain Rest and will take us there if we give him the rein. Are either of you familiar with the town?"

"Mountain Rest is a mining town," Gob replied. "The dwarven mines extend east from the West Gate of Nimrodell. The humans mine everything west of there. It is a small and dirty town - a mean town. No dwarves venture there anymore."

"How far is the West Gate from Mountain Rest?"

"An hour's march by foot. The horse cannot go where we must go, once we leave the town."

Suddenly, the lane curved to the left and they were upon the North road. The mist had lifted somewhat and the drizzle finally ceased. Although they could still not see the mountains, they could now see the road stretching out before them, a wide brown ribbon of hard packed dirt, slicing neatly through the tall green grass.

"I intend to leave the horse and wagon at the livery, with instructions to be returned to the owner. We'll leave from the livery and head straight to the West Gate," said Amos.

"At this pace, we can make the West Gate by nightfall," said Gob.

"How long will it take to assemble the army?"

"Oh, we can be marching back to the Twilight by dawn," Nob smiled. "With two thousand strong."

"Then we might just make it after all," Amos marveled.

The rest of the day passed by uneventfully. They met only one other wagon on the road and a couple of riders. By late afternoon, the mist had completely lifted. Ragged patches of blue sky began to appear and, every now and then, a beam of sunshine escaped through the dissipating clouds. By evening time, the sky was completely clear and the sun was turning the western horizon a brilliant mixture of oranges and reds.

"Turn there," said Gob, pointing at a small trail up ahead.

The trail, barely wide enough for the wagon, forked off to the left and wound gently uphill, through trees still dripping from the recent rains. At the crest of the hill, Amos pulled back on the reins and brought the wagon to a halt. Seemingly right in front of them, yet actually several miles away, the Iron Bone Mountains reared up stark and bare against the evening sky.

"There's the West Gate," said Nob, "that dark spot between those two peaks."

"And there's Mountain Rest," said Amos.

Down at the foot of the hill, in the small valley below, lay the mining town of Mountain Rest. The town was small and dirty and seemed completely devoid of any color except gray. Smoke curled from several chimneys, adding to the already dismal atmosphere that hung over the town.

"Let's get in and out of the town as quickly as possible," said Gob.

"Yes, quickly as possible," Nob agreed.

Amos clucked to the horse and the wagon began its slow descent down into the valley.

22 NIMRODELL

The main street of Mountain Rest was nothing more than two large muddy ruts, worn into the weary ground by the passage of time and countless wagons. The town was not crowded, but the people that were out and about did pause at whatever they were doing to ogle at the giant hairy man in furs and the two dwarves riding with him. As they neared one particular weathered old building, two sinister looking men sitting on crates in front of the establishment arose and went inside. A sign over the door of the building swung gently in the breeze, its rusty hinges squeaking to passersby, its faded letters advertising cold ale and hot stew for the weary traveler.

"I wonder what that was all about," Amos muttered.

"It can't be good," Gob replied. "This is a bad place. Dwarves no longer come here." Looking over his shoulder, he could see several men peering through the dirty windows and watching as the wagon passed.

"So I've heard," said Amos. "There, up ahead. That's the livery stable."

As the wagon rolled up to the front of the barn, Amos pulled back on the reins and brought the big draft horse to a stop. The barn was in a severe state of disrepair, battered by the elements like the bare and naked peaks that rose up behind the town. One of the double doors leading into the barn was gone and the other door hung askew from a solitary hinge of leather that looked as if it were hanging on a prayer, rather than a nail.

Amos did not like the look of the place. For that matter, he did not like the look of the whole town. There was something wrong here. Something that wasn't obvious, but something just below the surface and not all together hidden from sight either. A tension maybe? Or a danger? Or maybe both. It felt like seeing a poisonous snake lying in the grass, coiled and seemingly harmless, yet ready to strike in a flash. He called out from the wagon.

"Hello!"

A mammoth man, almost as large as Amos, appeared out of the gloomy recesses of the barn. He was bald, covered in soot, and was wiping his hands upon a long leather apron that hung down to his knees. He walked around to the side, then back to the front, looking the wagon and the horse over with a careful eye.

"Where did you come by that horse and wagon, mister?"

Nob noticed the man's biceps were like tree trunks and that his forearms were scarred and corded with muscle, from long hours at the forge. He slowly loosened the axe in his belt.

"We borrowed it," Amos answered. "From a farmer just a short piece off the North Road. And now we wish to leave it here, to be returned to him with our thanks."

"That's old man Miller's horse and wagon. He'd never lend them out."

"Well, he did not exactly lend them to us," Gob spoke up. "We paid him gold for the use of his horse and wagon. Good gold."

The blacksmith examined the two dwarves sitting beside Amos with narrow, venomous eyes then turned his attention back to Amos.

186

"Well, which is it? Did you borrow the horse and wagon, or did you pay gold for the use of the horse and wagon? Or did you steal it? For all we know, you may have murdered old man Miller."

"Thieves!" someone shrieked behind them.

"Murderers!" someone else cried.

Gob and Nob spun around on the wagon seat. Behind them, a group of fifteen men were beginning to encircle them. They were all carrying crude weapons. Some had pitchforks, a couple of them had shovels. Most of them were carrying clubs. Amos locked eyes with the blacksmith and sat calmly, not speaking, not moving. The silence in the small town was complete. Or at least it seemed so to Gob and Nob, who had their hands firmly upon their axes. Somewhere in the distance, a dog barked and the blacksmith finally looked away. He wiped the sweat from his brow and retreated a few steps back to the barn. Amos spoke slowly and calmly.

"As I said, we paid good gold for the use of the horse and wagon. We are leaving the horse and wagon with you so they may be returned to their owner, Mr. Miller. I had intended to pay you in gold likewise, to see that they are delivered safely and swiftly."

"We'll take your gold anyway!" someone yelled.

Gob and Nob rose as one and slid their axes from their belts, but Amos held his hand out and bade them to be still. Now that the mob was inching closer and getting ready to attack, the blacksmith regained his courage.

"Let's put them in the stocks," he shouted. "At least until we can verify their story."

The crowd surged forward, eager for blood and easy gold. Eager for anything to channel their anger upon. Anger built up through years of scraping out a living in this dismal little mining town. Anger that was almost palatable. And as they pressed in around the sides of the wagon, Amos stood, and as he stood, the air about him shimmered and he appeared to grow taller. The mob faltered, unsure now, and began to slowly fall back. Then suddenly, Amos spread his arms, threw his head back and roared. The effect was just what he was hoping for. The color drained from the blacksmith's face as he stumbled backwards into the barn, crossing himself and chanting some childhood spell, seeking protection from the evil eye.

"Witchcraft!" someone in the crowd screamed. The mob threw their weapons on the ground and fled down the street. The poor horse, however, was just as terrified as everyone else and sprang forward, tearing down the bumpy dirt road. Gob and Nob clung to the wagon with white knuckles, while Amos, still standing with arms outstretched, shimmered once again, then shrank back down to his normal size. As the horse thundered past the last building in town, Amos snatched Gob up under one arm, and Nob up under the other arm, and leapt from the speeding wagon. Amazingly, the big man kept his footing and safely deposited the two shaken dwarves on the ground with nothing wounded, but their pride. The horse continued down the road, the wagon bouncing madly behind it, spurring it on even faster. As the road curved away from the mountains, the wagon came loose from the harness and flipped end over end, disintegrating into hundreds and shards and splinters. In a matter of seconds the wagon was reduced to a pile of rubble and the only sign of the horse was a plume of dust rising over the next hill, where the terrified creature was probably still running for its life.

"I did not think a horse that big could run that fast," Amos exclaimed.

"Never again," said Gob, shaking his head. "Never again."

"I agree," said Nob. "No more horses for me either."

"That is well and good," Amos replied, "for we have no need of a horse now. Let's find our packs and get moving before that superstitious mob regains their confidence and comes looking for us."

"Yes," Nob agreed. "That mob will get the whole town riled up. And yes, they will come after us I'm sure, but I fear it will be more than fifteen or twenty people that do come."

"Well, we are closer to the gate now anyway," said Gob, looking up at the mountains before them. The West Gate, though still distant, was now visible on the slopes above. Nob started walking down the road, where the horse had disappeared, and Gob fell in behind him.

"Where are you two going?" Amos asked. "The gate is up there."

"There is a path that leads to the gate. It's just a short piece down this road," Gob called over his shoulder. "There will be many steps to climb and many switchbacks on the trail, but it will be much quicker than trying to go straight up the mountain."

Amos looked up at the mountains, studying the steep and rocky slopes leading up to the gate. He finally decided the dwarves knew best, this being their home, and hurried down the road to catch up with them.

When they came upon the path, the entrance was flanked on both sides by the remains of two very old towers. The roof was missing from the tower on the left and it looked like a broken, jagged tooth protruding from the ground. The foundation was all that remained of the tower on the right, a ring of stones, with a tree and a bit of grass growing in the center. Gob looked upon the ruins with great sadness in his heart.

"When our fathers were young, these towers stood strong and proud. The elves helped build them, you know. This tower on our left, was the guard house. There used to be a strong iron gate between the towers and the gate could only be opened from within the guard house. The tower on the right, was a storage room and barracks. Even though these were built during peaceful times, we always kept them manned with at least one regiment."

"And now," said Nob, "when it seems we are in perilous times indeed, they have fallen into ruin and stand deserted before the entrance to our very kingdom."

Amos smiled at the two dwarves. "Nothing is lost yet, my friends. How long from here to the gate?"

"Not long now," Gob replied. "Less than an hour."

Amos nodded, as the sun slipped down behind the tall peaks, taking the long shadows of evening with it. He glanced back down the road, toward town. All was quiet for now, but how long would that last? He shouldered his pack and started up the path.

By the time they reached the end of the path, it was dark and the rain-washed skies were ablaze with stars. The West Gate, sloping back into the stone wall of the mountain, was at least fifteen feet tall and twenty feet across. It was built from timbers that were rubbed black with pitch and bound together with thick rusty bands of iron. No hinges were visible and it was impossible to tell where or how the gate opened.

"What do we do now?" Amos asked. "Knock?"

"No," said Nob, "we just go right in. Follow me,"

Nob walked up to the side of the mountain, to the left of the gate, and pressed his hand against the rock wall. A thin line emerged in the stone, outlining what appeared to be an arched doorway, that was large enough for Amos to walk through without stooping.

"Why do we not use the gate?" Amos asked.

"This is the gate," Gob replied. "The West Gate."

"Then pray tell, what that is?" Amos asked, pointing over his shoulder at the hulking wood and iron gate set within the mountain wall.

"That gate is a decoy," Nob answered. "Back when Nimrodell and Mountain Rest had commerce, and there was no enmity between the dwarves and the men of Mountain Rest, the West Gate was a busy place indeed. However, we have always been suspicious of humans and their greed for gold, therefore only dwarves have ever been allowed upon this mountain. As a matter of fact, no man has ever crossed this threshold, nor even seen the true gate before us now. Bringing you through the gate is a great offense, but maybe it will add weight and legitimacy to the story we shall tell tonight, of the snaker invasion and the greater perils that lay before us."

"The decoy gate is meant to look imposing, like a gate of a great fortress," Gob added. "You see, a great fortress conjures up images of great armies, great armies conjure up images of great battles, and great battles conjure up images of great destruction and death."

"And should anyone actually raise an army and attack our gate," said Nob smiling, "they would only find the stone wall of the mountain behind the gate, and that wall, no army can raze."

Amos marveled at the two dwarves before him and began to regard them with a newfound respect and admiration. Gob gave the stone wall a gentle shove, and the door silently swung inward, revealing a dark tunnel leading down into the bowels of the mountain. Almost immediately, a drum began to echo and reverberate from within the depths of the mountain, a slow and steady beat that seemed to somehow throb with urgency.

"What is that?" Amos asked.

"That is an alarm," Gob answered. "It is announcing that the West Gate has been opened. The West Gate has been closed for many years now. When it was closed for the final time, an alarm was fashioned so that it would sound whenever the gate was opened. Even though our two towers have fallen into ruin, and the path to our kingdom is no longer guarded, we do not sleep, nor are we lax in the defense of our kingdom. Even though this mountain, even this very gate before us is no longer guarded, we have maintained an army within. Right now, that army, two thousand strong, is marshalling together and will soon speed this way."

"Two thousand to defend this one small door?" Amos asked. "I could defend this door against an entire army by myself!"

"The door is small, but Nimrodell is expansive. There is a great chamber, less than a mile inside the mountain, that will hold six times that number. Whoever holds that chamber, has a decisive advantage."

"Should we go inside and meet them?" Gob asked, peering around at Amos and Nob.

"No, I think we are better off to wait out here. If we go inside, they just might put an arrow or a spear into us before they recognize who we are. Especially, if they see Amos. Once they are satisfied that no army has invaded, they will send a small party up here to see what set the alarm off."

"Quite right Nob, quite right," said Gob, pulling on his long braided beard and peering down the dark tunnel. "Good thinking too, very good thinking. As a matter of fact, it might be a good idea if Amos hides until we speak to whomever arrives to investigate."

"Why thank you Gob, that is most kind of you, and a good idea on your part too."

Amos rolled his eyes and marched over to the other side of the fake gate to sit and hide in the shadows. Gob and Nob sat down to the side of the real gate and began to talk excitedly about returning to their dwarven home. As they discussed the adventures that lay before them, the drums, down deep in the mountains, continued to beat their ominous warning.

Boom... Boom... Boom...

23 STONE DOG

Louise had her arms wrapped tightly around Jonah's waist as the ground flew beneath them in a dark blur. Although they were traveling at break-neck speeds, the ride was smooth and easy. They raced over hills and valleys, through fields and forests, the great horses never slowing, never tiring. By dawn they reached a dusty, barren plain and the elves drew the weary horses to a halt.

"This is as close as we dare come," said Jonah. "Behold the Blight."

Nothing stirred on the plain before them. Tree trunks, sticks, and stems were the only remaining signs of vegetation that once grew here. A sickly gray mist covered the landscape that was brown and devoid of all other color. In the distance, a hill rose up from the plain and atop this hill sat a small, squat fortress with a lone tower jutting up from the center. The elves dismounted and helped everyone else down from the horses.

"There is Stone Dog," said Jonah, pointing toward the tower. He pulled an arrow from his quiver and handed it to Louise. "Strike out straight across the plain here and you will come to the road that leads to the castle. Lay this arrow in the road, pointing back to us. When you return from the castle, pick up the arrow and wave. We will be watching for you and will signal for you when we see you waving."

"Are you sure the castle is unguarded?" Louise asked.

"I am positive," Jonah replied. "The witch has no one but her shadow cat, and that demon is with her always."

The children walked up beside Louise. All three of them had a fierce look of determination on their faces. Joey was carrying an axe, that one of the dwarves had given him, and a small sack, from the Keeper, was tied at his belt.

"Well, I guess we'd better be on our way," Louise said.

"Be sure to come back with all twelve horns. We can use them to return to the Twilight."

"What do you mean by that?"

"I'll show you when you get back. Hurry now."

Louise and the children stepped out of the forest onto the blight stricken ground and the dead grass crunched beneath their feet. In a few minutes they came across the road, just as Jonah said they would, and Louise placed the arrow in the road, pointing it back to the place in the forest they had just left. From here, they could still see the elves on the fringe of the forest, standing as silent and still as the trees around them.

It took them half an hour to reach the castle. The walls were no more than twelve to fifteen feet in height and formed a square around a tower that rose thirty feet above them. Both the castle walls and tower were built of strange rocks, smooth and black like onyx, hewed in many different shapes and fitted together so precisely that it was hard to tell where one stone ended and another stone began. The road led them through the open gates into the courtyard and straight to a small door set into the base of the tower. Whether by magic or by might, the door was locked tight and would not budge. Louise and the children walked around the base and found no other point of entry, but they did count four windows at the top of the tower, one for each point of the compass.

"What do you think, Joey? Do you think you can climb up there?"

"I'm not sure, these walls are pretty smooth."

Meg peered up at the top of the tower. "The windows seem small too. I don't know if Joey could even fit through one."

Joey laid his axe down and untied the sack from his belt. Inside was a long thin rope with a strange looking device tied onto the end. According to the Keeper, this was a grappling hook and would lock onto whatever surface it struck. A hard yank would lock the hook in place and a gentle tug would release it. Joey coiled the rope into long, loose loops and everyone stepped back as he began to twirl the grappling device. The first throw landed far short of the window. Joey gave the rope a gentle tug to release it and then tried again. This time, the device locked onto the wall just a little above the window sill and slightly to the left. It was close enough. Fortunately, the base of the tower was much larger in diameter than the top, so that the tower wall, although steep, was not completely vertical. Even though the tower walls were smooth, the rubber soles on Joey's tennis shoes were able to get pretty good traction and Joey was able to make it to the window without much difficulty. However, he found the window barred from the inside and impossible to enter. They made their way around the tower, checking all four windows and each one, to their dismay, they found shut, locked and unopenable.

"What now?" Casey asked. It was now mid-morning and the sun was beginning to burn off some of the strange wispy mists that surrounded the castle.

"Let's see if we can force the door open," Meg replied. "That's the only option we have left."

The door was wooden and bound together with thick bands of polished steel. Joey took the axe and began hacking away at the center of the door but there were so many steel bands holding it together that, after a short while, he had accomplished nothing more than dulling his axe. He sat down in the shade of the tower to catch his breath while Casey, Meg, and Louise poked about in a pile of debris at the base of the tower. After closely examining what appeared to be the shattered remains of an old wagon, the three women huddled together and began excitedly discussing a new plan to gain access to the tower. His curiosity overcame his fatigue and Joey roused himself to see what they were talking about.

"It's a great idea, Meg," said Louise.

"What's a great idea?"

Louise turned to Joey. "We'll burn the door down."

"That won't destroy the tower?"

"No, the tower is stone. There may be a wooden structure inside, maybe a staircase or wooden floors but once we burn enough of the door to kick it in, we'll put the fire out. We can pile the timber from this old wagon up against the door. It's very dry and should make a nice hot fire. Once the door catches, it probably won't take long to burn through."

"That's a great idea, but how are we going to light the fire?"

Louise smiled as she reached into a pocket on the front of her dress and produced a pair of reading glasses.

"How are you going to start a fire with those?" Casey asked.

"You'll see. Right now, you and Meg start gathering tinder to start the fire; grass, small twigs, and stems. Pile it up in front of the door. Joey, I'll start moving small pieces of that wagon over here and you start moving the larger pieces."

In a few minutes, Casey and Meg had a large heap of dead grass piled up against the door. Louise knelt down and used her reading glasses to focus the sun's rays into a small intense point of light on top of the dry grass. Within a few seconds, a thin stream of smoke began to rise and the dried grasses burst into flames which began to hungrily devour the fuel. Next, she placed the small pieces of timber, from the wagon, onto the fire and when the small pieces started catching, Joey began tossing the larger pieces onto the flames. The fire roared against the door as it greedily consumed the old wagon and wisps of smoke began to curl out from beneath the eaves at the tower's top. Louise and the kids let the door burn until most of the wagon shards were totally consumed. Then Joey took his axe to the charred door and was able to hack through the burned timbers and gain access to the inside of the tower. Quickly, they set about beating down the fires that were burning around the entrance and once the flames were extinguished, they had to wait for the smoke to clear before they could enter.

The tower did indeed have a wooden structure within. It was divided into three levels and a wooden staircase spiraled around the outer wall between the levels. The first level appeared to be the living quarters, complete with a food storage area and a crude kitchen with a fireplace, tables and chairs. The second level was the sleeping chambers. On this level, there was a large bed near another fireplace, a wardrobe, and several chests. The third level had no furnishings at all. A twelve pointed star, that spanned the entire room, was painted on the floor and a unicorn horn was planted at each point of this star, with the spiral tip pointing skyward. In the center of the star stood the Merlin Tree, the portal to Pluton.

"Wow," said Joey, "no wonder the witch didn't have any problem finding the thing; it's right inside of her house!"

"This tree is different," said Louise. "Look at the opening. In the other trees, you can see through the opening."

Although it was very dim inside the tower, enough light shone through the shuttered windows that everyone could see that the opening in the Merlin Tree was pitch black. While everyone was looking at the tree, a thin tendril of smoke began to ooze from the dark opening. Rather than rising up to the rafters, this mysterious smoke crept across the floor, past Louise and the children. They watched in fascination as the smoke made its way to the edge of the room and tumbled down the staircase. Then Meg screamed.

Louise grabbed Casey by the arm and whirled around. Two long thick tentacles had emerged from the Merlin Tree. They were mottled pink in color and coated with a foul smelling slime. One of them was thrashing around, weaving back and forth, and probing the air as if searching for something. The other one was wrapped tightly around Meg's ankle and had yanked her off her feet. Joey, still carrying the axe, sprang into action and began madly chopping at the tentacle that was now dragging his sister across the floor. Though the axe was dull, he was able to hack the end of tentacle off with a few swift strokes. The injured tentacle, spouting an even fouler smelling liquid from the severed end, struck out in retaliation and flung Joey against the wall, while the other tentacle found Meg before she could escape, and wrapped itself tightly around her waist. Apparently, the creature these tentacles belonged to was now angry. Meg was violently flung to the floor and then very rapidly dragged toward the tree. Joey was dazed and unable to move. Meg was screaming. Casey was screaming. Then suddenly a crack of thunder exploded in the tower, blowing the shuttered windows open, and lightning arced across the room, searing the two tentacles to a smoking pile of lifeless ashes. Silence. Casey turned to look at her grandmother.

Louise was standing at one of the points of the star on the tower floor, with a unicorn horn in her outstretched hand. She did not remember picking up the horn. She did not know the word that formed in her brain, as she pointed the horn at the creature's arms. Even as she uttered the word, she did not know what to expect. She certainly did not expect lightning to shoot from the end of the horn and burn the creature to a crisp.

Meg scrambled to her feet and ran over the help her brother up.

"Grandma," said Casey in a shaky voice. "Are you okay?"

Louise slowly lowered the horn. "Yes dear, I'm fine."

"What just happened?"

"I don't know, sweetheart. We'll figure it out later. Right now, let's get these horns and get out of here. Joey, hand me your sack and then all of you go downstairs and wait for me by the door."

When Louise came out of the tower, the sack was bulging with the twelve horns she collected from around the tree. They used the roped to secure the horns within the sack and then Joey hoisted the bundle over his shoulder.

"Mission accomplished," Louise said. "Let's get out of here."

"Shouldn't we try to destroy the Merlin Tree while we are here?" Joey asked. "It wouldn't take much to burn the inside of the tower out."

"I thought about that," Louise answered. "And I don't think we should. If we destroyed the Tree, then Mordred would probably create another one and we might not be so lucky in finding the next one. Also, as long as he thinks the Merlin Tree is in Stone Dog he will think it's safe from attack. If we destroy it, he will probably try to fortify the next one."

"Was that Mordred that attacked us?" Meg asked.

"No, that was probably just a creature from the other side. Probably a guardian of the portal."

"Well, let's get out of here," said Casey. "This place has a sick feeling to it. It makes me feel like I need to take a bath or something."

Louise and the kids trudged down the road, until they came across the elfin arrow. They looked across the field towards the woods, where the arrow was pointing, but they could see nothing but trees. Louise picked the arrow up and began waving it over her head and four elves materialized from among the trees and began waving back. When they reached the elves, Joey handed the horns over to Jonah and then everyone retreated to a small glade a couple of miles into the forest to get further away from the Blight.

Jonah unbundled the twelve horns. He slid one horn into his belt and then handed each person a horn.

"Hold these tightly and do not drop them."

Next, he took the remaining four horns and slid one under each of the saddles so that the horns were in contact with the horse's flesh.

"The Keeper has instructed me in the art of creating a pathway. It is one of many things that Merlin shared with him. The wizards of old used these pathways to travel and all but Merlin needed their staffs to open these pathways. We have no staffs, but we each have something far more powerful."

Jonah cast a knowing glance at Louise and raised his eyebrow then continued, "Merlin was also the only wizard who could create a pathway and keep it open for others to travel. This feat I cannot do."

"Then how are we to get back to the Twilight?" Louise asked.

Jonah walked over to Casey.

"The Keeper believes that a spell-catcher will hold the spell and keep the pathway open. May I borrow your necklace, Casey?"

Casey reached behind her neck and unfastened the clasp. She held the necklace out and dropped it into Jonah's hand.

"You can have it, if you will get us out of here," she whispered.

Jonah pulled the spiraled horn from his belt and wrapped the necklace around it. He held the horn above his head and spoke a strange word under his breath that no one could hear. At first nothing happened. Then the air at the edge of the glade began to shimmer and suddenly, a black hole popped up in front of them. The hole was at least six feet across and hovered a few inches off the ground.

"I have to go through first," said Jonah. "Then Louise and the children shall follow after me. When you step into the hole, you will be in total darkness. You will be able to see through the portal behind you and you will be able to see the other portal that opens into the Twilight. Walk straight to the other portal and do not veer to the left or to the right. Understand?"

Louise and the children nodded. Jonah wrapped the reins in one hand and, holding the horn and the spell-catcher in front with the other hand, led his horse into the black hole and disappeared.

24 RAINING FIRE

Louise took a deep breath and stepped into the black hole. The darkness engulfed her, yet up ahead she could see a bright light shining like a candle in the night.

"That must be the portal inside of the Twilight," she thought. She started walking toward the light and glanced back over her shoulder. She could see the others in the small glade behind her, gathered around the portal and waiting their turn to enter. Casey was getting ready to step through now. Louise turned back toward the Twilight portal. She was much closer now. She could see Jonah and his horse on the other side, waiting for her to come through. When she stepped out of the pathway, she found herself beside the center tent. The Keeper had joined Jonah, and at his feet was an ornate box with two unicorn horns inside. Louise placed her horn in with the other two. Casey emerged next, then Meg, then Joey. The remaining three elves came through last, leading their horses. When the last horn was laid into the box, one of the elves that had accompanied them placed the lid on top and carried the box into the center tent. Marcus took the spell-catcher from Jonah and spoke a word of command to the jewel. The black hole snapped shut and he slipped the necklace into his pocket.

"It is a great thing you have accomplished today. With these horns, we believe we will be able to close the pathway we have created from Faerie to Pluton. We have reasoned that if the pathway we have created is destroyed, then the pathway Mordred created will be destroyed as well."

"What if you are wrong?" Louise asked.

"If we are wrong, then we must rely upon Ben to put an end to the witch, Mordred's only ally. And with the witch out of the way, we will be able to focus our energies on halting the spread of the Blight. However, should Ben's task prove unsuccessful, then we have at least delayed the coming of Mordred for many, many years."

"Well then, what shall we do next?"

"There is nothing to do for now, except wait and hope. However, you must be tired and hungry so Jonah will show you to your tent where you may eat and rest."

"And if you do not mind," said Jonah, "I shall eat with you today."

"We'd be delighted," Louise answered. "We have much to ask you."

"Actually, I am to keep company with you for the length of your stay here, so there will be plenty of time for questions. Let's eat first."

When they arrived at the tent, the meal, though a simple fare, was both delicious and satisfying and as soon as everyone finished, Louise began plying Jonah with her questions. Her first questions were about the Twilight, about Marcus the Keeper, the center tent, and the Merlin Tree. Jonah patiently answered all of those questions. From there, she moved on to the home world of the elves and Jonah, with much excitement in his voice, told of his homeland.

"Faerie is much like Camelot. Except in Faerie there is neither death nor decay, nor is there any sickness or disease. At least not until the Blight showed up."

"Why would you ever want to leave a place like that?" Meg asked.

"There are many of our own people that ask us the same question. They have never left Faerie and cannot understand why anyone would ever want to do so. Sometimes, we elves that are here in Camelot, lose sight of the very reasons that brought us here."

"Which are?" Meg prompted, feeling that Jonah did not answer her question.

Jonah smiled. "The original reason was nothing more than adventure. Some of us find many long years in paradise, tedious at best. We felt the need for new challenges and new experiences. Camelot offered that and more."

"If that was your original reason, then what are your reasons now?" Joey asked.

"There are two," Jonah answered. "The first, is to make Camelot a better place. There is much healing needed here. Not just in the land, but in the inhabitants as well. Here, sickness and disease abound and death is everywhere."

"Is there magic in Faerie too?" Louise asked, trying to steer the subject back to the elf's homeland.

"Oh yes, strong magic and much of it. That brings up the second reason we are here in Camelot. Elves are magical creatures. Magic is in our blood and we are drawn to it. When we discovered Camelot, we immediately felt the magic that existed in this world and we wanted to know more about it. What of your world? Is there magic in your world as well?"

"Yes," Louise answered. "But we have a very different magic in our world. It's called technology."

"Technology," Jonah repeated. "Tell me about your world and this magic called technology."

Louise spent the next hour telling Jonah about everything from airplanes to transistor radios. She told him about telephones and televisions. She told him about computers and microwave ovens. She told him about the bad things too, the weapons of war, from the small handgun to the great atom bomb, and Jonah listened to all of it with rapt attention.

"I would truly love to see your world some day," he exclaimed, when she finished.

Louise patted him on the arm. "If we ever get out of this mess, you shall." Then, she began to ask the elf questions about the current situation.

"Is Ben going to return safely?"

"Will the witch really be defeated?"

"How is the forest holding up?"

"How many snakers have been slain?"

"How many snakers are left?"

"Will the large snaker army get here before the dwarves?"

Jonah answered every question, as best as he could, then spent the remainder of the day trying to keep everyone's spirits up.

Outside of the Twilight, the snakers had lost many lives to the twisting and snapping limbs of the forest. Finally, they pulled back and began systematically attacking the forest in different places, searching for a weak spot. They kept this up all day long. By nightfall, they pulled back once more and began massing on the leeward side of the forest. All attacks had ceased and for several hours an ominous and foreboding silence hung over the forest like an angry black cloud. During this lull, Louise, Casey, Joey, and Meg did manage to get a few hours of sleep. Then, a couple of hours before dawn, it began to rain fire.

Scrambling from their beds, their first thought was that the forest defenses had been breached. Elves were fleeing from the tent city into the forest. Jonah came running up to them, concern and worry etched plainly upon his face.

"We need your help. We need every hand available."

"What's happening Jonah?" Louise asked, pulling Casey and Meg close to her side and wrapping her arms protectively around them.

"The snakers have been making bows and arrows during the night. They are shooting flaming arrows into the forest. The trees can extinguish many of the flames, but the arrows are coming fast and furious and some of the trees are catching fire. Grab furs from the bed and come with me. If the forest falls, we are lost."

Louise and the three kids grabbed furs, as Jonah instructed, and followed the elf to the river. Some elves were going up the river in swan boats and some were going down the river. Most of the elves were crossing the bridge and running into the forest with them. When they got closer to the perimeter of the forest, Louise could see bright flames streaking across the still dark skies and small fires were burning everywhere among the trees. They ran to the fires with the elves and began beating the flames out with the furs. Morning came and went and still the arrows rained down, but by noon they finally ceased. Either the snakers had spent all of their arrows or they had abandoned the idea of burning the forest down. There were still small fires burning in several different places, but they were all under control and well on the way to being extinguished. Louise and the kids were exhausted and trudged wearily back to their tent. Jonah met them there soon after, with wash basins, towels, and refreshments, but did not stay to eat with them. After they washed the soot from their hands and faces, they plopped down on the furs still remaining on their beds, too tired to eat.

"I feel as if I haven't slept a wink," Louise said.

"I think we should sleep if we can," said Meg. "Who knows what we will go through tonight?"

"Yes, you're right, dear. Let's eat too. We must keep our strength up."

When they finished eating their lunch, they did not get to sleep after all for Jonah returned and informed them that the Keeper had requested an audience with them. They followed Jonah to the center tent and then to the fire pit inside, where the Keeper was waiting for them. Marcus looked completely exhausted, but he stood and greeted them all before producing an emerald necklace from his pocket and addressing Casey.

"Casey, you have graciously allowed us use of your spell catcher and we have yet to return it to you. If we may impose upon you once more, I would ask that we could use it for a while longer. I don't think the forest can stand another attack like last night."

"Of course," Casey replied, "keep it for as long as you need it."

As Marcus clasped the necklace around his neck, another elf appeared at his side, whispered into his ear, and then hastily retreated from the tent.

"It is well that we have a spell catcher," said Marcus, "and it could not have come at a better time. Last night, while the snakers were attacking with the flaming arrows on one side of the forest, at least half of them were on the other side of the forest, pulling logs and brush from the river and piling it against the trees. It appears that this large band of snakers we are waiting on, have been felling trees around Long Lake and floating them down to the snakers that have besieged us. Last nights attack was just a diversion. The real attack will come tonight."

"What can we do to help?" Louise asked.

"The spell catcher is more help than you could ever imagine. Right now, we are waiting on three different armies to arrive here, the largest of which is an army of snakers. I pray the dwarves and our brethren from home get here in time. Either way, I fear the river shall run red tonight. So, to answer your question, what can you do to help? You and your companions may fletch arrows for our archers. We will have need for a great many tonight. Jerome will show you the armory."

Fletching arrows, Louise learned, meant putting the feathers on the arrows to make them fly straight. In addition to fletching them they also filled empty quivers - forty arrows to a quiver. It was a very tedious, repetitive, and mind-numbing task, but one that all of them performed gladly, for it helped them to keep their minds off the coming night. On the down side, time flew by quickly and night was upon them before they knew it. With the fall of darkness, the tented city once again came alive with the sounds of elves running and shouting. Louise and the kids ran outside the armory. The southern skyline, where the river entered the Twilight, glowed an ominous orange. Louise and the kids ran back into the armory and searched for short swords and daggers to arm themselves, then made their way to the river. In the commotion, no one noticed them follow the river north, away from the fires the snakers had lit.

"Grandma, why are we going away from the fire?"

"If the snakers breach the forest, we will try to escape on the other side."

"Don't they need our help?" Joey asked.

"We have helped all that we can," Louise answered. "We are not warriors, or soldiers, or fighters; we are just plain ordinary people. We're nice people. We don't know how to use these knives and these swords." Louise held her dagger up. "Do you children honestly think you could wield one of these against a snaker? Do you think you have it in you to kill one?"

None of the children could answer her and none would look up at her.

"That's what I thought. And that's not a bad thing. It means your parents have done a good job of raising you, and you should be thankful for that. Now let's go."

It took them a couple of hours to reach the perimeter of the forest. But when they got there, they were surprised to see flaming arrows raining down from the night sky. Fires were burning everywhere and the trees along the perimeter were in a frenzy, slapping at the flames burning up high with their limbs and stomping the flames on the ground with their great sandy roots. It was a full scale assault on all sides.

"Grandma," Casey whimpered. "What are we going to do now?"

"There are too many arrows and too many fires for us to do anything," Joey replied, shaking his head.

"Can we get out in a boat? Like Ben did?" Meg asked.

"No, dear. Look at the arrows coming down. There must be several hundred snakers out there."

Louise sat down upon the ground and began to cry. The children, though frightened, tried to comfort her. Suddenly, they heard the sounds of battle from the fields outside the forest. The arrows had ceased raining down their fires and they thought for a moment the elves had rallied and were attacking the snakers. Then, they heard the unmistakable roar of a very big, and very, very angry bear.

25 DING DONG

Gabriel and Hob screeched to a halt when Ben's cry rent the thick fabric of silence that hung over the aging forest. Before Ben's scream had completely escaped his throat, Gabriel spun around and let the first arrow fly toward the witch. Hob watched helplessly as the drama unfolded, in slow motion, before him. The witch wrapped an arm around Ben's chest and drew him close. Her free arm flew up, palm extended, and Gabriel's arrow transformed into a shower of dust that drifted harmlessly into the leaves. Then, the unicorn screamed. This broke Hob's paralysis and he hefted his axe over his head and charged toward the witch with a battle cry that would have frozen the marrow in her bones, had there been any warmth there to begin with. All thoughts of saving the unicorn were gone. Hob owed Ben his life and he was not going to let him down.

As Hob rushed to Ben's aid, Gabriel turned back to the unicorn and loosed a second arrow. The shadow cat had materialized in mid leap. The creature was terrifying to behold. A magnificent black mane framed the shadow cat's massive head and flowed down its powerful back. The claws were extended and it's teeth were bared. Gabriel's arrow caught the big cat just behind the front legs, piercing the heart and bringing it down. The big cat's mortal body reverted back to its shadow form, a lifeless shade that dissipated like smoke on the wind, as the unicorn fled away in terror.

Ben's immediate problem, however, was not the witch. His lungs were closing up fast. He had retrieved the inhaler from his pocket and brought it up to his lips. The witch snatched his wrist away and pulled the inhaler close to her face to examine it. Ben pumped it twice. The witch screamed and released Ben with one arm while she wiped at her eyes, but she maintained her grip on his wrist and, now, Ben could not pull free nor use his inhaler. Feeling the darkness closing in around him, he pulled his knife with his free hand and stabbed at the witch's hand that was clamped onto his other wrist. With a howl of rage, surprise, and pain, she loosened her hold on him and Ben was able to jerk free. As he was falling backwards, he was dimly aware of Hob screaming. It sounded as if the dwarf was at the end of a very long tunnel. He brought the inhaler up to his lips and fired two quick bursts before he hit the ground. As the cool sweet evening air rushed in to fill his aching lungs, Ben's panic subsided enough for him to actually take stock of his situation. Now he could see the witch. She was dressed in long black robes trimmed with white fur. The robes were adorned with all manner of bones and covered with many pockets, some large, some small. Some of the pockets even had pockets. The witch reached into one of the smaller pockets and produced, of all things, a dainty lace kerchief to wipe her eyes and her face. The absurdity of the scene made Ben feel as if he must either howl with laughter or go insane. At least, for now, the fear was gone and he was able to take a closer look at the witch, the creature that struck fear in the hearts of everyone in Camelot. In all of the stories Ben had ever read, witches were ugly creatures with big noses and warts, and they wore pointy hats and rode on broomsticks. At least, all of the evil witches were ugly. This witch, however, was stunningly beautiful. With eyes the color of a rain washed sky and hair the color of corn silk, she might have just stepped off a Viking ship, a queen from some snowy kingdom in the far north. Her visage, however, was one of bitterness, hatred, malice, and evil. If any beauty had remained, it fled from her face when she looked upon Ben. The unicorn was so close and this child, this stupid little boy, had foiled her plans. It could be years, even centuries before another unicorn came to Camelot. With a shriek of rage, she raised her arms over her head and brought them down, pointing all of her fingers at the child. Nothing happened.

As the witch brought her arms down, Ben threw his arms up to shield his face and tightly shut his eyes. He expected nothing less than lightning bolts to shoot out the witch's fingers. He imagined he was just seconds away from becoming a smoldering pile of ashes and, with the end upon him, Ben's thoughts turned to his mother. At least she would be spared the grief of his death. At least she would never learn of his horrible demise. Grandma would feel responsible though. Casey too. Ben felt sorry for them. And his poor dad. Ben imagined him getting another call. Except this time the bad news would be about his son. For that matter, Casey and Grandma might not survive either. What was taking so long? Ben lowered his arms and cracked open his eyes.

The witch was staring down at her hands with a puzzled expression on her face. Something had gone wrong. Snarling, she looked up at Ben as she reached into another pocket and slowly pulled out a wicked looking dagger with a serrated blade that curved like a sickle to sharp and deadly point. With a scream that made the hair on the back of Ben's neck leap to attention, she lunged at him with the knife. Ben was on his feet in a second, but before he could take two steps she was upon him. She grabbed him once again, this time by the hair on top of his head, and yanked his head backwards. Ben could hear Hob screaming, "NOOOOO." He closed his eyes and waited, but the blow never came. The witch still had him by the hair, but she was not moving and the forest was eerily silent. Ben cracked open an eye. Several yards away Hob was standing with the axe still poised over his head and a bewildered look upon his face. The dwarf was silent now and staring at the witch behind him. Ben opened the other eye too. Gabriel was approaching now with his bow drawn. Hob lowered his axe and came forward to stand in front of Ben.

"You never cease to amaze me, Ben Alderman from Atlanta Georgia. You defeated her! That inhaler of yours is a powerful weapon indeed."

Hob helped Ben pull free from the witch's grasp and Ben turned around to see what had happened. The hand that had grasped Ben's hair was still closed tightly into a fist and Ben's knife was protruding from the back of it. The other hand, the one with the dagger, was raised high above the witch's head. The expression on the witch's face, however, was not one of rage and hatred, but one of shock and surprise. Maybe even a little bit of terror. Ben reached up and rapped on her face with his knuckles. Solid stone.

"My inhaler couldn't have done this."

"You're right," said Gabriel. "It was your spell catcher."

"My necklace?"

"Ahh," said Hob. "Gabriel is right! She did not see that one coming."

"Could someone please explain to me what is going on?"

Gabriel reached down and pulled the necklace out from beneath Ben's shirt.

"This gem on your necklace, the gem you call an emerald, is called by another name in Camelot. It is a spell catcher. A magical gem, normally used by a spell caster to maintain a spell. This you have already heard. What you did not know, is that when you wear a spell catcher, one that is not carrying any spells, it will catch any spells that are cast upon you. When this happens, the spell is transferred to the next person that comes in contact with you."

"If you are wearing the spell catcher when they touch you," Hob added.

"Yes," Gabriel agreed. "You must have the spell catcher in your possession for the spell to transfer."

Hob laughed. "The witch tried to turn you into stone, Ben. Your spell catcher caught the spell she threw at you and then, when she grabbed you, her own spell came back on her. Serves her right."

"Is she dead then?" Ben asked.

"No," Gabriel answered. "Not yet. I have seen this spell before. It is an abomination, a cruelty beyond measure that should not be inflicted upon any living creature."

"She's alive!" Ben said incredulously, backing up a step and reaching for his inhaler again. "Can she see us or hear us?"

"She no longer has use of any of her senses," Hob answered. "She cannot see as we see. She cannot hear as we hear. She cannot smell, or taste, or even feel. She is truly stone, through and through."

"And yet, she is aware," said Gabriel. "Aware of everything around her. Aware of the prison her body has become. Time will pass ever so slowly for her now and she will have nothing to do but count the days as they turn into weeks, and then into months, and then into years. Madness will eventually take over, but even then, she will live on."

"I say that she has received her just rewards and the spell cannot be broken since she is the one who cast it. Let me take her home to Nimrodell. We will put her in dark places, deep beneath the roots of the Iron Bone, and then pull the mountains down upon her. It will be a fitting punishment for all of the lives she has destroyed."

Gabriel seemed to be considering Hobs suggestion, so Ben quickly spoke up.

"We can't do that guys, that's horrible! If we leave her like this, then we are no better than her."

The truth of Ben's words pierced their hearts like an arrow and an uncomfortable silence hung between them. Finally, Gabriel spoke.

"You are wise beyond your years, Ben, and you speak the truth. We cannot leave her like this. If we can shatter the stone the witch will cease to exist and perhaps find peace, or justice, in some other world."

Gabriel reached for Ben's knife and grasped the handle to pull it from the statue. The knife was stuck fast. Gabriel wiped his palm on his tunic and took hold of the knife again. He placed his other hand on the witch's marbled arm and pulled with all of his strength. The knife would not budge.

"Step aside and let me have a tug on that blade," Hob crowed.

Gabriel stepped back and Hob spat into has hands and briskly rubbed them together. Ben was not so sure he wanted the knife back now. The stout dwarf grabbed the knife with both hands and lifted up. He strained against the knife until the veins popped out along his temples and his face turned a purplish shade of red. Finally, he released the knife and threw his hands up into the air.

"Unless we can shatter this stone, I am afraid you have lost your blade, Ben Alderman. That knife is not coming out."

Hob then motioned for Ben and Gabriel to back up. The dwarf hefted his axe and began to swing it over his head in great long arcs. On the third swing, he slammed the axe into the witch's side. The impact was tremendous and the axe handle splintered and snapped in half. The witch however was unmarred, without even a scratch or a chip upon her torso as evidence that Hob had ever struck her.

"What now?" Gabriel asked.

Ben stepped forward and placed his hand on the hilt of his blade. With a gentle tug, the blade slid free of the stone and the statue cracked with a loud pop. Ben, Gabriel, and Hob watched in amazement while shards of stone began to fall away and the witch disintegrated into hundreds of little pieces. In a few seconds, all that remained of the witch was a pile of gray dust and rubble.

"I must have loosened the blade for you," Hob remarked.

Gabriel smiled down at the dwarf and clapped him on the shoulder.

"Is it over now?" Ben asked. "Is she dead?"

"Yes," Gabriel answered, "I believe she is quite dead."

"Then let the joyous news be spread, the wicked old witch at last is dead," said Ben.

"What was that?" Hob asked.

"A song from an old TV show," Ben answered.

"What's a TV show?"

Ben smiled at his friend the dwarf. "Later, I'll teach you the song and I'll try to explain to you what a TV show is, but right now I want to know what happened to the unicorn? Were you able to save it from the shadow cat?"

"The shadow cat has returned to the Dark Lands," Gabriel answered, "and the unicorn has fled to safety. We must return to the Twilight now and see how the war fares with the snakers." Gabriel looked down at Hob. "The horde will be upon us in two days time and it is at least two days march from Nimrodell to the Twilight. I know that the river sped them along for at least half of their journey, but do you think Amos and your two companions have made it?"

"Have faith, Gabriel. I am sure an army is amassing as we speak. The only thing a dwarf likes better than swinging a pick axe at a vein of gold, is swinging a broad axe at a horde of snakers."

"But I thought the witch was controlling the snakers," Ben pointed out. "Now that she is dead, won't they go back to where ever they came from?"

"That's possible," said Gabriel. "But we cannot be sure. If it were just a small band, then I would tend to believe that they would indeed flee. However, these creatures find courage in numbers and I'm afraid the witch, though she may have been responsible for getting them to war against us, had very little control over them at all. So, let us rest tonight. Tomorrow we will trek back to the river and we will have one more night to rest in the boat after it takes us home. After that, who knows what fates await us?"

Then, the three companions then raked leaves from the forest floor into three soft piles and spread their blankets over them. Night came swiftly and the darkness under the giant oaks was complete. Hob was soon snoring loudly and although Ben did not think he could ever fall asleep with all of the noise coming from the comatose dwarf, he too was soon sawing logs of his own. As for Gabriel, elves rarely sleep at all, yet that night, even he slept deeply and peacefully. That night, no one woke from their slumber and each one of them dreamed of sunny hillsides, green with soft summer grass and tiny yellow flowers that peeped up at an impossibly blue sky.

The next morning dawned bright and clear. Hundreds of birds greeted the rising sun with song, each one trying to out-sing the other. Circling the patch of ground where the party slept were tracks. A visitor in the night had watched over them while they slept. The tracks were hoof prints.

26 BATTLE AT THE RIVER

Louise, Casey, Joey and Meg ran through the forest. The trees were busy slapping at flames and they had to duck and dodge the whipping limbs and thrashing roots. When they came to the edge of the forest, the grisly battle that was taking place in the field before them, stopped them in their tracks. Although it was dark, the night was lit from above by the stars and the moon, and from below by several hundred torches that were flung to the ground once the battle began. On this side of the river, hundreds of dwarves were hewing through the ranks of the snakers, while hundreds more were constructing a bridge across the river. The bridge was going up so fast that it was almost like a living thing, growing before their eyes. But that was not the most amazing thing about the battle. The most amazing thing was the tornado of activity on the other side of the river. There, an army of one, a monstrous bear was mowing down the snakers like a wild fire in a dry straw field. Nothing could stand before the bear's wrath and fury. Eventually, the snakers on the other side of the river threw down their weapons and fled in terror, hoping to regroup with the main army. Louise made the kids turn around. She did not want them to see the death and destruction that was taking place in front of them,

218

but she could do nothing to keep them from hearing the battle cries of the dwarves and the death cries of the snakers as the battle raged on. Thankfully, in a matter of minutes, the battle was over and the bridge was complete. The dwarven army then split into two units, one unit crossing the bridge and pursuing the snakers that had fled from the bear, the other unit circling around the forest in the other direction. Louise spotted Amos, back in his human form, at the top of the bridge. He was speaking with two dwarves.

"Come on children, let's make a run for it," she cried.

Louise and the kids burst from the forest and sped to the bridge. All of them were shouting for Amos who, upon seeing them, ran to meet them and snatched all of them up in his great hairy arms and hugged them tightly.

"I am so glad to see you," Amos cried. "When I saw the forest in flames and under attack, I feared the worst."

"We feared the worst as well," said Louise, wiping here eyes with the sleeve of her dress. "If you had not have got here when you did, I think it would have been the end of us, the Twilight, and everyone in it."

"The elfin army isn't here yet?"

Louise shook her head. "Not yet. Messengers have been sent, but we have no way of knowing when the army will arrive."

"What about the big snaker army? When are they expected?"

"I'm not sure now. They have been delayed. It seems they have been felling trees up around Long Lake and sending them down the river. The snakers here have been pulling the trees out and piling them up against the forest. This whole attack is nothing but a diversion. I expect the real attack will come when the big army gets here. My guess is that they will light the wood they have piled against the trees and try to burn a road into the forest."

"Then we need to push back the snakers that are here and remove that brush pile."

"Do we have enough dwarves to do that?"

"We have enough!" said Nob proudly as he and Gob walked up behind Amos.

"Gob! Nob!" Louise and the kids cried together. The dwarves bowed low to everyone, just as if this were the dance floor at some formal ball and not a battlefield strewn with bodies and soaked with blood.

"You have come just in the nick of time and have saved the day," said Louise.

"Perhaps," said Gob. "The battle is not over yet though and I feel that my axe needs to separate a few more snaker heads in order for me to feel better about our odds."

"He's right," said Amos. "If the forest still holds, you and the kids need to return there. It's the safest place for you right now. I'll accompany you, along with Gob and Nob. The dwarven army has divided and the plans are to drive the snakers to the river on the other side of the forest. Once there, they will push the snakers as close to the forest as they are able and we will be waiting within the forest with elfin archers. If all goes according to plan, we should be able to crush these snakers before the big army arrives. And hopefully, the elfin army will be here by then."

"You're right, Amos. Let's get these children out of here."

Louise placed her arms around the children protectively and ushered them back into the forest, with Amos on one side and Gob and Nob on the other side. Once inside of the forest and away from the carnage, Amos, Gob, and Nob took turns recounting their adventure; from acquiring the horse and wagon from Mr. Miller, to the standoff with the blacksmith at Mountain Rest, to the mustering of the dwarven army. It turns out that the mob in Mountain Rest did regain their courage and managed to whip the town into a frenzy, with talk of witch craft, black magic, murder, and dwarven gold. The whole town turned out to storm the gates of Nimrodell and as they marched to the Western Gate with their torches, clubs, and pitchforks, they were met head on with an army of grim faced dwarven warriors. Needless to say, the townspeople lost their courage and, throwing down their torches and weapons, fled back to their homes in the darkness and barred their doors and windows. The dwarven army marched right down the main street of Mountain Rest unchallenged. They marched all the way to the North Road and then straight to the Twilight. They marched all night and all day, without tiring, and now they were faced with another sleepless night, this one of battle, fast and furious.

Gob wrapped up the story as they arrived in the tent city where things were still in a state of panic and confusion. Amos led them straight to the center tent and the two guards at the tent door admitted them at once. Marcus was waiting for them at the fire pit and Amos briefly retold their story and their plans to crush the remaining snakers.

"We are indebted to your people," said Marcus to Gob and Nob. "You have saved the Twilight and, perhaps now, our army will arrive in time to repay the debt when the hive arrives."

"The hive?" said Amos.

"Yes," Marcus replied. "We have sent out scouts and have confirmed that this horde is not just a large hunting party, it is an actual hive. The numbers are so large that the queen fears nothing and travels with the hunters."

"Does the estimate of five thousand still hold true?" Louise asked.

"Yes, there are at least five thousand marching this way. They will be here by nightfall."

"How many of those five thousand are queen's guards?" Amos asked.

"One thousand. One thousand of these snakers are queen's guards."

"God help us," Louise whispered.

"You are right to be afraid," said Marcus. "But we do have a plan. For now, though, we must deal with the snakers at our door."

Marcus nodded to one of the guards. The elf went outside and blasted three long notes upon his horn. The notes echoed clear and sweet throughout the forest and all who heard them felt their spirits lift and began to make their way to the center tent. Soon the tent was filled with elves and more kept coming. Marcus climbed to the top of a nearby hill and addressed the assembly.

"Brothers, as many of you now know, a dwarven army has arrived from Nimrodell to aid us in our hour of need. This army has already battled and defeated the snakers on the north end of our forest. There, they have split into two units, each unit one thousand strong. One unit is flanking our forest on the east and driving the snakers south, while the other unit is flanking our forest on the west and also driving the snakers south. The plan is to drive the snakers to the river and, then, as close to the forest as possible. There, we shall be waiting within the forest with our bows and arrows to greet them. This army must be defeated before the hive arrives or their numbers will be too great for us to overcome."

Marcus's voice somehow carried throughout the entire tent and everyone present heard him clearly, though he did not shout. Now, however, he rose up taller and thrust his arms skyward and his voice echoed like thunder.

"Hear me, oh elves of Faerie! This is a call to arms! String your bows and fill your quivers! Go now to victory and go quickly! Listen for the Keeper's horn then let your arrows fly. Faerie!"

"Faerie!" the elves shouted in return, thrusting their bows and their swords skyward. "Faerie!" they roared.

All of the elves present then sped from the tent, their faces grim, and their eyes glittering dangerously. Some of them already had their bows slung across their backs, with full quivers hanging from their sides, while others hurried to the armory. Amos sent Louise and the children to the armory to help fill quivers and to get them out of harm's way. Then he, Gob, and Nob ran to the southern end of the

Twilight, where hundreds of elves were hiding behind the trunks of trees and hundreds more were hiding in the branches up above. Amos and the two dwarves, not having bows and arrows, hid further back and waited.

"I have a question," Gob whispered to Amos.

"Yes?"

"When we arrived here by boat it took us a while to reach the tent city, but just now we have traveled from the tent city to the edge of the forest in a matter of minutes. How is that so?"

"The forest is always changing," Amos replied. "Maybe it has grown smaller because it is under attack. Or maybe the Keeper is shrinking the forest so the elves may easily patrol and guard the borders. That is my guess anyway and that is all that I am able to tell you, my friend. Listen, I hear the sounds of battle!"

The sounds were faint at first, but grew steadily louder. The snakers on the western side of the river arrived first. The dwarven unit pursuing them had split once again, this time into two units of five hundred. One unit slowly followed the snakers around the forest, while the other unit hastily looped around to get in front of the snakers to prevent them from fleeing up the river. Once the snakers realized that they were trapped, they retreated as close to the forest as they dared and there, they prepared to make a final stand. However, the dwarves did not advance and waited patiently until the unit on the other side of the river arrived. They too had divided, one unit slowly pushing the snakers south, while the other unit sped around to cut off any chance of escape.

"This is it," said Amos. "Get ready."

The snakers on both sides of the river had their backs to the forest, waiting for the dwarven armies to advance. Two age-old enemies faced one another down, both sides knowing that there would be no survivors for whoever lost the impending battle. The tension and silence of the moment was maddening. The wind had ceased and even the river seemed to be sliding by noiselessly. Then suddenly, an elfin horn pealed forth from within the forest. The snakers did not even have time to turn around before a rain of arrows descended upon their heads, killing hundreds where they stood. At that instant, the dwarves rushed forward with a mighty cry, wielding their broad axes and long knives with deadly precision. The elves too poured out of the forest with their long spears and their terrible and shiny swords. The snakers were crushed in the middle and the battle ended as quickly as it had begun.

"It's over," exclaimed Gob. "I've never seen an army defeated so quickly and so thoroughly!"

"Yes," Nob agreed excitedly. "There shall be many songs of this battle for many years to come."

"Do you think we'll be in any of the songs?" Gob asked.

"Most certainly," Nob replied. "We shall be heroes, no doubt."

"Not if the hive gets here before the elfin army," Amos reminded them. "Come, we have much work to do and I fear none of it shall be pleasant."

Dwarves and elves worked side-by-side into the night, dragging the logs and brush away from the forest. They piled the debris far enough way from the forest, so that the heat from the flames would not harm the living trees. Then, they gathered the dead snakers from the battlefield and heaped them upon the pile. Once the pile was lit and the smoke was rolling skyward, the elves and the dwarves retreated into the Twilight to rest and regroup.

Amos, Gob, and Nob, stopped by the armory to get Louise and the children.

"Is it over?" Louise asked anxiously.

"It was a decisive victory," Nob declared.

"A total rout, I might add," said Gob. "I'm working on a song about the battle now. Would you like to hear it?"

"Not now," Amos interrupted, smiling at the dwarves and their indomitable spirit. "But you shall definitely sing us your song when this is all over." Then he turned back to Louise. "We are on the way to see Marcus. We have to make plans for the battle against the hive."

Louise nodded and gathered the kids together. They followed Amos and the two dwarves out into the night. With the battle over, the night noises had returned. Cicadas, crickets, and katydids composed a symphony under the stars that no orchestra could match while fireflies provided a light show, winking their greenish-yellow lights by the hundreds. The cool night air was refreshing too, bearing the fragrance of honeysuckle and wild holly on a gentle breeze. On the way to the center tent, everyone began to feel their worries and tensions slowly melt away. Upon arriving there, one of the elfin guards opened the tent door for them to enter. Louise went inside first, followed by Casey, then Meg and Joey. Gob and Nob entered next with Amos coming in last. When they came upon the fire pit, Marcus was there waiting for them. He was huddled about the fire pit, in deep conversation with three other people. Casey gasped, then suddenly shot past Louise, running for the fire pit.

"BEN!" she cried.

27 THE HIVE

"Ben!" Casey cried again. Louise then realized the three people speaking with the Keeper were Ben, Gabriel, and Hob. It must have dawned on Gob and Nob at the very same instant, for, suddenly, they too dashed by her with Joey and Meg right behind them. Crying tears of joy (and relief), Louise ran to Ben and swept both him and Casey up into her arms, squeezing them tightly.

"Thank goodness you are okay," Louise cried. She turned to Gabriel and Hob. "Thank you two for looking after him."

"No," said Hob. "You need to thank him for looking after us."

"What happened?" Amos asked. "Did you save the unicorn?"

Hob at once began to dance and sing, "Ding-dong the witch is dead! Which old witch? The wicked witch. Ding-dong the wicked witch is dead!"

"What is the matter with Hob?" Amos whispered to Gabriel. "Did the witch cast a spell upon him?"

"No," Gabriel laughed. "It is a song that young Ben Alderman has taught him and I fear that we shall be hearing that song for many years to come. But the witch is dead and the unicorn is safe as well."

"I wish we had time to tell one another our stories," Marcus interrupted, "and perhaps we will, sometime in the future. But for now, we need to make plans on how we shall deal with the queen and the hive."

"What is the news on the hive and the army from Faerie?" Amos asked.

"There are about seven hundred warriors coming through the Merlin Tree right now. It is not as many as we had hoped for, but it will have to be enough."

"The hive," Gabriel reported, "is making way overland. They are following the same path you took when you came here and they have already passed the place where the troll attacked you."

"That does not leave us much time," Amos remarked.

"All the more reason for us to make haste. We will set up a defensive line of two hundred of our best elfin archers in the fields, so that we may target the hive as soon as it leaves the protection of the trees. We will position one thousand dwarven warriors two hundred yards behind the archers. The dwarven warriors shall be in plain view, while the elfin archers shall be hidden among the grasses. The snakers will be emboldened by their sheer numbers. The dwarves will appear to be outnumbered five to one and the snakers will more than likely charge recklessly into what they perceive to be an easy victory. Once the charge has begun, we will wait just long enough for most of the hive to get out into the open and then, we will stand and start firing. Many hundreds will die in that first charge, but that will not halt the surge. Before the snakers get within striking range, the elfin archers will hastily retreat half the distance to the dwarven army and turn and fire again. This second volley of arrows will be the signal for the dwarven army to advance. The dwarven army should reach our archers the same time as the oncoming snakers. At that point it will be hand to hand combat with sword, knife, spear, and axe."

"What of the other half of our army?" Hob asked.

"And the seven hundred elves coming through the portals now?" Gob added.

"The other one thousand dwarven warriors will hide from view within the Twilight, until the battle is well under way. Then they will form a phalanx and drive through the center of the battle, dividing the snaker army into two smaller armies. If one thousand snakers are slain by elfin arrows, then there will be one thousand dwarves and two hundred elves against three thousand snakers. When the second dwarven army divides them, there will be two armies of one thousand dwarves and one hundred elves against two armies of fifteen hundred snakers. Much better odds."

"And what of the queen's guards?" Louise asked.

"The queen's guards will be in the rear of the hive with the queen. Gabriel will lead the seven hundred elfin warriors from Faerie up the river and will come in behind them. They will deal with the queen's guards and keep them out of the battle. That's our best chance of winning this – dividing their forces and keeping their strongest soldiers out of the main fray."

"A brilliant plan," said Hob. "I like it. Gob, you lead the first wave. Nob, you lead the second. I'm going with Gabriel for a swing at the queen's guards. Who knows, I may even get a swing at the old queen herself."

"Well, that's not fair," cried Nob.

"Yeah," added Gob. "Why do you get to have all the fun?"

"There will be plenty of action for the two of you," Amos remarked. "I'm going with Hob and Gabriel as well. Maybe the three of us can focus on the queen, while her guards are engaged in battle. I would like to pay her back for invading my woods and wrecking the fountain at the fairy glen."

"An excellent idea," said Marcus. "And look, here comes the army from Faerie. Gabriel, you and Amos and Hob take that army and get started up the river now. You have a lot of ground to cover in order to get behind the queen. Don't attack until the second dwarven army charges. Then hit them hard."

Gabriel nodded, then trotted over to meet the approaching elfin army. Amos gave everyone a quick hug, then he and Hob fell in with the army that was quickly filing out the tent door. Marcus then turned to Gob and Nob.

"Our archers should be moving into place. Now would be a good time for you two to get your armies situated as well. Louise, you and the children will stay with us. While the battles are taking place, we are going to attempt to close the portal from Faerie to Pluton. If all our plans go awry, those of us who are able, will escape to our homeland. I know it is not your home, but you and the children are welcome there."

"Thank you, Marcus."

"Do not thank me yet. Know this; if we must retreat then the portal from Camelot to Faerie will be destroyed to keep the snakers from defiling our homeland. You and the children will be stranded there until a new Merlin Tree can be constructed and that may be years."

"That's okay," said Joey. "Time does not pass by for us in our world while we are here in this one."

Marcus smiled. It was a sad smile. "When I speak of years, I speak of decades. It may be a hundred years before we get the portals opened back up. Time may not pass by for you in your world, but it does pass by for you in this world."

Joey's face fell as the Keeper's words sank in. Meg began to quietly weep and he protectively put his arm around her. Ben and Casey clasped hands and Louise pulled them close.

"Let's not worry for tomorrow just yet," said Amos, patting the children on their shoulders. "There are worries enough, for today."

The morning sun beat fiercely down upon the steel helmet on Gob's head. At least it was not in his eyes. It had taken him about an hour to get his troops into position. They were lined up, five hundred across and two deep, grim couriers of death, clad with leather and steel, armed with broad axes and short swords. Gob stood far enough in front of the army of dwarves, so they all could see the flag he was holding up. At the right time, he would drop the flag and that would be the signal to charge. He looked over his shoulder at the army behind him. They were all waiting patiently. Behind them, hidden within the strange trees of the Twilight, Nob waited with another army of the same size. Gob strained to see them, but could make nothing out among the dark leaves. Checking the position of the sun, to mark the time they had been out here, he spotted a hawk circling lazily overhead. Eventually, it caught a warm updraft and soared up out of sight.

"Soon, there will be buzzards and all manner of carrion fowl circling overhead," he mumbled.

As if that were a signal, the snakers appeared. At first, it was just movement in the trees at the edge of the field. Then they came pouring out, like ants from an anthill that has been disturbed. They came and came and kept coming. When they spotted the dwarves, there was much pointing and waving as their ranks swelled and as they milled about on the fringe of the forest. Finally, because of their numbers and the inability of the field to hold them all, they could do nothing but advance. They advanced slowly at first, but as more poured forth from the trees, they began to pick up speed like an avalanche. Gob gripped the flagpole with white knuckles, waiting, waiting. Then an elfin horn pealed out, rising above the clamor of the oncoming snakers and as one, two hundred elven archers sprang up out of the grasses and started raining volleys of arrows down upon the oncoming snakers. The bodies began piling up, but the mass only slowed for a short time. Soon they were surging forward again and a for second time the elfin horn rang out across the field, this time signaling retreat. The elves began to hastily fall back, fleeing toward the dwarves. This encouraged the snakers, leading them to believe they had the elves on the run now. The third and final blast on the elfin horn brought the archers around for another volley of arrows. Gob threw down his flag and one thousand dwarves charged forward with axes in their hands, a battle cry on their lips, and murder in their eyes.

Gabriel, Hob, and Amos led the seven hundred elves from Faerie up the river toward Long Lake. The tall grasses and bushes, that grew along the edge of the river, concealed them from the view of the dwarves lined up in the field to their left. The trip up the river went smoothly and uneventfully and they entered the forest unchallenged. Normally an army of seven hundred could not sneak about undetected, but these were elves and they passed over hill and dale, through field and wood, with no more than a quiet rustle in the grass. They continued to follow the river for a couple of miles into the forest and then they turned left, leaving the river behind them. Gabriel led them a mile further into the forest and then, turned back toward the Twilight. He led them unerringly to the rear of the queen's guard. The queen herself was in the very rear, while her guardsmen were hovering about the edge of the field, anxious to join the fighting that was well under way. Hob crept to the front where he could see the queen. Tall and gangly, she looked more like an insect than a reptile. She was unprotected and nervously pacing back and forth, pausing every couple of steps to survey the battle. She did not like what was taking place. Another dwarven army had just emerged from the Twilight and was slowly, but surely, dividing her army.

Suddenly, from the midst of the elves, a giant bear shot forward, toward the queen. It happened so fast that everyone, snakers and elves alike, stood there with their mouths agape. In an instant the giant bear had snatched up the queen by the back of her neck. The queen screeched loudly and flailed about helplessly. She beat at the bear's head and kicked her feet to no avail. The bear gave a quick shake of his head and snapped her neck, killing her instantly. The elves stared at the bear with the queen hanging limply from his jaws. The snakers stared at the bear. Hob saw a bee buzzing about the ground, the only living thing that was actually moving in the entire forest. Then, the bear dropped the queen and the forest exploded in battle.

Back on the field, the dwarves had successfully divided the snakers and were hewing them down left and right. The two hundred elfin archers had retreated from the battle, when the second dwarven army began their charge. A couple of hundred additional archers had joined them from the Twilight. They now stood back from the battle, on the side furthest away from the river, steadily picking away at the snakers with their arrows. Although it seemed to go on all afternoon, the battle was actually over in just under three hours.

Gob walked across the battlefield, stepping over bodies, searching for Nob. The dwarves and elves had divided into three groups. The largest group was about four hundred elves, most of them archers who fought in the battle. This group set off at a brisk trot across the field to aid in the fight against the queen's guards. The other two groups were mostly dwarves. One group was set with the task of helping the injured, while the other group was set with the task of tending to the dead. Finally, Gob spotted Nob across the field, helping an injured comrade. Nob happened to glance up and saw Gob at the same time. He threw up his hand in a signal indicating that he was okay and Gob waved back. Now that he knew Nob was okay, he turned his attention to the forest, wondering how Hob was faring. The elves were almost there. If there were any fighting going on, it was all taking place within the forest. Hob would be fine he told himself. Hob would be fine.

When the elfin archers entered the forest, they found the dead queen lying on the fringe of the battle that was taking place in front of them. Their brothers from Faerie were in hand-to-hand combat with the queens guards, who were madly fighting for their lives. In the middle of the melee, a dwarf sat astride a giant bear, swinging his broad axe left and right and felling the queen's guards one after another. The bear was a killing machine too, batting them aside with his huge paws and snapping them into with his powerful jaws. The elfin archers formed a line and once again began picking off the enemy with deadly precision. Very soon after that, the battle was over and the snaker invasion was crushed. Now, the grisly task of clearing the battlefield was at hand.

Although everyone was exhausted, all worked into the late evening hours, piling the dead snakers to be burned. There were casualties among the elves and dwarves as well, but surprisingly few considering the size of the battle that had taken place. The elves took their dead back into the Twilight to be transported back to their homeland for proper burial, while the dwarves buried their dead upon the battlefield. They excavated a single grave that was large enough to lay their dead out side-by-side and then piled the broken weapons of the enemy at their feet. Once the dead were covered, the dwarves worked late into the night constructing a cairn with rocks hauled up from the river. The elves helped them build the cairn and by the light of the fire, from the burning snakers, they worked silently, side-by-side, under bright stars which glittered coldly above them.

28 CELEBRATION

Louise and the children woke to a day, dawning bright and clear. With the exception of the thin column of smoke rising above the treetops, it was hard to believe that the Twilight had ever been under attack. Beneath their feet, the dew-beaded grass sparkled brightly, while morning glories of pale blue and white shimmered in the golden sunlight along the river. However, the thing that really amazed them was that there was only three tents left standing in the city. Sometime during the night, the elves had taken down all of the tents except three – the tent Louise, Amos, and the kids were staying in, the center tent, and a tremendous red and orange pavilion tent that had been erected by the river. The pavilion tent reminded Ben of the big-top tent of an old traveling circus show his grandparents took him to see last summer. Except the elfin tent was bigger and brighter. Much bigger. There appeared to be a lot of activity around the tent too. Elves and dwarves were bustling about everywhere. As they all stood gawking, Amos strode up with a big grin on his face. Gabriel was beside him and he too was smiling.

"Good morning," said Amos. "I hope you all slept good and are well rested."

"We did," said Louise. "Now, can you tell me what's going on here and why you're wearing that silly grin?"

"Let me explain," said Gabriel. "First of all, the Keeper was able to destroy the pathway from Faerie to Pluton and, once destroyed, the Blight immediately began to dissipate in our home world. The Keeper then used a pathway to travel to Stone Dog and found the Blight had lifted there as well, and the tower was in ruins. The Merlin Tree and the pathway to the Pluton could not be located among the ruins either. So, as you can see, this is a joyous day for all, both here in Camelot and back home in Faerie too."

"Where did all of the elves go?" Meg asked.

"Why, home of course," Gabriel answered with a smile.

"You guys are not leaving Camelot for good, are you?" Meg asked.

"Oh no – far from it. We are returning to our homeland to start plans for a more permanent residence here in Camelot. A fortress if you will, with towers, ramparts, and parapets. The dwarves are going to help us with the stonework and Hob, Gob, and Nob have graciously agreed to oversee the project once it gets underway."

"Awesome!" said Joey.

"Awesome?" Gabriel repeated. The elf paused a few seconds, reflecting on the word. "Yes, I believe that it will indeed be awesome," he said smiling. "We already are deeply indebted to the dwarves so, in return, we are going to open the smithies here when the fortress is complete. Dwarves are excellent craftsmen at the forge but we are masters. We will teach them secrets of the craft that will allow them to take their gold and precious gems and create things of rare and magnificent beauty."

"That's really nice," said Louise. "But what is the big tent for? And I still want to know what Amos is grinning about."

"The tent," Gabriel continued, "is for a special occasion. Tonight, all of the elves that are here in the Twilight, and the remaining dwarves, will feast together and celebrate the defeat of the snakers and the downfall of the witch. Amos is grinning because he, Gob, Nob, and Hob, along with you, Ben, Casey, Joey, and Meg, are to be the honored guest of this celebration."

"You said the remaining dwarves are coming," Casey noted. "What do you mean by that?"

"More than half of them left to return to Nimrodell early this morning. Their West Gate is well guarded by only a few stout dwarves and they prefer to have the doors to their kingdom heavily guarded. They were especially worried about the townspeople of Mountain Rest rising up against them."

"About this honored guest thing," Ben interrupted. "I'm not going to have to make a speech or anything like that am I?"

Gabriel looked at Ben for a few seconds then threw his head back and laughed. It was an infectious laugh and after all the stress of the previous days, Amos joined in and soon they were all laughing. Louise finally begged them to stop before her sides split open. Ben didn't see what was so funny and began to turn a bright cherry red. Gabriel saw his distress and rescued him.

"Ben," he began, "You will not have to make a speech tonight. Forgive me for laughing, but I was not laughing at you. Yesterday, we feared for our lives and yet today you fret over making a speech. I laugh because, after all you have been through, you appear to be well and that gladdens my heart. As guests of honor we will sit at the table with the Keeper. A toast shall be made to our health and we shall most likely have to recount our adventure many times before the night is over. There will also be gifts. though I do not know what they may be."

"What time does the celebration begin?" Louise asked.

"The party begins after sundown. Today is a day of rest. I'll have food brought to your tent. If you have need of anything, send for me."

Somehow they made it through the rest of the day. Although everyone was looking forward to the feast tonight, they were all anxious to get back to their homes as well. The sun had set below the tree tops some time ago and the long gray shadows of evening were soon lost to the purple shades of dusk. The pavilion tent was lit from within and a steady stream of elves and dwarves were now entering. Amos, Louise, and the kids waited patiently for Gabriel, who soon appeared, and motioned for them to hurry.

Everyone followed Gabriel down to the tent and when they entered, there were a few moments of dizzy disorientation. This tent, like the center tent, opened up into a place much larger than the Twilight. However, when you entered the center tent, you could at least turn around and see the tent wall, fading into the darkness overhead and disappearing into the horizon on the left and right. As disarming as that was, it did manage to keep you somewhat oriented. But here, in the pavilion tent, there were no tent walls to be found anywhere. When you entered the pavilion tent and turned around, you expected to see a tent wall like the one in the center tent. What you saw, though, was the exterior of a very small tent, very similar in fact to the center tent. So, upon entering the pavilion tent, that was standing in the Twilight, you immediately exited from this small tent that was standing in ... well, some other place.

Once the initial shock of what had just happened wore off, everyone began looking around and started taking in their surroundings. If the Twilight was beautiful then, there were simply no words to describe the place they were in now. Here, it was daytime. The sun, bright and yellow, was riding high in a cloudless sky of dazzling blue. Although it was a little warm, a cool gentle breeze stirred the soft green grass beneath their feet and bore sweet smells that made each of them remember something dear to them. Amos smelled the fragrant pines around his cabin and Louise smelled the fresh cut hay in the fields at her farm. Ben and Casey both smelled a fragrance that reminded them of a perfume their mother used to wear, while Joey and Meg could smell the honeysuckle that grew along the bank of the fish pond behind their house. They were standing on a grassy knoll in the center of a forest of strange trees. The trees had smooth gray bark with no spots or imperfections. The leaves were of a green so dark they looked to be black, but that was all they could tell of them for the tree tops were high above their heads.

"Where are we?" Casey asked.

"This is Faerie, isn't it?" said Ben.

"Yes and no," Gabriel answered. "This is only a reflection of our homeland, like an image in a mirror – very close and lifelike, but not the real thing. This was the Keeper's idea for the celebration."

"Then where are we?" Casey asked again.

Gabriel laughed. "Forgive me; I see I did not answer your question. Actually I cannot tell you where we are physically. This magic is beyond my powers and beyond my comprehension. We are probably within the Twilight and inside the pavilion tent. At any rate, do not worry yourself with such matters. Now is a time of celebration."

At that moment, a horn rang forth, high and sweet, and the sound of many bells began to fill the air. Gabriel ran down the grassy knoll and called over his shoulder.

"Come. Follow me quickly, lest the party begins without the guests of honor!"

Everyone scrambled after the elf, who led them down a winding path through the strange trees. The path brought them to an arched doorway within a stone wall that surrounded the forest. They passed through the arch, into a great field, where row after row of tables stretched out before them. A tremendous roar erupted as hundreds and hundreds of elves and dwarves stood up from the tables and cheered and clapped. Gabriel led them through the center of the celebration, to a platform that had been erected in the midst of the tables. They mounted the stairs to the platform to find one large table heavily laden with food and drink.

Marcus was there along with Hob, Gob, and Nob as well. The Keeper rose from his chair and bade them to sit. After they were all seated, he raised his hand for silence and addressed the assembly. Through some bit of elfin magic his voice carried across the field to every table and everyone present heard him clearly.

"Friends, today is a great day in the history of Camelot and Faerie. Today, thanks to the bravery and valor of our friends from Nimrodell, we celebrate the defeat of the largest army of snakers ever assembled and forged a new, lasting alliance with our dwarven allies."

At this point, there was another eruption of cheers from the crowd, especially from the dwarves who were beating their mugs upon the tables and shouting "Hear, Hear!"

Marcus held up his hand again for silence. When the dwarves settled down, he continued.

"Because of this, we honor today, Amos, Nob, and Gob, for bringing our dwarven friends to our rescue."

More cheers and more applause. This time Marcus clapped as well. When the applause finally quieted, Marcus continued.

"Today we also honor Louise, Casey, Joey, and Meg. These four ventured forth into the witch's lair to retrieve the horns of the unicorns. With these horns, we were able to close the pathways to Pluton from both Faerie and Camelot, foiling once and for all Mordred's plans to escape from his exile."

Marcus paused. More cheers, more applause, more toasts and blessings.

"Eight hundred and thirty seven years ago, the first unicorn was slain in Camelot by the hand of the witch. Since then, eleven more have died by her hand and with each death, the witch grew stronger and moved one step closer to breaking the spell that prevented Mordred from returning to Camelot. Today is a great day in both Camelot and Faerie because the witch's reign of terror has come to an end."

The applause was thunderous. Elves and dwarves came to their feet and cheered. "And so today, we also honor Ben, Hob, and Gabriel for bringing about her downfall."

The crowd was once again on their feet and once again, the applause started and began to build into another deafening crescendo, but it quickly died down into an eerie silence. All heads turned toward the arched doorway in the stone wall that surrounded the forest. A disturbance was taking place and the murmurs of the crowd began to rise as whatever was causing the disturbance approached the platform where the honored guests were seated. Ben, upon the platform above everyone's heads, was able to see everything. A soft white nimbus parted the crowd as it came nearer. Like ripples from a stone tossed into a lake, the elves bowed as the creature passed them by. Ben was speechless. His memory, only a few days old, did nothing to recall the actual beauty and majesty of the unicorn that was slowly making its way toward him. Gabriel, with Hob in tow, walked up beside Ben.

"Come, Ben. This creature does us great honor with it's visit."

Ben, unable to speak, just nodded and followed Gabriel and Hob down the steps to meet the unicorn. The three companions lined up side-by-side, with Ben in the middle, and waited nervously.

The unicorn came to Hob first. It paused in front of the dwarf and gazed into his eyes. Hob nodded, then reached up and touched the tip of the spiraled horn. There was a gasp from everyone around who was able to see. The unicorn then moved to Ben and gazed into his eyes. Ben, like Hob, nodded and then reached up and touched the unicorn's horn. Finally, the unicorn moved to Gabriel and gazed long into the elf's eyes. Gabriel however, smiled sadly and shook his head. The unicorn lingered for just a moment then turned and left them, slowly making it's way back to the doorway that lead into the forest. Soon, it was gone and everyone had the feeling as if they had just awakened from a dream. Gabriel led them back up the platform. The Keeper acted as if nothing out of the ordinary had happened, but everyone else was full of questions. Everyone, that is except Amos, who just sat at the table and stared thoughtfully at them.

"What was that all about?" Joey asked, grabbing Ben by his sleeve. "It looked like you were communicating with the unicorn."

Ben pushed his glasses up on his nose and scratched his head. "Yes and no," he replied. "I did not communicate to the unicorn, but the unicorn did communicate with me – inside my head."

"Well what did it say?" Louise prompted.

"It didn't speak with words," Ben answered. "I don't know how to describe it, but the unicorn wanted to show me something and I had to touch its horn to see it."

"What did it show you?" Meg asked.

"Just a flash of a dream I have often," said Ben, looking down at his shoes. "It's not something I really want to talk about." Then he looked up at Hob. For the first time since Ben met him, the dwarf was strangely silent. "What about you, Hob? What did the unicorn show you?"

The dwarf looked at Ben and pondered the question for several moments. "I suspect the unicorn was just showing us our hearts desire. It's probably nothing more than a pretty trick."

"Then why did you refuse it, Gabriel?" Ben asked, looking up at the tall elf standing beside him.

"It was not just a pretty trick," the elf answered. "The unicorn was showing you something significant in your future."

"Something that will come true?" Hob asked with a glimmer in his eye.

"Nothing in the future is written in stone, but whatever the unicorn showed you will in all likelihood come to pass."

"Elves have an annoying habit of avoiding a direct question," Hob snorted. "Why did you refuse?"

Gabriel smiled at the dwarf. "I have lived many years and seen many things. If there are any new joys or sorrows in my future, I wish for them to be a surprise."

Hob eyed the elf suspiciously. "I feel there is more to it than that, but I will let it go so that we may get on with our celebration."

"Truthfully there is more to the story as you say, but thank you for not pressing it," said Gabriel. "Perhaps another day we may talk more at length, but now is not the time."

"Ben?" Louise called. "Ben, what's wrong dear?"

29 GIFTS

Ben hastily wiped the tears from his eyes then put his glasses back on.

"Are you crying, dear?" Louise asked.

"No, I'm not crying."

Louise stared at him for a few moments and Ben was terrified she was going to press the issue. However, she must have sensed how uncomfortable he was because she relented and turned her attention back to Amos. Ben felt a hand on his shoulder and looked up to see Gabriel smiling down at him.

"Are you sorry for what the unicorn has shown you?"

Ben thought for a moment then shook his head.

"Do not worry, Ben, I do not wish to know what you have seen. The unicorn's gift is a personal one and if you choose not to share your vision, then you need not feel bad about it."

"What I saw," Ben began. "Will it really come true?"

Gabriel gazed over the tables, at the forest where the unicorn had disappeared, as he pondered Ben's question. Ben began to think that Gabriel had not heard him and started to ask his question again when the elf began speaking.

"I used to believe that nothing is ever written in stone and that we choose our own fates and to some extent that is true. But sometimes fate chooses for us a destiny we have no control over. The prophecy concerning the witch, for example - I believe the Keeper saw you in that prophecy because it was your destiny to play a part in her downfall. Does that help?"

Ben shook his head. Gabriel smiled and folded his arms across his chest and tried to rephrase his answer.

"What I am trying to say, is that the Keeper saw a point in time where you played a role in the prophecy of the witch's demise. He saw multiple paths that led to that point in time, but that was only a few of the many hundreds of possible paths. However, in each path that he did see, you were present. That, Ben, is destiny. Do you understand?"

Again, Ben shook his head. "What's that got to do with what the unicorn showed me?" he asked.

This time Gabriel frowned. He cupped his elbow with one hand and began to stroke his chin with the other hand, while he tried to think of a way to explain his thoughts to Ben. Finally, he clapped Ben on the shoulder and leaned down to speak in his ear.

"I believe the vision the unicorn showed you will come to pass. Let's go eat."

The feast was magnificent and there was much merriment at all of the tables. Soon after everyone had eaten, Marcus stood and held his hands up for silence. When all was quiet, he called the guests of honor forward. After a brief speech, he presented each one of them with a slender silver chain to wear around their necks and dangling from each chain was a gold leaf made in the likeness of the leaves on the trees of the Twilight.

"There is magic in the golden leaves we have given you. These leaves are keys to the Twilight. As long as you have them in your possession, the trees will let you pass and you may come and go as you please. We hope that you will return often and visit with us."

244

"What about Gabriel?" Ben piped up. "He can already come and go as he pleases. Why did he get one of these too?"

"Gabriel's leaf contains a different magic. As Nob and Gob will be overseeing the construction of our fortress here in Camelot, Gabriel will be training the dwarven smiths and teaching them the secrets of our craft. The leaf he has received, bestows upon him the knowledge and skill of all of the masters of our race that have ever wrought things of beauty and magic in an elfin forge."

Amos thanked the Keeper and promised to return often and invited them to visit him at his cabin in the pine woods. Gob and Nob said their thanks and Hob even promised to look in on them from time to time to make sure they were doing a proper job. Finally, it was Ben's turn to thank the Keeper for his gift.

"I would love to come back and visit sometime," he said. "But I'm not sure when I'll be able to. Maybe before the summer is over Grandma will bring us back." Ben looked over his shoulder at Louise, who smiled and nodded at him. Then he turned back to Marcus. "But when the summer is over," he continued, "I have to go back home and I live a very long ways from here."

"I know that your home is in another world, just as our home is in another world. I also know that you live far from the Merlin Tree in your world. That's why your leaf and Casey's leaf are special."

Ben looked down at the gold leaf hanging from the silver chain around his neck. It looked no different from the others.

"Your leaves," Marcus continued, "will bring you straight to the Twilight from your home world. But it will only do it once and then the magic will be spent, so use it wisely."

"Wow," Ben exclaimed. "How does it work?"

Marcus smiled. "Just hold the leaf in your hand and say 'Twilight'."

"That's all?"

"That is all."

"Will the leaf still work as a key to get in?"

"The leaf will always work as a key, it just cannot bring you here from your world more then once."

"Gee thanks," said Ben. "It's an awesome gift."

"Awesome?" said Marcus. "Hmmmm. Yes, I suppose you could say that. It is an awesome feat of magic to accomplish that."

Ben laughed and soon everyone was laughing with him. The party continued on late into the evening and as darkness began to fall, lanterns were lit on every table and the party quieted down considerably. When things slowed down, everyone realized that they had just had two full days of daylight back-to-back and now they were growing extremely tired and sleepy. Gabriel whispered something to Marcus, who nodded in response, and then he came over to speak to Louise.

"I can see that you and the children are tired. Come with me and we will return to the Twilight where you may rest. I suspect you will be returning home tomorrow and from what Amos has told me, it is no small journey that you must make."

Louise and the kids followed Gabriel through the fields to the stone archway and into the woods. Although no moon could be seen, the woods were alight with a silvery glow and they followed the path with ease to the clearing where the small tent sat perched upon the hill. The tent appeared to be lit from within. They followed Gabriel up the hill and into the tent. As soon as they stepped through the door into the small tent, they stepped out of the door of the big pavilion tent and they were back in the Twilight.

"I'll never get used to that," Meg remarked, holding her stomach. "It makes me queasy."

"It helps if you close your eyes," said Joey. "That keeps you from getting disoriented."

"Hey, it's still dark here," Ben noted. "I figured it would be daytime back here by now."

"No time has passed here since we left," said Gabriel. "Would you like for me to explain that?"

"No," said Louise over her shoulder as she marched toward their tent. "I couldn't understand it if I was wide awake and right now, I can hardly keep my eyes open."

Gabriel laughed. "Rest well then. Tomorrow we shall say our farewells."

The next day, everyone slept late into the morning. Hob, Gob, and Nob would have slept all day, but Amos was finally able to rouse them by telling them they were going to miss breakfast if they did not get out of bed. Outside of their tent, a table was laid with breads, meats, cheeses, and an assortment of fruits and juices. The sun was shining brightly and a gentle breeze was blowing up high, stirring the leaves in the tops of the trees back and forth. Other than that, the only other movement in the Twilight was the slow, quiet passage of the river below their tent. It reminded Ben of one of those lazy Sunday afternoons in the summertime when parents would take naps after lunch and children were banished outdoors to play. Everyone was enjoying their meal and dreading their goodbyes yet at the same time, anxious to be returning home. They all ate without speaking – not wanting to break the silence of the day as if it were something sacred not to be disturbed. Gabriel and Marcus appeared soon after they had finished their meal.

"I hope you are refreshed for your journey," said Marcus.

"We are," Louise replied. "Our breakfast was wonderful."

"Then, if you are finished, come with us."

Everyone followed the elves to the dock. There were two boats moored there. One was a swan boat, like all if the others they had seen, and the other one was the boat that Gabriel had given to Hob, Gob, and Nob. The elves had provisioned the boats with packs that were full of supplies that they would need for their journey.

"Hob, Gob, and Nob may ride in their boat back to Long Lake. We have provided one of our boats for Amos, Louise, and the children to travel in as well and we have placed the same enchantment upon that boat as is upon the other boat, that now belongs to the dwarves. The swan boat, however, will return to the Twilight as soon as the last person steps off, so be sure to leave one person on board until the boat is completely unloaded."

"I'm not sure how to thank you," said Louise.

"It is we who need to give thanks to you," said Gabriel winking at Hob, "and for once, we elves do not know what to say!"

"Ahhhh, enough of these mushy goodbyes," cried Hob. "It's not like we'll never see each other again. Let's shove off now before someone starts blubbering."

The three dwarves bowed low to the Keeper and Gabriel and then piled into their boat. Hob hastily untied the boat from the pier and used a paddle to push the boat out into the river. The boat spun around until it's prow was parting the oncoming waters, then slowly began moving upstream. After several hasty handshakes and hugs and promises to return, everyone else climbed aboard the swan boat and followed after the three dwarves. The swan boat sped up the river until it was even with the dwarve's boat and then slowed down to the same pace, so that the boats were traveling side-by-side and only a few inches apart.

"How long will it take us to get to Long Lake?" Amos asked.

"Once we exit the Twilight, if we maintain the rate we are traveling at now, we should be there in about four hours," said Nob.

For the next thirty minutes, they watched the forest slide by as the boats steadily made their way upstream and then suddenly they were out of the trees and back into the bright sunshine. Now that they were really on their way home, their spirits lifted and they laughed and talked and told tales and sang songs to pass the time until they reached the rapids. As the rapids approached, the swan boat dropped back behind the dwarve's boat and followed it safely through the rushing currents. After successfully navigating the rapids, the two boats sailed into the calm still waters of Long Lake. The boats turned and began to make their way toward the far shore where the dwarves kept their boat on a small sandy beach. When they had run aground, the three dwarves hopped out and pulled their boat up on the beach. Remembering Gabriel's advice, everyone in the swan boat pitched their packs onto the shore before leaving the boat. Meg was the last one to step off the boat and as soon as her feet were on solid ground, the swan boat backed away from the shore and slowly turned to begin the return trip back to the Twilight. Everyone stood on the shore and watched the boat until it was out of sight, then picked up their packs and headed up the hill to the dwarve's cabin.

The front door to the dwarve's home was busted off the hinges and lay splintered on the porch. The inside of the house was a wreck too. The large band of snakers had found it and although the house itself was still intact, everything inside of it had been destroyed. Amos, Louise, and the kids decided to stay and help them get things in order before they left. The dwarves set about mending the broken furniture, while Louise and the kids started cleaning the kitchen. Amos took his axe into the forest and returned dragging a tree behind him to chop up for firewood. By evening time, the house was back in order. A merry fire crackled and popped on the hearth and food from the packs, along with some fresh fish from the lake, simmered in pots and pans among the coals. After eating supper and cleaning up the dishes, the three dwarves sat down before the hearth in their mended chairs and lit their pipes. They had graciously offered their beds to Louise, Casey, and Meg and all three of them had thankfully accepted the offer and were deep under the thick woolen covers, nodding off to sleep.

"I'm so sorry we have delayed you," Nob called over his shoulder while puffing on his pipe. "I know you are anxious to be home."

"Don't be ridiculous," cried Louise. "We wouldn't have it any other way. Besides, we are all tired and one more good night's rest will make the journey tomorrow more bearable."

As a matter of fact, all of the kids were already asleep. Louise could hear Casey and Meg breathing deeply in the soft straw beds beside her and she had not heard a peep out of Ben and Joey who were curled up tightly in warm blankets before the fire. Louise was beginning to nod off herself. Amos had disappeared outside shortly after eating and the dwarves were now in some deep conversation about black gold or black dragons or black hills. Louise listened for a little while, but the hushed voices of the dwarves and the flickering shadows cast by the firelight had a mesmerizing and tranquil effect upon her. She simply could not stay focused on the conversation and finally gave up and surrendered herself to sleep.

30 HOME

The next morning everyone woke up early, eager to get
started. Louise sliced bread from a loaf baked the previous
day for supper and sliced cheese from a block the elves had
provided them for their journey. She arranged the bread and
cheese on a grill and placed the grill over some hot coals she
raked out onto the hearth. Hob, Gob, and Nob watched her
prepare the food with keen interest.

"What are you making?" Gob asked.

"It's called cheese toast," Louise replied. "You'll like
it."

As a matter of fact, the dwarves did like it and got into
a very heated debate about which was better for breakfast –
cheese toast or ham biscuits. After everyone finished eating,
they prepared for the remainder of their journey. Hob
announced that he and his partners would accompany the
others through the tunnel to the ledge. What they really
wanted to do, however, as soon as the others were gone, was
check on their treasure.

"Are we ready?" asked Amos, as he slung a sack across
his shoulder with one hand and stuffed an axe into his belt
with the other hand.

"Yes!" the children shouted.

"Well, let's head home," he called over his shoulder as he followed the dwarves into the round chamber. Gob lit a torch and the dwarves led them across the chamber and through the door into the tunnel. Everyone hastily marched, without pausing, until they reached the secret door that opened up inside the crevice on the ledge where Ben first met the dwarves. Gob placed the torch in a sconce on the tunnel wall and opened the stone door into the tunnel. Even though the tunnel door was at the back of the small crevice, the daylight that streamed in through the open door seemed exceptionally bright. They eagerly passed through the door and crevice in single file, with Amos bringing up the rear on his hands and knees. Once outside on the ledge, everyone sat down to rest and enjoy the warm sunshine. Since they had got an early start, it was still mid-morning and the day promised to be a good one for traveling.

"Will we make it back to your cabin today?" Louise asked.

"Oh yes," Amos answered. "We are not returning the way we came. We are going back to the Fairy Glen by the shortest route possible and then following the path from there to the cabin. We should be able to travel at a nice leisurely pace and still get there by late afternoon."

"How is that possible?" asked Ben. "It took me longer than that to get from the Fairy Glen to this ledge and I was definitely not moving at a leisurely pace."

"No," Amos laughed, "I guess you were not. However, when the snakers caught you they were carrying you in the opposite direction. When you escaped, you ran in the opposite direction and when you followed the stream it brought you here, but it did not bring you here in a straight line."

"Oh," said Ben. "I didn't think about that."

"Is everyone rested? I'm ready to be off," said Joey.

"Me too," Meg added. "I'm ready to just be at home."

"Then let's get moving," said Louise, as Amos gave her a hand and pulled her to her feet. "Cause I know just how you're feeling sweetheart."

At that point, Nob cleared his throat.

"I'm afraid this is where we say our farewells, friends. It has been a most exciting adventure and even though we'd love to continue on with you, we really must take our leave now."

"We understand," said Louise. "We would welcome your company, but we really did not expect you to accompany us for the entire trip."

"We would be thrilled to escort you all the way back, but there is still much work to undertake and many repairs to be made yet at our home," Gob added.

"Repairs?" Hob exclaimed. "I thought we were going out to check on our treasure."

Gob and Nob immediately began to kick him in the shins and Amos gathered Louise and the kids together and led them down the small stairs that were carved into the stone wall while Hob howled with pain behind them.

"I'm going to miss them," said Ben quietly.

"We will all miss them, dear," said Louise. "But we'll see them again some day I'm sure."

Soon, they came upon the small stream, with the path beside it. They followed the path for a while and then Amos turned and led them away from the stream and up the side of a very steep hill. Thankfully, they were under the shade of the forest because the day had grown warm. As they climbed higher, the hardwoods began to give way to pines and they soon found themselves in a pine forest with a soft quiet carpet of brown needles beneath their feet.

"These are the pines in my forest," Amos called over his shoulder.

Not long after entering the pines, the ground began to level out. Eventually, they reached the summit of the hill and there they found a large outcropping of rock overlooking the valley on the other side. A cool refreshing breeze blew up from the valley below and spread about them the sweet fragrance of the small white flowers growing between the stones. They chose this spot, to sit and eat a small bite of food for lunch.

"What is that," Casey asked, pointing at a clear spot in the valley below.

"That's the Fairy Glen where this whole mess began."

"How far away is it?"

"Not far. It should only take us a couple of hours to get down there from here. Is everyone ready?"

When they arrived at the Fairy Glen, they were surprised to find the fountain repaired. The red slab of granite was back in place and the spray from the water splashing against the stone created a beautiful rainbow that encircled the fountain. Below the rainbow and across the glen, the flowers that had been trampled by the snakers were thick and vibrant and blooming profusely. Hundreds of fairies were flitting back and forth and for a while no one spoke, each person caught up in the enchantment of the scene before them. Ben finally broke the silence.

"Who did this?"

"I don't know," replied Amos. "But if I had to guess I would say that it was the elves. They love all things of beauty and all creatures of magic. They knew of this place and were distressed to learn that the snakers had destroyed it. I suspect that the Keeper also sent guards to watch over us to make sure we made it home safely."

Everyone looked around at the hills surrounding them, half expecting to see elves hiding behind trees and keeping their watchful eyes on them. No one saw any elves, but Casey saw something glittering on one end of the granite slab. At first she thought she was seeing one of the fairies out of the corner of her eye, but when she looked at the slab she was able to look directly at the shiny object and it did not disappear. She went forward to get a closer look. It was a necklace. An emerald necklace. Casey remembered that she had loaned her necklace to the elves. Amos and the others walked up behind her.

"It appears that I was right," said Amos.

Casey took the necklace and placed it around her neck.

"Come on guys," Joey shouted. "We're almost home!"

The hike back to the cabin was the most exciting part of the entire adventure for Ben. Amos and Louise walked out front, followed by Joey and Casey, with he and Meg bringing up the rear. Meg walked close to Ben and a couple of times their hands touched while they were walking. Ben finally got up the nerve and grabbed her hand the next time it touched his. He clasped her hand gently, half expecting her to pull away, but to his delight she intertwined her fingers with his and squeezed. He was holding her hand! Now he did not want to go home. Now he did not want to go back to the cabin. He wanted this walk to last forever and now, to his great disappointment, they were back at the cabin. Meg squeezed his hand tightly and smiled at him before she pulled her hand away. Amos was holding the door open and waiting for them to enter. He winked a knowing wink at Ben as he passed by and Ben immediately felt the heat starting to rise in his neck.

"I can't believe we're back," said Louise, sitting down at the table. "It seems we've been gone for months."

"Don't sit down, Grandma," said Casey. "Let's keep going. We can be home in five minutes."

"Listen, children. I know you are anxious to get home. So am I. But we have hiked all day long and we are all exhausted. Remember, when we go back through the Merlin Tree we will be going back to the same timeframe that we left. Why don't we stay here tonight and rest. We'll eat a good breakfast in the morning and return home refreshed and full of energy. We're going to need some energy too, because as soon as we get back home, all of us have to take a shower, or a bath, to get clean and I will have to wash everyone's clothes. Look at how filthy you all are."

The kids looked at each other and realized that Louise was right. Amos must have been thinking the same thing for he brought a bucket of water in and plopped it down on the table.

"You kids can wash up with this. I'll get supper started and after we eat, I know a place not far from here where a family of talking monkeys live. Would you kids like to go see them?"

"NO!" they all shouted in unison.

The big man through back his head and laughed a long, hearty laugh. Louise thought she was too tired to laugh, but soon she started laughing too, more at Amos's merriment than his joke. The kids, however, did not see the humor in it at all and scowled as they began to scrub their hands and faces. After eating, they moved the table and benches outside and spread two great furs on the floor before the hearth. Joey and Ben slept on one fur and Meg and Casey slept on the other one. Louise slept in Amos's cot and Amos, after loading wood into the fire, went outside to sleep under the stars.

The next morning was overcast and gray. Dark puffy clouds hung low in the sky and blotted out the sun. A chill was in the air and not long after finishing breakfast, a heavy rain began to fall. Outside the cabin window, a thick curtain of water flowed from the roof and over the eaves.

"It looks like you all might be staying a little longer," said Amos. "This rain has really set in. I expect it will probably rain all day today."

Louise could tell that the kids were not happy with this news. She wasn't happy with this news. As much as everyone loved Amos, his cabin was too small for all of them to be cooped up within for any length of time.

"What do you kids want to do?" she asked. "Do you want to wait this out or do you want to go for it?"

"Let's go for it," said Ben.

"Yeah," said Joey. "It was hot and dry when we left home, so we'll only be in the rain for a few minutes."

Casey and Meg nodded. Louise turned to Amos. "I guess this is good-bye then."

"For now," the big man smiled.

Louise threw her arms around him. The kids encircled him and wrapped their arms around him too.

"Bye, Amos."

"We'll miss you."

"I hope we'll get to see you again."

Amos wiped his eyes with the back of his hand and then stooped down to look at the kids. "I want you all to come visit me, okay?"

They all nodded.

Amos smiled and then pointed toward the door. "Well, get going then. I'm like Hob – I don't like mushy farewells either."

Ben and Joey nodded and walked over to the door, where Louise was waiting. Casey and Meg, however, gave the big man one more hug before joining them.

"The rain is cold, kids, but we can't run or someone might slip and fall. Besides, I can't run anyway. But we can walk really fast, can't we?"

The children smiled and nodded.

"Then let's go!"

Louise threw the door open and they all stepped out into the downpour. The cold rain immediately took their breath away and they all began to hastily walk through the woods. When they got to the edge of the woods, the rain was coming down even harder and the wind was starting to blow. Visibility was dropping fast, but they could still see the bamboo patch in the meadow at the base of the hill, a green island in a stormy sea of gold. Before they made it to the bamboo, the wind had begun to howl. The rain was now being driven sideways by the storm and the force of it stung their skin. Everyone had to turn their backs to the wind and walk sideways to reach the bamboo. As soon as they arrived at the patch, a great clap of thunder made everyone jump. Louise rushed the kids into the patch and then fell in behind them. Before she got too far into the patch, she turned and looked over her shoulder into the meadow. Through the driving rain she caught a glimpse of a dark object sitting in the meadow, unaffected by the storm raging around it. It looked like a bear. Louise smiled.

Getting through the thick bamboo was difficult on a calm day. During a storm, with the wind whipping the canes around, it was almost impossible. However, they finally made their way to the middle of the patch. Lightning flashed in the darkness and revealed the thick canopy over their heads heaving and surging as the storm raged about them. There, in the center, still and calm, unaffected by the elements through centuries of time, stood the Merlin tree.

When they emerged from the Tree, everything around them was dry and an eerie green light was all about them.

"Where is that light coming from?" Casey asked.

"That's sunlight," Ben answered. "Remember, it was sunny when we left."

"Well, keep going. I want to get out of these wet clothes."

They started back into the thick part of the canes again. The closer they got to the outside of the patch, the thicker the canes became. Finally, after much twisting and turning, they stumbled out into the bright June sunshine and landed in the backyard of George and Louise's home. They were back on the farm. They were home.

31 SPECULATIONS

The kids grabbed hands and began running around in circles, laughing with joy. They tried to get Louise to join them, but she made them stop.

"Listen up, children. We don't have time for this right now. We have to get inside and get cleaned up before George gets home. Meg and Casey, you two get upstairs and take a quick shower. Joey and Ben, you can use the shower in our bedroom. Joey and Meg, you two go first. I'll get you a robe to wear, because I need your dirty clothes as fast as possible, so I can get them washed and dried. Let's hurry!"

The kids ran around to the front porch and scrambled up the steps, with Louise right behind them. Meg and Casey ran up the stairs and Ben and Joey hustled into the back of the house. Within half an hour, the kids and their clothes were clean. Louise took the clothes out of the washer and threw them in the drier, then hurried off to get herself a shower too. By the time she had dressed and dried her hair, the kids were sitting at the kitchen table drinking milk and eating cookies.

"Oh my, that looks good," said Louise.

She poured herself a glass of milk, grabbed a handful of cookies from the cookie jar, and then leaned back against the counter to eat them.

"Is it really over?" Ben asked.

All of the kids stopped eating and waited for Louise to reply. Louise finished chewing the cookies in her mouth and then washed it down with a sip of milk.

"Yes, dear. It's over. Thank goodness, it's finally over."

"What do we do now?" Ben asked.

"Why don't we all just take it easy for the rest of the day? We've been through a lot and I think we all need a few days to recuperate, don't you?"

Ben nodded.

"Let's put the dishes away and I'll take Joey and Meg home. I have some canning jars that I need to return to Rebecca anyway."

The kids rinsed their glasses out, placed them in the sink and headed outside. Louise came out behind them, with her purse on her arm and her car keys in her hand. She got Joey to pick up a cardboard box by the door that was full of pint size Mason jars and opened the trunk of her old Galaxy. Joey sat the box in the trunk and closed the lid and they were on their way.

Rebecca was kneeling in the front yard, weeding one of her flower beds, when Louise pulled up in front of her house. She laid the small hand spade down and brushed the dirt from her knees then walked out to greet them.

"Hello, Louise. Is everything okay?"

"Oh yes, nothing's wrong, dear. Ben and Casey wanted to show Joey and Meg their goats and then they wanted to come back over here to play the Play Station. I had some jars to bring you, so I just gave them a ride, that's all."

Louise opened the trunk for Joey to get the box of jars and the kids hurried off into the house, while she sat down at the picnic table to visit with Rebecca. The two women chatted for an hour or so about flowers and vegetables and the proper way to grow them. Finally, the kids came out of the house and Ben came over to the table to speak to Louise.

"Grandma, Grandpa is home now. He just called and said we all needed to come home too."

"Is something wrong?" Louise asked with concern in her voice.

"No, I asked him if anything was wrong and he said no. He said he had some important news for us and didn't want to tell us over the phone."

"What do you think it is?" Rebecca asked.

"I don't know. But I guess we'd better get going and find out."

"Call me if you need me for anything, okay?"

"I will, thanks Rebecca. Ben, Casey, let's go find out what's going on."

Ben and Casey said their goodbyes and crawled into the front seat of the car with Louise. When they got back to the farm, Louise stopped about halfway up the driveway, where the car could not be seen from the house. She switched the car off and turned to the kids.

"Children, I have a story to tell you. Do you remember that fall when your mother had her car accident?"

Ben and Casey nodded. Ben's pulse quickened.

"Do you remember coming up here to visit at the end of your summer break, right before school started back?"

Ben and Casey nodded once more.

"Okay. Do you remember going to the cattle sale with your father and your Grandpa?"

"Yes, Grandma, we remember," said Casey. "Why are you asking us all of these questions?"

"That day you went to the cattle sale, your mother was not feeling well and had lain down to take a nap. While she was asleep, I slipped out and went through the Merlin Tree to Camelot. I was going to pop in on Amos and say hello. I hadn't seen him all summer."

Louise paused for a moment, staring through the windshield, while calling up some painful memories from long ago. The car windows were rolled down and Ben could hear the small stream that ran parallel to the driveway gurgling over some rocks nearby. Other than that the afternoon was quiet, until Louise continued her story.

"I saw the unicorn when I was returning to the bamboo patch. It was grazing in the tall grass. At first I thought it was a white prairie stag, but as I got closer I could tell it was a horse. Then it raised its head and I saw the spiral horn. And then, suddenly, I saw the shadow cat materialize behind the unicorn. I threw my hands up and shouted and the unicorn sped off with the shadow cat in hot pursuit."

Louise paused for a moment and began fumbling around in her purse for some tissue.

"I thought a unicorn had not been seen in Camelot for a very long time," said Casey.

Louise nodded. "I don't know why the elves did not know of this one. Or maybe they did know. Maybe they know everything and that's why they didn't say anything."

"What happened next, Grandma?" Ben whispered. He was beginning to put the pieces together now himself. Louise dabbed at her eyes and continued with her story.

"That's when I heard the witch scream. She had been hiding in the tall grass nearby and now she stood up where I could see her. She was fit to be tied, that's for sure. I knew who she was; I just couldn't believe that she was standing there in front of me."

"What did you do?" Casey asked.

"I ran. She had reached into one of the pockets on her robe and pulled out a wand. She started waving it over her head in a big circle and chanting some kind of gibberish. When I got to the bamboo patch, I looked over my shoulder and saw the witch pointing the wand at me and shaking it. I remember that she had a confused look on her face and before I disappeared into the bamboo I saw her take the wand and snap it in half. She didn't pursue me into the bamboo, because she was not sure why her spell did not work. I thought I had escaped unharmed."

"But you didn't," Ben said. "Did you?"

"No, sweetheart, I didn't."

"What are you guys talking about?" Casey asked.

"You were wearing a spell-catcher, weren't you?" asked Ben, ignoring Casey's question.

Louise nodded and dabbed at her eyes again.

"Would someone please tell me what's going on?" said Casey.

"Back in Camelot, the unicorn showed me a vision of something that would come to pass," said Ben. "Something in the future." He turned to look at his sister. "The vision was one of you and me sitting at the table and eating dinner with Dad. And Mom." Ben waited a few seconds for this to register with Casey.

"You mean Mom is going to be okay?"

"I think so. I think the witch cast a spell at Grandma and her spell-catcher caught it. And then Mom was probably the next person grandma touched and the spell was transferred to her."

"Is that true, grandma?" Casey asked, tears welling up in her eyes.

"I think so, sweetheart. When I came out of the bamboo I went back into the house and started breaking beans. When your mother woke up from her nap, she came and sat down at the table and I felt of her forehead to see if she was running a fever. I believe that the witch's spell was meant to paralyze me, but my spell-catcher caught the spell and transferred it to your mother when I touched her. The spell must have been slow acting because it was working in another world and not the world in which it was cast."

"And now that the witch is dead," Ben continued, "the spell should be broken. Is that right?"

Louise nodded. "That's the way I understand it."

Louise pulled the necklace out from beneath her blouse. The jewel dangling from the end of the chain had saved one life and destroyed another.

"But Mom had a car wreck," said Casey. "You guys know that."

"Yes, Mom had a wreck and I think the wreck was just enough to weaken her to the point where the witch's spell could take hold. I don't think Mom has been in a coma for two years because of the wreck. I think it was because of the witch's spell. Think about it Casey, it makes perfect sense. The doctors have never been able to explain why Mom is not physically wasting away. It has to be magic."

"So you think she is okay now?" Casey asked, with tears streaming down her face.

"I think so," said Ben. "Don't get your hopes up too high but yes, I think Mom is okay now. I don't know if she'll recover immediately or if it will take time, since we are in another world. But I think she will recover.

"Maybe that's what Grandpa called us about!" said Casey.

"We hope so," Louise replied. "But let's quit guessing and go find out."

Louise pulled the gearshift down into drive and they made their way up the long gravel road, with Ben and Casey sitting on the edge of the car seat. When they came around the curve they saw George's truck parked beside the barn. George had let the tailgate down and was sitting there waiting for them. He hopped off the rear of the truck as Louise drove by to park the car under the magnolia tree. Louise and the kids jumped out of the car and ran to him.

"What's going on, George?" Louise asked. "What is so dog-gone important that we had to drive all the way back over here for you to tell us?"

"Charles is coming home."

Now Ben and Casey crowded around him, pulling on his sleeves and asking him questions.

"When's he coming home, Grandpa?"

"Did he say why?"

"Is he okay? Is anything wrong?"

George held his hands up in the air.

"Everybody calm down and I'll tell you exactly what he told me. Alright?"

Ben and Casey nodded. Louise patted George on the arm.

"As I said, Charles is coming home. He called this afternoon and said that something had come up that required him to be at home. His company is flying someone else up to Chicago to run the project he was working on and he is flying into Greenville this evening. He wouldn't tell me what it was, he just said for you kids to be packed and ready to go by the time he gets here."

"Well for heaven's sake George, when is he going to be here?"

"Should be around eight o'clock."

Ben and Casey ran for the house.

"Where are you kids going?" George called after them.

"We're going to pack," they called over their shoulders.

George watched them scramble up the porch steps to the front door, fighting over who would be first inside the house. He glanced at Louise who was watching the kids and smiling.

"What are you so happy about?" he mumbled. "It looks like those kids can't wait to get out of here."

"It's not that, George, they're just anxious to see their father and find out why he's coming home. That's all."

"Hmmph. I'll be in the barn if you need me."

Ben and Casey were packed in fifteen minutes. Now they had about seven hours to wait. Ben's stomach growled noisily and they had not eaten lunch. Down in the kitchen Ben fixed a tomato sandwich with Dukes Mayonnaise and Casey made a grilled cheese sandwich. After eating they tried watching TV to pass the time, but found that they could not sit still or stay interested in anything that was showing. Finally, Ben suggested they go for a walk. They first walked up to the goat house to pet their goats. Then they walked back to the fish pond and skipped rocks across the smooth green surface. Time crawled by slowly, but somehow they made it through the rest of the day. That evening, Louise cooked a big supper. She made Charles's favorite – pork chops, mashed potatoes and gravy, green beans, and homemade biscuits. After eating, she fixed a plate for Charles and put it in the refrigerator. Then, everyone helped clean up and put the dishes away. Afterwards, they retired to the front porch, where Ben and Casey had placed their suitcases earlier. Because George and Louise's house was situated in a small valley, the sun had already set behind the hilltop, but a golden soft warm glow still lay about them. In another hour, lightning bugs would be flashing all over the pasture and bats would be swooping around the night light catching big fat juicy moths. Ben had a small pang of regret that he and Casey did not catch any lightning bugs. Every time they visited in the summer, they would catch all that they could and put them into jars. Then they would take the jars into their room, when they went to bed, and watch the little bugs flash on and off, while they drifted off to sleep.

"Someone's coming," said George, rising to his feet. Since their driveway was gravel, you could always hear a car before you could see it. In a few seconds, Charles's Honda rolled out of the woods, speeding up the driveway raising a plume of gray dust behind it. Everyone walked out into the yard to meet him.

32 A JOYOUS REUNION

The Honda rolled to a dusty stop. When Charles hopped out, Ben and Casey rushed to his side and threw their arms around him. Charles pulled the kids close and hugged them tightly. George and Louise tried to wait patiently for Charles and his children to finish up with their hugs and kisses. Louise, however, reached a point where she simply could not take it any longer.

"Okay, Charles, that's enough! You've got to tell us what's going on."

Charles let the kids go, swooped his mom up in his arms and spun her around.

"Heaven's sake, Charles, put me down! What's got into you, son?"

Charles set his mother down and put his arm around her and his father.

"I need to eat a bite, first. I haven't had a single bite of food all day today. I'm so excited it seems I've lost my appetite, but I know I need to eat something, because I'm a little light-headed too. Or maybe I'm just a little light headed, because I'm so excited, I don't know. Let me scarf down a sandwich and then I'll give everyone the good news."

"You don't have to eat a sandwich," said Louise. "We had a late supper and I saved you a plate. It's your favorite too."

While Charles ate everyone plied him with questions, but he refused to answer a single one. As soon as he was finished eating, Louise whisked his plate away and everyone walked out to the front porch.

"Sit down, Son," said George, pointing to the old wooden swing. "Louise can put on a pot of coffee, if you like?"

"No, Dad, I can't stay and visit. I'm going to give you my good news now and then we will have to be off."

"Well, I don't see why you have to rush off like that. You could at least have a cup of coffee with us."

"No, I really can't. You'll understand why in just a moment. But you and Mom and the kids need to be sitting down for this – it's big."

George and Louise sat in their old rocking chairs and Ben and Casey plopped down in the porch swing. Charles stood between the porch columns, on either side of the steps, where he could see his parents and his children. He cleared his throat and took a deep breath.

"Last night, about nine o'clock, I was in my hotel room getting ready for bed. I had a long exhausting day at work and I was dead tired. Just as I crawled into bed, and turned the lights out, the telephone rang. At first, I thought it was work related and I started to just lay there and let it ring. But then I started thinking that something might have happened to one of the kids and someone was trying to get in touch with me. You know how I am."

Louise nodded. "You always expect the worst."

"Well, anyway, I answered the phone and it was Newberry Downs calling about Carol."

George and Louise quit rocking and Ben and Casey stopped swinging. Time froze, and everyone's attention hung on the next words to come out of Charles's mouth. Finally, Ben spoke and time started back.

"What did they say?"

"They said," Charles's voice cracked and he paused a moment to wipe a tear from his eye. When he regained his composure he continued. "They said your mother is awake."

Ben and Casey sat there stunned. They heard their father clearly, but they were afraid to believe him. They were afraid it was all a dream and that they would wake up and nothing would have changed.

"Did you hear me, guys? Carol is out of her coma now. She is awake and talking too."

Ben and Casey jumped from the swing and ran to their father. Charles dropped to his knees and the children sobbed on his shoulder. Louise and George came over and they too were crying.

"Is it really true? Is mom really awake?" Casey cried.

"It's true, sweetheart. That's why I'm here. To get you two guys and take you home. Are you ready?"

Casey nodded.

"Good," said Charles. "Grab your suitcases and let's go get your mother and bring her home."

George helped Charles and the kids load their luggage into the trunk. Ben and Casey hugged their grandparents and climbed into the Honda. Louise leaned down and yelled through the window as Charles was cranking the car.

"You call me when you get home and give me an update, you hear?"

Charles nodded and blew her a kiss. He then backed the car, turned it around, and sped off down the driveway, tooting the horn and waving his arm out the window. Casey and Ben waved at their grandparents, until their car rounded the corner and disappeared into the woods.

"I can't believe it," said Ben. "I have dreamed of this day for so long, I just can't believe it's finally happened."

"I know, Son. I have been praying for this day for two years now. I have been praying the same prayer over and over and over. I've prayed the same prayer so many times that it has just became some kind of ritual, without any meaning or thought behind the words. Do you know what I'm saying?"

"Yeah, I think so. Casey, are you okay? You are awful quiet."

"I'm fine. I guess I'm just kinda floored by the news. It's been so long since we've had a mother and I've just been sitting here thinking and trying to remember what it was like. And I've been wondering what it's going to be like. Is she going to be the same? Or will she be different now?"

"She's going to be fine," said Charles, leaning over and patting Casey on the knee. "I've saved up a lot of vacation time over the past couple of years. I'm going to take some time off to help your mother get back on her feet. I'm going to need your help too. Both of you."

Soon, they were on Highway 11 and Charles pushed the little Honda up to seventy. After a while, Ben spotted a big sign – Sparky's Fireworks was just half a mile ahead. He remembered his dad had promised to stop there on the way home, to buy them some fireworks. He didn't want to stop now, though. He didn't want to stop for anything and he smiled to himself as Sparky's big metal building flashed by the car, on the left. Almost to the interstate now. Almost home.

Back on the farm, George and Louise had watched Charles and the kids, until they were out of sight and then they went into the house to sit and digest this turn of events. Louise had been crying ever since Charles had given them the good news, and could not stop. George could not understand why she kept crying and finally decided that it must have something to do with being a woman, so even though it was now getting dark, he promptly declared that he had some work to do on his tractor and left. Louise pulled the last tissue from the box on the end table and wiped her eyes once more. She then pulled the necklace out from beneath her dress and yanked it from her neck, then went into the kitchen to fix a pot of coffee. She paused by the kitchen door and dropped the spell-catcher into the garbage can, and then took the carafe over to the sink to fill it with water. As the pot was filling, she looked out of the window at the bamboo. It was finally over and she had her family back. She smiled and then filled the coffee maker.

On the interstate, Charles pushed the Honda up to eighty. He wasn't worried about getting a ticket, because even though the speed limit was sixty-five, everyone was driving seventy-five and eighty. Even at that speed it seemed to take forever to get to Newberry Downs, but they finally made it. Charles did not even bother to park the car. He pulled up to the front of the building and killed the engine, right at the steps leading to the front entrance. All three raced up the sidewalk and burst through the double doors, into the waiting room. There was Carol, sitting in a wheelchair across the room with a suitcase at her side. Charles and the kids froze, as Carol put her hands on the arms of the chair and slowly rose to her feet. A tear slid down her cheek as she smiled and opened her arms to her family. Charles ran to her and swept her off her feet. The two clung to each other tightly and then Carol pulled away and motioned for her children. Ben and Casey ran to their mother and flung themselves into her arms. After many tears, and many hugs and kisses, Charles led his wife over to a sofa to sit. Ben sat beside her on one side and Casey sat beside her on the other side. Charles pulled an old wingback chair out from the corner and dragged it over so that he could sit in front of her.

"How do you feel, Mom?" Ben asked.

"I'm a little weak, but other than that I actually feel pretty good. The doctors are amazed at my recovery and wanted to keep me for a couple of days to observe me, but I wouldn't have it. I'm ready to get out of this place."

"Do you know how long you've been here?" Charles asked, picking his wife's hands up and squeezing them gently.

"Two years," Carol answered. "Two long, miserable, horrible years."

"What do you mean by that?"

"I don't think I was in any kind of coma, Charles. I was aware of everything that went on around me, I just couldn't respond. It was more of a paralysis than anything."

"You could hear us when we talked to you?" Casey asked.

"I heard every word, honey, but I couldn't move a single muscle. I couldn't even open my eyes. If you guys had not come as often as you did, I would have gone insane in just a few weeks."

"And the doctors still don't have an explanation for what happened?" Charles asked.

"None. All I can tell them is that one moment I had no feeling anywhere in my entire body and the next moment, it was like someone turned on a switch and every nerve, every fiber, every cell within me cried out; I'm alive!"

For a few moments, everyone sat there in silence. Finally, Carol spoke again.

"So what do we do now?"

Charles stood up and pulled his wife to her feet.

"Come on, sweetheart, let's go home."

"Home," Ben whispered. There was more magic in that one word than existed in all of Camelot; Home.

THE END

ABOUT THE AUTHOR

W. D. Newman is the pen name for William Dale Porter.
Dale lives on a farm in upstate South Carolina with his wife
Melody and their two children Kyle and Isaac. Dale has a
passion for horses and spends as much time as possible
enjoying the great outdoors.

A NOTE TO THE READER

Thank you for reading The Thirteenth Unicorn. If you enjoyed this story I would love to hear from you. Email me at dale339@bellsouth.net and if you are on Face Book, be sure to look up "The Thirteenth Unicorn" book page and add it to your likes.

I am currently working on book two in the Ben Alderman series; "The Black Dragon". In this story, Ben and his sister Casey will return to Camelot with their Grandma to help Amos, Gob, and Nob rescue Gabriel and Hob from the gnome mines. Hob has found Merlin's staff, and Zoltan, a black dragon from Crag, will stop at nothing to obtain the spell-catcher that adorns the staff.

Made in the USA
Lexington, KY
18 June 2014